CW01572888

By Chance

By Chance

E. Denise Billups

Prologue

February's thick snow silences Boston's Back Bay area and heightens frightful screams inside seven-hundred-eighty Boylston Street. Annoyed tenants, arriving home from work, hasten inside and swiftly close their apartment doors. Several minutes later, shuffling and whispering evolve in front of apartment 20A. Tom, worried neighbors reported the noise, looks through the peephole, finding an attractive brunette and several men staring back. He takes a deep breath, clears his throat, and opens the door a crack.

"Yes. May I help you?" He asked, tempering remnants of anger in his voice.

As the door opens wider, Ellen, his wife, joins his side. Immediately, aware of the camera crew, and their disheveled appearance, they both step back. Ellen brushes her hair in place and rolls a crinkled sleeve over newly formed bruises. Tom conceals a contused fist with his left hand and forces a grin. Unaware of the rampage moments ago, the television host and camera crew believe they're witnessing a couple surprised and nervous from unexpected events.

"Congratulations! You're the new winners of the AHD Dream Home Sweepstakes," the woman squealed, waiting for a response, only receiving wide-eyed silence.

Now, curious neighbors spy through slit doors.

Unprepared for the fortuitous moment, Tom flinches when the lively Alcott Home and Design's (AHD) TV host places the intrusive microphone at his mouth. She steps aside, directing the cameraman to move in and capture the winner's excitement. With a curious glance, she gestures her hand to induce some emotion from the straight-faced couple. "Are you excited?"

"What? Is this for real or some hoax?" Tom asked. Shock, embarrassment, disbelief, and a mixture of emotions swell through their minds.

"This is real," the animated brunette said. "You and your family are the winners!"

Only entering his name twice in the sweepstake, and never taking it seriously, Tom can't believe his name was chosen out of millions of people. "You're kidding … Right?" Moments later, realizing their reality is about to change, elation replaces incredulity.

* * *

A week later, they're chauffeured from their two-bedroom apartment in Boston to their new million-dollar home in Vermont. For a weekend, AHD's Dream Team treats them like royalty and proclaims, "Your life just changed for the better." When the magical weekend concludes, they're given three sets of keys attached to a geometric keychain—a bronze triangular home inside a gilded circle and square—the keys to their beautiful Mountain Home. Boxes packed, old items discarded, they leave their two-bedroom apartment and never look back. Although Tom realizes the Dream Home might be too expensive to maintain, he vows to make their new life work.

Two years later, remembering the Sweepstake Dream Team's promise of a new and better life, Tom stares at the elusive dream crumbling around him. "All lies, lies, lies … What do they think; they can give us this dream then take it away? No, they won't, not from me," he mumbles with anger burning in his eyes. Reeling from the loss of his high-powered career, and pondering the uncertainties of his life, disillusionment soon turns to anger, vengeance, and now madness as he paces back and forth in his office.

A sudden dizzy spell claims his balance. He holds his head and rubs his temples to contain swelling pain. For a moment, he pauses, takes a deep breath, and turns his attention to the layout in front of him, wondering if he can pull off his plan. Uncertain of the outcome, he merely understands the need to strike their hearts with fear. *They must know what they've done,* he affirms while staring at the circular trail of photos surrounding a picture of AHD's headquarter.

His desk resembles a small-scale FBI crime lab. Photos of three females and one male are numbered one to four in executable form. Internet printouts from Google maps and other miscellaneous information are strategically placed beside each picture. Given the sweepstake team's celebrity, he's amazed he'd found all the information needed on the Internet. With a little cunning, he'd pretended to be the new architect for the 2016 Dream Home, acquiring the team's cell phone numbers from the ill-advised receptionist, Rebecca. As a gatekeeper, he couldn't believe how gullible she was, making no effort to confirm the real name of the architect. *She will be useful as my plan unfolds.*

Magazine clips from personal interviews provide more intimate details about AHD's team. Tom scrutinizes the layout on the table and reassesses each picture and item of significance. Several photographs surround an image of AHD's headquarters. The first photo displays an attractive, African-American woman with massive waves of brown hair and almond-shaped hazel eyes. Below her picture lay two printouts from the web—a townhouse surrounded by cobblestone sidewalks and gas lanterns, adjoined to a photo of the Bakehouse Bakery Cafe with the caption *Morning Coffee Stop.* The second picture of a striking strawberry blonde with mesmerizing bluish-green eyes is stapled to a blue velvet ribbon. Underneath the photo, lays a printout with a red bullseye in the middle of a sprawling home labeled *Alcott Estate.* The third photo of an enchanting raven-haired female with piercing green eyes is surrounded by letters copied from AHD's blog site. Similarly, an image of a modern townhouse with massive oak trees sits under her photo.

Tom ponders the picture of the only male, an African-American with hazel eyes, a strong jawline, and closely cropped brown hair. He wonders why he couldn't find personal information on AHD's Producer and Home Planner. His image sits alone with a bold red question mark he'll undoubtedly answer with time.

On the table sits four silver gifts wrapped with blue velvet bows. He wonders if they'll understand the message the gifts contains. One last time, he scans the large graph paper and wonders if the information is enough to carry out his plan. *It has to be,* he affirms. With meticulous hands, he rolls the paper like an architectural blueprint and places it inside a black satchel with the silver packages. Tom sweeps his office from corner-to-corner, to confirm clues aren't left behind.

Sadly, he glances around his home, wondering how life spun out of control so quickly. *This is not my life, and won't be my children's,* he maintains firmly. His vision blurs. Tom reels forward and clutches the desk's corner before black spots claim his sight. With a tight grip, he holds the desk's edge until dizziness elapses. A veil rolls over his eyes, like shades enclosing him in darkness. And with the same alacrity, his sight returns—spotty globs dissipate to light.

With the return of sight comes another bout of anxiousness. The permanent dweller in his head taunts relentlessly. *You can't handle this, Tom. How can you live with the pain you'll cause your family? Look at you; you can't even pay your bills. How do you expect to feed your family and keep this house? You can't! What sort of man are you! You're just like your father.* He glares at stacks of bills hidden from his wife and snaps at the voice in his head. "You'll never understand what I'm capable of. I'm not my father!"

A guttural sound escapes his mouth. Clenching his teeth, he tries to silence the noise rattling inside his head. Momentarily, the voice subsides, but anger reappears with the elusive dream fading around him. A delusional sense of entitlement and paranoia invades his mind. Sickness clouds his logic. No longer comprehending his personal difficulties, he blames others, not his illness for his troubles.

A sudden surge of nausea overcomes him. Quickly, he runs to the master bath and dry heaves over the toilet bowl, but the bitter liquid refuses to surface. For several minutes, he sits on the floor, fearing another bout of nausea. Slowly rising to his feet, he heads to the medicine cabinet, rummages through multiple prescription bottles, and finds the mind-altering pill. Inadvertently, he catches a shocking, gaunt image staring back in the mirror. He's never been this thin. Unwilling to tolerate another listless moment, he disgustedly spits the tablet into the sink. "No more ... I have to feel like myself again," he affirms. Willfully, he empties the entire bottle into the toilet.

With quiet steps, he exits the bathroom, pauses, and stares at his wife fast asleep under the down comforter. Backing toward the door, he makes his way to the children's room, standing over his four and five-year-old nestled fast asleep in the bunk bed. A lump forms in his throat as he fathoms the fragile security of their world. A few minutes pass before he snaps out of his reverie and he leans over and kisses them on the forehead.

"I won't let them take this away from us."

With brevity, he hurries to the dining room and writes a note to his wife.

> *Ellen*
>
> *There's an opportunity for work that involves travel. If I'd told you I'm going away for a while, you would have protested and I don't want to fight about this. Sorry for sneaking out. I'll call you when I reach my destination. Please give the kids my love. See you soon.*
>
> *Tom*

Tom envisions Ellen's morning routine as she proceeds to the fridge for a glass of water. He's certain she will see the note pinned to the refrigerator door. He takes his five-year-olds' favorite black and white spotted dog magnet and posts the note for Ellen's eyes. One last time, he heads to the master suite and watches Ellen's peaceful slumber. He remembers her joy when they moved into the home, and can't bear the thought of her pain and loss to come.

With a heavy heart, he leaves his family in tenuous comfort. Steering the car out of the driveway, he glances back at the home's deceptive beauty and the mountain's perpetual grandeur. Determined to reach South Carolina, Tom exits Vermont and heads onto I-95 South, realizing he may never see his family again.

PART 1

Chapter 1

Tara

December 15, 2014, Charleston, SC

In South Carolina, Mother Nature overlooked winter and soared full-fledged into spring, blitzing December with unusual warmth and balmy breezes. Along Charleston's Battery Promenade, Palmetto trees sway from coastal winds, and early risers, though stunned, welcome tropical weather as they start their morning ritual.

In the French Quarters, harbor winds whip around Tara McPherson's townhouse and through an open window, banging blinds rowdily across the windowsill. Bolting from sleep, Tara stumbles downstairs in a somnolent trance, closes the window then plods heavy-eyed through the dark, bumping into the hall credenza. "Owww!" She squeals, stoops, and grasps her stubbed toe, sucking air through clenched teeth until the pain subsides.

Slowly, rising from the floor, she shuffles one-sided, eyes down to the top of the stairs, and then abruptly stops when a strange light glimmers above. Rubbing sleep from her eyes, she steps onto the landing, glances about the window-less space, circles, and waves her arms about for the source, but finds nothing.

Much too tired to solve the baffling light, she shuffles into the bedroom.

"Darn," She grumbles.

Catching time on the clock, she realizes the alarm will chime in two minutes. Tara sighs and deliberates jumping back in bed. With a deeper sigh, she drags her weary body to the shower; unaware the glow trails behind.

* * *

Thirty-five minutes later, Tara's bedroom appears a hurricane's aftermath. With clothing strewn pell-mell about the room; she searches for a suitable outfit to wear in the unseasonable weather. Fretfully standing undressed in the middle of the room, hair flying in voluminous curls, she sighs and peers toward the large walk-in closet. At the back, she spies her spring wardrobe and ponders two dresses suitable for the temporary warm spell. *Improvise; improvise.*

Finally, she tugs a simple tan dress around her narrow hips and slips into a pair of suede pumps, wishing she could wear a pair of jeans and T-shirt. *Maybe it's time for a new dress code at work—casual dress, jeans and a blouse; no sneakers or flip-flops.* "Hmph," she deliberates with a smirk. However, Southerners prefer formality and she's certain casual attire is unacceptable. Anyway, as Managing Director, I must dress accordingly.

Standing at the vanity mirror, her father and mother's features appear dominant this morning. Never one to wear much makeup, she applies modicum lipstick, blush, and mascara, stares at her massive curls, and toys with the idea a simple ponytail. But instead, she wears it loosely about her shoulders. At first glance, Tara appears a Southern Belle, that is until her northern dialect reveals her native origins. Her nationality isn't always apparent given indistinct facial features. With honey brown skin and wavy chestnut hair, she borders on African, Indian, and Latin-American. She abhors racial labels and will never deny her mother's African American heritage or her father's Irish roots. She realizes the appropriate representation is biracial, but she prefers African-American for the sake of simplicity.

Tara scoffs at laws prohibiting interracial marriages, prevalent in South Carolina before the 1970s. *Life is so absurd.* If she'd been born in Charleston, the probable outcome would have been imprisonment or worst for her parents. The thought infuriates her; the ignorance makes her boiling mad, but she appreciates what her parents endured to make their lives possible. Although years ago, racial mixing was forbidden; she's certain it was merely concealed in Southern towns like Charleston. Nonetheless, neither race nor anti-miscegenation laws prevented her parents from marrying, but at the cost of uprooting themselves from their beloved Charleston. Moving to New York City, they married in 1975, several years after interracial marriages became legal in South Carolina. The McPherson's made a life in New York, and Tara grew up a city girl, which was probably for the best.

With her father's connections, she entered New York University's Business School and two years later, acquired her Interior Design degree from Parsons School of Art and Design. She recalls Nyla's surprise when she decided to enter business school. *"You're just like your dad."* However, Tara suspects she's more like her mom than she lets on. Tara perceives she inherited her business acumen from her father, an astute Corporate Lawyer, but she also inherited her mother's aesthetics for architecture and interior design. Nyla postponed her career to raise her daughter, wanting to give Tara a healthy home environment and the relationship she'd had with her mom. Aware of her mother's decision to abandon a cherished career in Interior Design, she'd often ponder Nyla's success if she hadn't been born. Nevertheless, Nyla always upholds, *"Honey, you're my greatest piece of work, and nothing else compares."*

At the age of fourteen, Tara sensed her mom's desire to resume her career. She laughs at her futile attempts to prove her maturity. *"Mom, I'm old enough to take care of myself,"* hoping to persuade her to restart a stunted career. Finally, when Tara turned sixteen, Nyla took a position as an Assistant Interior Designer with a small design firm where she worked many years before leaving New York City.

Tara's parents loved and missed the South's simple lifestyle and longed to move back. There wasn't a single day she didn't hear about their beloved Charleston. She grew up eating her mother's Southern cooking of butter beans, fried green tomatoes, buttermilk biscuits, bread pudding, pecan, peach, and blackberry pies, and her favorite—blueberry cobbler. Just thinking about her mother's cooking makes her mouth water. *It's a wonder I didn't grow up porky,* she thinks while glancing in the mirror. Tara's relieved she'd not only inherit her dad's business acumen but also his long, lean figure.

Years later, at twenty-four, Tara made her first trip to South Carolina. A grandfather she'd never met and who had no interest in meeting her was her parent's impetus to move back to Charleston. Her father, James, inherited the entire McPherson estate. There was no inkling of her family's wealth and prestige in Charleston. Because of her grandfather's animosity toward his marriage, dad spoke of him rarely and usually in a disparaging tone.

One poignant morning, her father was hesitant to take a call from his dad. His semblance of defiance swiftly dispersed to uncertainty, reverence, and then tears. *"Hi, dad..."* His composed voice reverted to an unexpected boyishness. *"It's been a long time, but I'm happy to hear your voice."* His powerful figure softened as Tara hid, listening in the hallway. Swiftly, James' pained expression warmed to affection. Never had she heard her father's voice so light. Years of anger vanished with one phone call, a conversation so intimate, Tara felt uncomfortable watching.

That unexpected call settled her parent's decision to return to Charleston. She'd heard James say, *"Nyla, the old man must have forgiven me for running away from the family business and marrying you."*

Nyla had summed it up as aging. *"Sometimes age and mortality give one a better perception of what's important. James, he never stopped loving you. He just made peace with your decision."*

Tara hated her grandfather's callous disregard of their marriage and will never make peace with his racist thinking. She'd never possessed any interest in visiting the South, given the disdain for racial mixing and her family's ordeal. However, Tara instantly fell in love with Charleston's lifestyle and architecture. When she'd decided to join her parents a year later, her father's name and connections landed her a position with Alcott Home and Design (AHD), where she'd worked her way up to Managing Director.

Tara glances at her image in the mirror. *Something's missing ... Too much brown.* Her skin tone melds with the tan dress, creating one brown monotone silhouette. She glances at the jewelry box on top of the dresser, pondering seldom worn gems it contains. She's never been one to wear much jewelry, sometimes, perhaps simple earrings and a necklace. Inside the silver box, she stares at various rings, pendants, and crystal charms Nyla gave her over the years. The most recent addition to her collection is the blue Lapis-Lazuli stone necklace. She remembers Nyla telling her of the gems unique powers. *"The crystals will help develop your intuition."* Tara wore the gift once, and Nyla scoffs whenever she's without it—as if the stones hold some magical power.

The Cabochon Chakra pendant catches her attention. The different abilities of each stone and their vibrant colors always fascinate Tara. Her mother, the guru on crystals and stones, is never without some beautiful crystal necklace or ring. She remembers what Nyla told her about chakras and the seven points in the body circulating energy or prana. But she can't remember the unique abilities of each stone. One day, she thought she'd find time to learn more about crystals and gems, but with her demanding schedule, there's no time. Dangling the necklace mid-air, Tara admires each stone. *Well, if Nyla says they will clear my chakras I believe her.*

Just as Tara wraps the chakras necklace about her neck, the sacred-seven-stone pendant sparkles brightly in the jewelry box. *How could I forget the pendant?* The last time she wore it was in New York. The colors always soothed her. She'd memorized each gem—Amethyst, Quartz, Rutile, Goethite, Cacoxenite, Lepidocrocite, and Smokey Quartz Crystal. The pendant was a twenty-fourth birthday present from her father, but she'd immediately recognized Nyla's role. James would never buy her jewelry. Nyla would always affirm, *"The stones will help you become who you're meant to be,"* words of her all-knowing mother. *Has it worked yet?* She wonders.

She places the chakra pendant back in the box and replaces it with the sacred-seven pendant. The stones glow radiantly, catching the overhead light. She takes another look in the mirror, touches the stones, and wonders if they indeed hold some magical power. "I hope so. I'll need all the help I can get today." From the antique dresser's top drawer, she takes a striped indigo and ivory silk scarf, double wraps it around her neck with the pendant dangling at her heart.

Collecting her bags and turning off the foyer light, the mysterious glow appears again, shimmering like an illumined body of water at night. An unusual electrical aura surrounds the space, causing hairs along her arms to prickle. Unnerved, Tara swiftly leaves the foyer and exits the front door. From the porch of her townhouse on Gillon Street, strong harbor winds knock her off balance. Like an accordion, the newspaper whips back and forth at her feet. Picking up the paper, the front page unfolds to Marion and Anson Alcott's picture. Headlines herald:

Real Estate Donated For Medical Research Facility By Alcott Foundation

Hmmm, another philanthropic venture ... She's not surprised. The Alcotts are always involved in some major affair. Curiously, Tara glances back at the foyer. Her intuition screams, *something's wrong.* If she believed in the supernatural, she'd say the townhouse has a visitor this morning. Tara closes the door and hopes the glow is gone when she returns.

Lifting her head toward Charleston's Harbor, a sunrise painting splays spectrum of colors, signaling a glorious December day in the Palmetto State. Savoring the unusually warm breezy autumn day, she decides to walk to the office. Charleston's French Quarters stir with morning noise. But she relishes Charleston's morning calm, a drastic contrast to New York City's rush-hour. Cautiously, Tara passes private homes, wary of cars backing out of side alleys. From horse-drawn carriages, curious tourists spy on Charleston's antebellum architecture.

A few minutes later, on Cordes Street, Tara's heels sink into jagged cobblestones. "Darn, I've forgotten my flats," she mumbles. Finally, arriving at East Bay Street, she makes her way inside her favorite morning haunt—the Bakehouse Bakery Café. Coffee is Tara's foible. She can't start her day without the bitter aroma brushing her nose, filling her mouth, and jolting her senses awake. She's tried almost every coffeehouse in Charleston, finding the Bakehouse Bakery Café makes the perfect cup of Joe. She considers many customers she's referred to the coffee bar and muses; *I could be their marketer* as she walks through the door.

"Morning, Tara. Will it be your usual?" The barista asks in a thick Southern drawl.

Tara loves Southern hospitality. She's more at home here than she'd ever been in New York. "Hank, one of these days I'm going to surprise you and order a triple-mocha latte," she says with a smile.

"Well, you're one of our favorite customers. If you ask for something different, I'm going to do my best to please."

Playfully, and she feigns a Southern drawl with a wink. "Al' righty Hank, I'm sure you'll do your best."

A hearty laugh escapes Hank's mouth as he prepares the coffee. "Almost there, Tara, just work on your drawl a bit more, and for sure, no one will know you're a Northerner," he says with encouragement.

Tara prefers her own dialect, but now and then, resorts to her family's vernacular. "I'm working on it, Hank." She picks up the extra-large coffee and redistributes her bags to one shoulder. Looking down at her feet; she wishes she'd brought her flats. With a wobble, she prays her heels won't catch in the cobblestone, sending her careening flat on her face. *What an embarrassment that would be.* She frowns at the image of her body splayed on the ground—dress up exposing her underwear, and bags and coffee flying in the air. A chortle escapes her mouth. *Now that would be a comical sight.*

"Happy thoughts?" Hank asks.

Tara winks, trying to contain her laugh. "Always. Have a good day, Hank."

Outside the café, she pauses, takes a sip of coffee, and stares at the unassuming three-story structure across the street. McGrady's, a social gathering spot for prominent Charlestonians, has been around since 1778. She takes another sip, and cast a dubious peek at her high heels, wondering if she'll make it to work without a blunder. Relishing the glorious weather, she decides to chance it and continues with careful steps past Rainbow Row—colorful eighteenth-century townhouses painted brilliant pastels. In the distance, she spies AHD's headquarter and expects her staff is busier than usual. The sweepstake period began only five days ago, and the entries have been staggering.

Taking another sip of coffee; she stares at the Pink Lady several homes away. There's a sense of déjà vu as she grows closer to AHD's headquarters, an old colonial built in the late 1700s. She feels she'd seen AHD long before she moved to Charleston. *Perhaps in a dream,* she ponders. The first time she saw the home, she named it the Pink Lady. It felt as if she'd been saying that name all her life. The appellation prevailed. Soon, the entire staff dubbed headquarters the Pink Lady.

She wonders why the Alcotts, with their considerable real estate, donated this particular home. An Architectural Digest article explained the home was granted to AHD with hopes of furthering their passion for architecture. However, every article she's read about the Alcotts' affluence, failed to mention fortunes their ancestors made as slave-owners. As much as Tara wants to forget slavery, she's finding it difficult in a town steeped in history.

The uncanny familiarity lingers as she makes her way closer to AHD's gate. The home's immense Southern charm always causes her to stop and gape at its quintessential antebellum design. The three-level home, bound by a dark wrought iron gate, old-world gas lamps, Palmetto Palms, and tall Angel-Oak trees, sits at a distance from the street. Tara especially likes the oak trees in spring and summer—dripping with Spanish moss. Painted a pastel pink, the home's steep white columns and sweeping white piazzas give it an old-world charm. Suddenly, there's a tinge of recollection in her memory.

A vibrating sensation tickles her hip. Stopping a few steps from AHD's gate, she quickly retrieves the vibrating cell phone from her tote. "Tara McPherson."

Silence …

Glancing at the phone, there's no call or text. *That's odd.* Suddenly, the sun catches the phone's silver rim. She squints and quickly places the phone back in her bag.

Tom

After two weeks of sleepless nights and planning his trip to Charleston, sheer vengeance is the only force driving Tom. Parked a few blocks from AHD's headquarter, he waits anxiously for a glimpse of the Dream Team. Dressed in clothing he's worn two days, hair unkempt, face unshaven, he appears vagrant as he sits idly waiting.

Across the street from AHD, he watches vigilantly from a bench. Moments later, he notices a tall, slender woman walking slowly while sipping coffee. A striped silk scarf adorns her neck, and a knee-length, honey twill trench coat, displays long slender legs accentuated by brown suede pumps. She's every bit the cosmopolitan woman with a large tan leather tote hanging from her shoulder and a laptop bag in her hand. She's a balancing act in motion as she manages coffee in the other.

Discreetly, Tom snaps a picture of Tara approaching AHD's front gate. Just as he snaps the photo, she pauses across from him, pulling a cell phone from her tote. Sunlight catches the phone's silver rim, altering her quizzical frown to a flinch. Tom squints at the luminous light, pondering the sudden radiance circling Tara's body. With the same alacrity as the light, Tara replaces the phone in her bag.

Unwaveringly, Tom watches Tara open the large gate with difficulty, pick up her laptop case, close the gate with one foot, and saunter wobbly on the cobblestone pathway until AHD's front door closes behind her. He stands, crosses the street, and stops at the gate. Frozen, he hesitates before making his next move.

Inside ADH's foyer, there's a sense of past and future converging. Two massive white columns flank the foyer and open to cantilevered marble stairs lit by a cupola. A large floor medallion etched in stone and crystal inlays, sit at the stairwell's center, glistening from ceiling lights. When leaning over the stairs above, the geometric symbol lay prominently as if the home was designed around it. Tara always wonders if the circle enclosing a square enclosing a triangle holds any significance. Perhaps it holds special meaning for the Alcott family. However, it looks curiously cultish.

Pausing a second, Tara peers past the stair hall toward a reception area boasting historic and modern features. Decorated with plush oversized white sofas and two sleek black leather chairs at opposite ends, marble floors span the entire first floor, creating opulence. As she does most mornings, she cast a glance about the room; ensuring miniature architectural models are in their perspective places. Four flatscreen televisions hang on the wall, broadcasting various AHD TV programs.

Adjacent to the fireplace, a large, glossy, mahogany desk swallows a young, copper-haired woman busy manning the phones. Quickly, she answers one call after another. "AHD, how may I help you Sorry, ma'am, you'll need to visit our website to enter the sweepstake. You'll find the address and information online," Rebecca says in a soft, lilting drawl. "You're welcome, ma'am. Have a pleasant day. Good Morning AHD…" Besieged with incessant calls, Rebecca is oblivious to Tara's entrance.

Too anxious to speak with staff this morning, Tara rushes past Rebecca through the foyer and up the stairs on quiet staccato steps. One long black and white blur forms as she sweeps past former sweepstake homes showcased in dark frames. Similarly, at the top of the staircase, pictures of the Sweepstake Dream Team hang prominently, enclosed in antique mahogany frames.

Endearingly, Tara greets her colleague's pictures. "Good Morning Cody, Laura, and Leanne." Cody Darling, Producer and Home Planner, Laura Alcott, Senior Interior Designer, Leanne Davis, Website and Blog Coordinator and Tara McPherson, Managing Director of AHD Sweepstakes, hang etched in time. The photos, placed under the cupola above, glow an angelic halo. *Angelic,* she smirks, knowing the Alcotts arranged the pictures in that spot intentionally. Her photo is a reminder of a younger self eight years ago—eager and driven, and she wonders if she still has the same drive.

Stifling warmth and a strange glow greets Tara at her office door, presumably morning light streaming through the windows she thinks. Oddly, the luminosity resembles the glow in her townhouse. Setting the coffee and bags on the desk, she opens the door leading to the piazza. Outside, she takes off her trench, unravels her scarf, and breathes the warm, welcome breeze, while viewing waterways and Fort Sumter in the distance. In her periphery vision a man stands dazed, and then suddenly recovers from stillness. As he starts to open the gate, a bright light illuminates his face, causing him to flinch and glance upward. A frightening chill cascades down Tara's spine as her eyes lock with Tom's.

Tom

A few minutes pass before Tom shakes off dizziness that once again claimed his sight and balance. Finally, he finds the strength to open the gate unaware Tara stands above on the second-floor piazza. Just as he reaches for the iron knob, sunlight bounce off vibrant hues of Tara's sacred-seven pendant, catch his wedding band and blind his eyes. At that exact moment, Tom squints upward, Tara peers down. Surprised, he freezes, uncertain whether to enter or flee. Tara's odd expression and chilling stillness heighten his alarm.

Tara's gut knots. She ponders the man's startled expression and his quick retreat in the opposite direction. "Hmmm … Odd," she mumbles. Gripping chills presage something malevolent. The last time she had chills like this was on the night of Daniel Alcott's death. Hours before the accident, she felt something horrible was about to happen, sending chills through her body. And seconds before the fatal accident, a formidable chill ran down her spine.

All women on her mother's side of the family possess the gift of foresight. But she's reluctant to call it a gift when it feels like a curse. Tara's insight has always caused her unease, and she seldom shares her forebodings. Knowing something bad is to happen, but not knowing how, when, or where is frustrating. The dilemma is to alert someone and risk ridicule, or keep silent and endure guilt if they're harmed. A double-edged sword Tara has yet to reconcile.

Again, glancing at the front gate, she wonders why the man walked away so quickly. *Maybe it's nothing.* But in her mind, an alarm sounds. If I'd only warned Laura that fatal day, maybe Daniel would still be alive. *Is my intuition trying to warn me again?*

Inside the office, the phone rings. Tara rushes from the piazza, throws her trench coat and scarf on the chair, and grabs the phone quickly. "Good Morning, Tara McPherson."

"Good morning, Tara. How's lovely Charleston today?"

For several days, she's anticipated Cody's call. Worry melts with his mellifluous voice. "Cody, you won't believe the weather we're having; feels like summer." She glances at the caller I.D. and ponders the 530 area code. "Where are you calling from?"

"I'm in beautiful Lake Tahoe. We're getting ready to shoot the promo for the new Dream Home location. You're going to love it, Tara. Right now I'm looking at the Sierra Nevada Mountains. The view is gorgeous!"

"Lake Tahoe..."

"Actually, the location is Martis Camp, one of the many residential villages surrounding Lake Tahoe."

"Sounds fantastic; I can't wait to see the promo."

"Tara, it's going to be awesome! We decided to shoot the preview with the fresh snowfall."

"Cody, hurry up. Let's get this shot before we end up like the Donner Party," the cameraman yells in the background.

"Man, don't be so morbid," Cody shouts with a loud chuckle. "Tara, check your inbox. I emailed info and photos on the new site. Gotta go; we'll speak soon."

"Thanks, Cody. Hey, what's the Donner Party?"

Cody laughs again. "There's a bit of history there, Tara, but I'll give you the short version. Back in the late 1800s, a wagon train became lost in the Sierra Nevada Mountains, and the group resorted to cannibalism to survive."

"Yikes, sorry I asked. Okay, Cody, keep me updated, and good job with the new location. Have fun with the shoot."

Checking her email, a picture of Lake Tahoe in big bold words declares, "This is it, the next site for the 2016 Dream Home." Clicking the link, a small community of Martis Camp materializes—a community of luxury mountain homes surrounded by the Sierra Nevada Mountains and Lake Tahoe as the center of attraction. Tara squeals in delight. "Yes, another Mountain Home!" AHD's last Mountain Home in Vermont was one of their best projects, and their fans were hoping AHD would give them a similar architectural design. Tara responds to the email.

> *Cody,*
>
> *Congratulations on finding the site of our 2016 Dream Home; and, as usual, it's a beautiful place. Our fans will love the way Tahoe looks in the wintertime. Have*

you met with the developers and builders yet? Let me
know when you find the lot selection and the builder's
management contract. Hopefully, we can get the pre-
liminary budget signed and approved. Let's make this
a seamless process. Keep me posted Cody.

TM

"Yahoo! Here we go again," Tara yelps quietly. Her mind is already spinning with ideas. Tara reaches over to make another phone call, but the phone rings in her hand. Recognizing the number, she swiftly answers, "Mom, you're calling early."

"Honey, I was just thinking about you and thought I'd give you a call ... Anything happening this morning?"

Tara's always possessed an uncanny ability to sense her mother's emotions. At this instant, she detects a little concern in Nyla's voice. "No, business as usual ... I just got off the phone with Cody. He's found the new location for next year's Dream Home in Lake Tahoe. I'm so relieved. Now I can start the building process."

"Honey, you'll be fine. You stress about this every year, and the project always turns out beautiful."

"I know, but the building process can be so tricky. You realize it takes anywhere from six to eight months just to get contracts signed, and preliminary budget approved, the architect and home engineer's documents—"

"There you go again, Tara," Nyla interjects, "stop stressing. So, it's definitely Lake Tahoe this year?"

"I just got the news, mom."

"I've never liked the place much myself. It gives me the chills."

"Why? It's such a beautiful area of the country?"

"I wish I could explain, but it's just one of those places I dread."

"Well, wait until you see the beautiful home we build, maybe you'll change your mind."

"Tara, has your intuition been telling you anything this morning?"

"That's a strange question. Should I be feeling something?" Noticing the long pause, Tara wonders why Nyla's concerned with her intuition. She never mentions it unless something's wrong. "Mom?"

"Honey, just be aware of your surroundings today. Heed any feelings or intuitions you may have, okay?"

"I usually do."

"Of course, but today, just be more alert, sweetie. I have to go, but I'll call you this evening."

"Okay, bye, mom."

Why didn't I tell her about the strange man at the gate *and the cascading chills?* Tara realizes every time she's had a major intuitive warning, her mother somehow knows as if they're connected spiritually. Well, after Daniel Alcott's accident, I'm heeding my intuition.

"Okay, Tara, get to work," she mumbles. Taking a sip of coffee, her face contorts in disgust as she spits oily, tepid dregs back into the cup. Suddenly hot from vents spewing heat, she grabs a folder and fans her face and neck. With the warm weather, she's surprised the heat is still on.

Staring at the Lake Tahoe picture, she mulls over the 2015 fiasco, hoping project 2016 will be problem free. Just as she remembers the previous year's setbacks, her left eyelid flutters. *Hmmm … Does a twitch in the left eye mean bad luck, or is it just an old wives tale.* She hopes the twitch's inauspicious timing is mere coincidence, not bad luck. Dispelling worries, she tries to concentrate on the new Dream Home site, but her mind drifts again. *How'd I managed so many years without burnout?* Overseeing the sweepstake project and its diverse group of talent isn't easy. It can't be just my *keen sense of business. Maybe it's some other God-given talent? Perhaps my intuition is stronger than I believe.*

Fanning her face, she glances around at the eerie glow. The room has never appeared so unreal. For better words, the office feels ghostly. Another chill fills her spine, and a sudden thought scratches her consciousness. She clicks an icon on her desktop. On the screen, a list of esteemed Tahoe architects appears and a particular name tugs her gut. Inadvertently, she highlights an architect named Michael Anders and types a brief note to Cody.

> *Cody,*
>
> *See the attachment. These are a few architects you might consider in the area. Please let me know the outcome. I'm excited about your choice. I'll contact Laura and tell her about the new site. Cody, good job! Let's get this ball rolling!*
>
> *TM*

Momentarily tranced, Tara clicks send and stares at the screen. With the room's eeriness and the prompt decision to email the architect list, unease fills her mind. *Was it my intuition again, or did something else trigger my actions? Get a grip, Tara. What else can it possibly be?*

With a shoulder shrug and head roll, she tries to dispel growing worries. But a sudden thought enters her mind. *Today makes thirteen years—the thirteenth Dream Home sweepstake. Thirteen … Another omen* she wonders … *First, the eye twitch, and now the dreaded number thirteen.* She's never liked that number but shirks the thought and superstitious beliefs. As much as she wants to stifle ominous warnings, she can't, not after Nyla's phone call.

Before Nyla rang, Tara was about to call Laura Alcott, AHD's Senior Interior Designer, with news of Lake Tahoe, but instead, she sends an email. In the subject line, Tara types in large caps, LAKE TAHOE. With worries of finding a new Dream Home site behind her, tension starts to fade. But with the room's eeriness and the strange man at the front gate, a new concern invades her mind.

Chapter 2

Laura

December 15, 2014, Alcott Estate

The tap of fingernails on laptop keys resound throughout the sizable master suite, as Laura Alcott delete tons of junk email accumulated while on assignment in Maine. Annoyed, she considers deleting all, but fears she'll erase important messages. Sitting with her laptop in the four-poster bed, surrounded by soft pillows and textures, Laura wants nothing more than to relax in the comfort of her space. However, disassociating emotions from her last assignment, the beautiful interior design for the 2015 sweepstake home, is challenging.

After months of watching her designs come to fruition, the beautiful Maine home was hard to abandon. And as usual, like every assignment she's completed, separation anxiety will subside when a lucky sweepstake winner claims the new home. Laura diverts her yearnings back to reality. *The reality of a widow,* she thinks while rubbing the empty space that once cushioned her husband. Quickly, she focuses on her present life.

Home for two weeks, she ponders the approaching Christmas holiday and her plans for Christmas Eve with the girls. Sammie, her Bichon Frise, sitting at the bottom of the bed glares expectantly with sporadic barks at the laptop. Laura recognizes that face. Sammie knows the laptop means less attention for him. "Just a minute Sammie, I'm almost done," she placates and brushes her well-manicured toes against his white fur.

Appeased for a moment, Sammie stops barking and lowers his head on her ankle. With the sullen expression, a stab of guilt invades Laura's mind. *Look at those sad eyes.* She ponders the many months away from him and can't bear ignoring him any further. Resolute, she closes the laptop. "This can wait." With the click of the latch, Sammie's head pops up with an inquisitive stare. "Come on Sammie, let's get some breakfast."

Jumping off the bed, Sammie follows Laura to the staircase, hopping and pausing between leaps. Laura turns around with a chuckle and scoops him up, making her way down the long, winding staircase. At the stairwell, crystal inlays on the large floor medallion twinkle, catching light from the chandelier. Respecting the Alcott family crest, she veers around the colophon as she always has. Something about the symbol is so sacred. She's noticed over the years every home owned by the Alcotts contains this medallion—even the Sweepstake Dream Homes.

"*It's a family thing,*" her husband Daniel had revealed their first night in the home. She remembers his warm, engaging voice as he explained in detail. "*The symbol represents a harmonious balance between heaven and earth.*" Circling the outline, he'd deferentially stated, "*The three symbols—circle, square, and triangle—together represent the persistent effort required to achieve a supreme goal.*"

This always fascinated Laura. Over the years, she'd learned the espoused symbol belongs to the Gowan women, her ancestors. Curious about the medallion, she'd researched and studied the importance of the combined symbols. The circle represents a sacred space of unity, wholeness, and female power. The square symbolizes a quest to find one's true path in the world. And the triangle's three points signifies the past, present, future—mind, body, and soul, and the process of growth, and attainment of spiritual transformation.

As she makes her way past the stairwell, the home's sweltering heat sends her veering toward the thermostat. She lowers the temperature then circles to the back door of the veranda—letting in the warm breeze off Charleston's Harbor. A strong gust rushes through the door, brushes her face, and ruffles Sammie's fur. He squirms and leaps from her arms, scampering with delight onto the veranda. For an instant, Laura glimpses the multicolored skyline inspiring sensations of a new day and new possibilities. She watches Sammie scamper to the backyard, running around trying to catch the breeze. *If only life were as simple as that.*

Down the hallway, at the main entrance, Laura hears a male voice say, "Thank you."

Jennie, the maid, responds, "Have a good day."

A few seconds later, gravel crunches under a vehicle moving down the private road. Jennie pauses at the kitchen, unsure whether to stop or continue down the hallway. "Good Morning, Mrs. Alcott," she says in a high-pitched voice, which sounded like a question rather than a greeting.

"Good morning, Jennie. Who was at the door?"

"Ma'am, Rob from Janelle Launderette made his usual weekly pickup."

"Oh, Jennie, that's right. Time is going so fast I can't keep up with the days," Laura says with a smile. Laura loves the sound of maids in the home, even though they work only half a day. However short, Laura feels more secure hearing someone else in the vast estate.

Laura senses Jennie still standing behind her and pictures her eyes transfixed in a daze. She feels Jennie's unease and hears her thoughts of not wanting to intrude on her privacy.

Why can't the girl learn to relax?

Laura hired Jennie because she adores her innocence and admires her sincerity. Her youthful insecurities remind Laura of her own at twenty. She realizes motherly instincts overshadows her role as employer, but she can't help feeling protective of Jennie. Again, Jennie's queries fill Laura's mind.

Her face is so flawless and fresh in the morning. She couldn't possibly be a natural strawberry blonde. All the Gowan women are brunettes. Well, she's nothing like the wealthy women I've worked for, so humble and sweet. Is she truly clairvoyant?

Laura considers replying, but instead, she turns, interrupting her reverie. "Jennie, I'm so glad to have you here. You've been invaluable the last two years. I hope you realize that. I don't know what I'd do without your help."

Realizing she's been gawking, Jennie states bashfully, "Thank you, ma'am," and rushes down the hallway.

Tickled by Jennie's obvious embarrassment, a grin rushes across Laura's face. She's caught her staring on several occasions and understands Jennie's interest in the Alcott family and the Gowan gift. It always makes her laugh knowing her Gowan bloodline causes such curiosity in the maids. Their inquisitiveness doesn't bother her. On the contrary, she tries to ease their concerns. She refuses to be the boring, privileged-socialite cliché she's met over the years—only concerned with money and prestige. Born of a different cloth—the Gowan blood—she never tolerates the spoiled, pampered women she's seen around Charleston.

However, piqued by Jennie's musings, Laura glances across the hallway at her reflection in the mirror—not a strand of hair out of place. At forty-five, Laura is grateful the wrinkles she's seen on women of her persuasion and age have yet to appear. With not a drop of makeup, her skin is flawless. She throws herself a wink, pushes hair behind her ears, and studies her face from side-to-side. "Hmmm, you're a perfect Southern Belle," she mumbles, then chides her vanity with a shake of her head.

Southern Belle, yes indeed, she affirmed. Laura loves her Southern roots and Charleston's lifestyle. Although well-traveled, she can't imagine living anywhere else. But Laura always ponders the ease in which she acquired her wealth. Born of modest financial means, she married into one of Charleston's wealthiest families. Unexpectedly, affluence found her.

Laura wanders out of the kitchen through a separate hall leading to the pantry. She recalls the disorientation she'd felt the first day in the Alcott estate. The hallways are so tricky and disjointed; one wrong turn can lead to a separate wing of the home or to another hallway leading to other corridors. In the long, well-stocked pantry, she browses rows of bagged, bottled, boxed, and can goods. Laura's mind roams to the day she'd become lost in the corridors, blushing at embarrassment she'd felt venturing from one hallway to the next in search of the kitchen. All the while, she'd called out to Daniel, as a clue to her whereabouts. How stupid she'd felt when he'd rescued her from the maze. Daniel appeared red-faced and apologetic for laughing at her confusion.

Laura married the man of her dreams and raised her beautiful daughter Callie in this home. Now, twenty-three years later, she can't believe this all belongs to her. She grabs a box of cereal from the pantry and glances at the sharp turn made years ago. The enduring memory reminds her of what she's lost. She peers at her bare feet taking, familiar, sharp steps into the kitchen. Ghostly sounds greet her from the past—metallic rattle of pots and pans, utensils clanking on plates, and happy chatter of Daniel and Callie enjoying countless homemade meals. The many hours spent with her family around the kitchen island, are now long gone. Their favorite spot, the beautiful kitchen, is desolate without them. At the island, she pauses wistfully. The humming stainless steel refrigerator and gurgling coffee pot never sounded as loud as they do now. Laura's heart sinks, and she aches a little more.

Obliviously, Laura pours cereal into the bowl, while recalling the first time she'd met Daniel. Till this day, she wonders why the Alcotts hired her fresh out of school. *Of all the established Interior Designers in Charleston, why had they chosen me?* She couldn't believe her first commissioned assignment was with Daniel Alcott—a prominent architect. She recalls the nervousness she'd felt whenever their eyes met. Instantly, she'd sensed his attraction. All his thoughts and emotions flooded her mind and body. His steamy sentiments had caused her to blush and made concentration incredibly difficult. One day, she'd said flippantly, *"Now how do you expect me to get any work done with all your gawking?"* Daniel, caught off-guard, stammered inaudibly and walked away. She'd laughed when he turned like a pup with his tail between his legs. She'd made the mighty Daniel Alcott stammer.

Daniel believed Laura's nervousness stemmed from efforts to impress him with her designs. But he'd failed to realize it was both his prominence and strong attraction that aroused her, although she hadn't let on. Laura played ignorant of his attraction and feigned the eager designer, merely looking for approval. A year after they married, he'd confessed, *"Laura, I cared less about the interior design. I was so captivated by your charm, you could have painted the house black, and I wouldn't have objected."* Of course, Laura already knew. A month after completing the assignment, Daniel's family secured her a position at AHD. Several years later, they granted one of their prime real estates as headquarters.

A whipping breeze rushes through the French doors. The glass panes vibrate under its strength, reminding Laura of nature's cruelty. She closes her eyes, remembering the terrifying hurricane two years ago when Daniel tried to make it home. "So stupid of you, Daniel," falls off her tongue. She's still angry with his hapless decision but feels partially responsible for his actions that fatal day. She's recounted their brief conversation many times, wishing she'd been more forceful and fearless of being alone during the storm.

"Laura, don't worry; you're safe. I'll be home shortly."

Laura remembers listening to the weather report as she'd spoken with Daniel on the phone. *"Daniel, the weather channel says the hurricane won't hit land for a while, but I still believe you shouldn't drive home."*

"I'll be al'right, honey. I've driven in storms worse than this. Besides, the drive is only thirty minutes from the office."

"Daniel, are you sure—"

"Laura, stop worrying," he'd retorted, unwilling to listen to her concerns. *"I'll see you soon. Batten down the hatches for me, darling."*

She'd perceived his doubt but hadn't stopped him. If only I could go back in time and change his actions. *Maybe he wouldn't have gotten in the car if I'd been more persistent. He might still be alive.*

Laura stares beyond the great oak and palmetto trees, toward the boathouse, remembering the storm like it happened yesterday. Coastal winds lashed about the home and century-old oak trees bowed under its pressure, bumping against the walls. The boat heaved with choppy waters and tidal winds, banging a dull drum on the boathouse. Alone in the home, she'd listened to eerie winds wail like human voices through crevices. Frighten from the hurricane's force, she'd curled beneath the flannel throw praying Daniel would make it home. For an eternity, she'd sat by the fireplace, watching flames cast shifting shadows along the walls, and trying to dispel ominous warnings.

Seconds and minutes crept by as she'd listened for crunching gravel and watched for shining headlights on the private road. With every noise, she'd rush to the window, staring at the driveway. A vestige of fear, an instant pain, slowing breath, and then blackness gripped her senses. She'd felt the impact of the car tumbling off the road and the tree as it squashed the car, killing Daniel instantly. The moment his life slipped away, she'd sensed his last breath and lay motionless, hoping the storm would take her with him. Twenty-one years of a blissful marriage cut short by a hurricane.

Laura closes her eyes and whispers into the air, "Daniel, I can't believe it's been two years without you," as if he were in the room.

Wistfully, Laura swirls the spoon around the cereal bowl. Leaning over the kitchen island, she sighs and thrusts thoughts of Daniel from her mind. Through the massive dining room windows, beyond the boat dock, and across Charleston's Harbor, she fixes her gaze on the horizon. A horizontal shade lifts with sunrise, revealing Charleston's Battery Promenade and historic homes glistening along the waterfront. In the distance, long spiraling steeples of the Holy City—St. Matthews and St. Michaels—dot the skyline, protecting the city from harm. With a piercing squint, she detects the Pink Lady shimmering among historic homes.

Laura loves this view of Charleston and begins most mornings staring at the harbor. She recalls the moment Daniel blindfolded, guided, and positioned her in front of the massive windows. When he'd removed the blindfolds, Laura gasped at the treasure bestowed her. Instantly, she fell in love with the home and gorgeous views beyond.

On their wedding day, Marion and Anson Alcott gave Daniel the keys to their sprawling estate as a marriage gift. Laura still hears Marion's words and sensed she'd known of her and Daniel's special bond long before they'd met. Laura recalls her surprise when Marion reached skillfully in her bag and placed the keys in Daniel's hand. Laura had heard the words in Marion's mind before they escaped her lips.

"Fill this house with warmth and magic."

Shocked by the Alcott's generosity, she'd stood frozen, mouth agape, and a stupid expression of astonishment on her face. Twenty-three years later, she's still living in this massive twenty-thousand square feet palatial home, situated on fifteen acres with one-hundred-eighty-degree waterway views of downtown Charleston. *How will I manage here alone?* With thirty rooms, four separate wings, plus the carriage house, Laura realizes the house is too immense for just her and Sammie. She's considered selling many times. However, thoughts of Daniel and his love for the home prevent her from doing so. She swears Daniel's presence is still in the house. *How can she possibly sell it?* Their history is here. The thought of selling is unbearable. Besides, Callie gets so obstinate whenever she mentions putting the house on the market.

She still hears Callie's adamant cry several weeks ago when she'd broached the topic. *"No, no, no mom! You can't. This is our heritage. Dad wouldn't approve of complete strangers living here."*

Although Callie is grown with a small place of her own near the University, regularly, she runs back home, finding security and comfort in the place she grew up. The Alcott estate will always be their heart which makes selling it excruciating.

Sammie's sharp bark startles Laura from her reverie. She's surprised he's inside so soon. He jumps up and down on her leg and circles his bowl. "You hungry, darling?" Laura opens the cabinet and pulls out a can of his favorite food. "There you go, boy," she muttered, filling his bowl.

Watching Sammie eat, she's surprised he's grown so fast. He was just a pup when she left for her last assignment. *Marion fed you well while I was gone,* she thought. Laura recalls Christmas a year ago when Callie pulled a tiny, white puppy out of her bag. *"Mom, you need company in this home. I thought about getting you a bigger dog, but I know you've always loved this breed."* Laura fell in love with Sammie immediately. She dreads the thought of leaving him for her next assignment, wishing it possible to bring him along. Thank goodness for Marion Alcott's love of animals. She welcomes Sammie until she returns.

Down the hallway, Laura hears Jennie humming a tune. The washer and dryers swirl and bang. White noise drones from the vacuum cleaner in another wing. The cacophony of housecleaning noise is disturbing. Collecting her coffee from the granite island, she heads to the foyer, collects the morning paper Jennie left on the sideboard and escapes to her office in the old guest wing at the far end of the home. At a distance from the rest of the house, it seems separate, its own contained space.

Down the long hallway, Laura strolls barefoot in her silky blue pajamas. At the end of the hall, a light glows brightly through the window. She stares admiringly; failing to realize the sun never shines through windows at the northern end of the home. Oblivious, and lost in thoughts of Daniel, she ignores this fact. Down the stairs to the ground level, she enters a long, narrow corridor of windows and stone-tiled floors. Five large hanging glass cloche pendants light the area. Windows run along the entire corridor, providing views of the swimming pool, and the guesthouse. Laura loves the way natural light floods the hallway during the daytime, however, at night the passage is frightening. She laughs at childish thoughts of ghost and ghouls lurking in the dark—fears embedded from countless horror movies watched as a child. At night, the corridor brings back those images as darkness turns the interior view inside out. She believes some ungodly figure glares from the opposite side of continuous glass panels. Most nights, she rushes through the corridor to her office.

Arriving at two massive barn doors, she slides them open to a large white room with a sparkling chandelier and floor to ceiling windows running corner to corner. The room's white walls and furnishings accented with blue, red, and tan stimulates her creative mind. Standing at the threshold, she stares beyond French doors framing oak trees, lush gardens, and Charleston's waterways. The room appears part of the outdoors.

Pensively, Laura glides to the sitting area across from her desk and flops onto the white sofa adjacent to the fireplace. Calm tinged with sadness invades her mind, but the feeling is fleeting. Before long, restless and bored, she'll deliberate how to fill her vacation days—unable to bear sitting around idly twiddling her fingers. She places the coffee cup and newspaper on the large oak coffee table and rests her eyes on the blue velvet chair directly across from her. Blue velvet, a vestige of her childhood, always soothes her. She remembers the blue velvet throw she'd cuddled as a child. The blanket's protective warmth forever calmed her anxious mind.

Over the fireplace, the painting reminds her of another incredible day with Daniel. It seems only yesterday she'd dragged him to a yard sale, where they'd found an abstract painting lying among various artworks. The moment she'd noticed the enigmatic painting, she'd visualized it hanging on the walls of her office. Daniel thought the painting odd but approved when he saw the colors in the white room. *You have a good eye, Laura. I wouldn't have chosen this painting for your office, but it works,* she hears Daniel say in a rich, honey-laced voice she loved.

Across the room, Laura stares at the lengthy white seesaw desk and the blue velvet wing-back chair. She smiles at the framed picture of Daniel and Callie shadowed by red and white stripes of Morris Island Lighthouse, sparkling in the background. *That was a perfect day.*

With the coffee cup suspended to her lips, she steps toward her desk. At the barn doors, an apparition of Daniel bringing her coffee appears, turns, and then fades through the entrance. Memories of him flood the room—a shadow of him on the couch, standing at the fireplace, everywhere watching over her. Finally, she takes a delayed coffee sip and glances at Dream Home 2015 sketches lying cluttered on her desk. She's not ready to file them away just yet and lingers momentarily on another accomplishment.

She stacks them neatly, and then thoughts of Daniel, toasting champagne to the 2012 Sweepstake Dream Home, enter her mind. *"To another successful project and my beautiful wife,"* rings in Laura's ears. A much-needed tear escapes, falling to the corner of her mouth. *Does this get any easier?* "Okay, Laura, get a grip."

Laura grabs the Post and Courier; removes the rubber band and unfolds the newspaper with an instant sigh of admiration. *The Alcott Foundation made the front page again and* "Another donation," she mumbles. Remembering Daniel's fondness for his parents, she smiles at the picture of Anson and Marion Alcott sitting in the backyard of their massive estate in downtown Charleston. Casually dressed in a navy dress, Marion sits in a lounge chair next to Anson wearing similar colors as if they'd coordinated their attire. Wrinkles in both their faces set deeper than she remembers, but she still sees features of their younger years. They will never age in her eyes. She wonders if Daniel would have aged the same as his father at seventy-five. *Yes, he would have*, she believes. Daniel was the spitting image of his father—tall, dark, and handsome. Everyone in Charleston recognizes the Alcott men's signature strong jaw, dark brown hair, and sky-blue eyes. They're unmistakable.

The newspaper article speaks of the Alcott's wealth and yet another philanthropic gift of land for a new medical research facility. *Callie will appreciate their donation.* Her daughter's passion for medical research is tantamount to her love for her family. Laura never doubted her calling as a doctor. Now, after many years of watching her passion bloom, Laura can't believe her baby is a first-year medical student. *Daniel would be so proud.* Laura stares at the pile of sketches again. "Well, it's time to put away all things old." *But I will never discard memories of Daniel.*

Opening the middle drawer of her desk, files spanning the last eleven years of Dream Homes greet her. She places sketches of the twelfth Dream Home in a new folder and inadvertently glimpses the Vermont Dream Home file. An unfamiliar pang nips at her senses. She runs her hands over the folders. "Ow!" escapes her lips. Blood oozes from her finger, smearing the folder a bright sanguine. "Darn," she murmurs while searching for the culprit. A corkscrew staple sticks out of the folder. She examines her finger, wondering how such a small cut can be so painful and bloody. The sight of blood makes her queasy. She reaches for a tissue, wraps it gently, and watches the white tissue saturate a ruby red.

Irritably, eying the spiky staple, she pulls the Vermont folder from the drawer. Just as she does, the chandelier grows brighter, as if about to explode—casting an eerie glow around the room. The light bounces off the French doors, then onto the photo. For an instant, she thought she'd seen a figure. She swings her head toward the backyard, but nothing's there.

The chandelier grows dimmer then lighter. Unease settles in Laura's mind, overshadowing temporary pain. The bloody tissue falls to the floor, releasing a bullseye drop of blood on the Vermont home photo. A sudden tingle runs across her hand. A chill invades her spine. She takes another tissue and wipes the blood from the picture, leaving a smear of brown. She peers at the chandelier and deliberates its sudden brightness. With an immense fear of electrical fires, she wonders if she should have the wiring checked. Once more, she examines the Vermont file and then pushes it aside. Disquiet invades her mind.

Tom

Tom peers at his car hidden on the roadside, hoping no one notices specks of red through the bushes. Slumping low between sculpted shrubbery and a large oak tree, he hides and waits near

Alcott Estate's massive gate. He's perturbed by Tara's appearance at AHD. His attempt to leave packages for the team foiled. But more so, he's bothered by her odd glare. *Was it a glare of recognition?*

If she hadn't been on the piazza, his trip would be going as planned. At first, the idea of leaving packages with the receptionist seemed simple, but now he realizes it was a stupid move. He couldn't possibly go back to AHD. It's much too risky. His only choice is to leave packages inside the Dream Team's homes.

He studies the gate's height, certain there's no way to climb it. Outside the entrance, a big oak tree with broad branches, too high to climb will serve no purpose. On the other side, another large oak tree teases him with its long, oddly curved branches sitting closer to the ground. And he wishes the tree was on the opposite side. The only way in, he determines, is through the gate—to wait for a car to enter and rush through unnoticed. He studies the area carefully. The estate is in a secluded area—miles from the nearest home; no one will see him enter or leave the premises.

Waiting patiently, he realizes it could be a while before a vehicle enters or exits. Seeking the perfect angle, he wriggles awkwardly between tall, sculpted shrubs. The sound of crunching gravel signals an approaching vehicle. He turns swiftly, colliding with pointed limbs. Grimacing, he pushes the bush aside.

"Perfect timing," he mumbles, noticing the brown van approaching down the private road. Tom prepares to move. Stealthily, on hands and knees, he inches closer to the gate, ready to crawl through when the vehicle passes. Janelle's Launderette Service is illustrated in big bold letters on the side of the van. *They must have dropped off or picked up laundry at the estate, which means someone's home.* The van comes to a complete stop, waiting for the slow-moving gate to open. Tom moves behind the wide oak tree, certain the driver can't see him. Finally, the van moves forward inch by inch as the gate opens slower than flower petals unfolding in sunlight. Before moving on the main road, the driver looks left then turns right, driving away from the estate.

In disbelief, Tom stares at the plodding gate, realizing he can walk right through before it closes. But before he does, he checks for cameras. "Well, that's unusual," he mumbles, amazed the Alcott's would forgo surveillance around such a wealthy estate. "Big mistake," he mumbles with a chortle. With haste, Tom examines his surroundings and cautiously saunters through the gate. Pondering the home's distance, he warily makes his way along the private tree-lined road, edging toward his destination.

At the front of the home, the private road ends in a circular pattern. Without trees or shrubbery to hide, he heads toward a brick path at the side of the home. A salty breeze greets him as he makes his way along the trail. Carved, granite stones lead to a boathouse on the waterfront, forking left behind the home toward a garden and a pond.

Choosing the left fork toward the backyard, he spies for interior access, when a reflection jolts an alarming step backward. Slowly, he peers around the corner through a facade of French doors. At the center of the room, Laura pulls a folder from her desk at the exact moment the chandelier flickers, casting light in his direction. Blinded, Tom squints at a familiar glow, the same radiance that had circled Tara McPherson at AHD's gate. Laura glances in his direction and Tom jumps back. Warily, he waits a few seconds and then peeps around the corner again.

He ponders Laura's odd expression as she stares at a folder. She fumbles for a tissue and then wipes something reddish from the file. Bothered by the odd glow surrounding her body, he heads to the west end of the home. On the veranda above, sits an open door. With ease, Tom enters a low lying gate near the back porch, wanders up patio stairs toward the kitchen entrance, and listens for the right moment to enter. All the while, he ponders the white light that had circled both Laura and Tara.

As she waits for the MAC to power on, Laura notices Sammie has found her in her favorite spot and moves to his usual spot beside her desk. He jumps onto a pillow three times his size, turns in several circles, lies in a ball, and settles his gaze on Laura. Clicking the envelope icon on her desktop, an email from Tara exclaims in large-capped letters, LAKE TAHOE!

"Lake Tahoe," Laura murmurs, recalling ski vacations with Daniel in the region and luxurious mansions surrounding the Sierra Nevada Mountains. She already knows the Dream Home architecture will be Mountain style and visualizes an interior design to complement the new Tahoe home. "Laura, what are you doing? You're on vacation. Stop it now," she chides and turns off the computer. She looks down at Sammie's big-eyed stare. "Not today, Sammie, we're going for a walk."

The consummate Southern Belle, Laura wouldn't be caught dead without her makeup—even if she's only going for a stroll along the waterfront. Her hair and face must always be sheer perfection. Callie would laugh at her as usual, believing her mom looks beautiful without makeup. Raised in the ways of the old south, Laura always upholds her physical appearance, even in the privacy of her own home. "There's no telling when a guest will drop by," she would tell her daughter. Laura often wonders how Callie blossomed from a tomboy into a beautiful young woman who's passionate about medicine, not fashion and makeup. Raising her eyebrows, she wonders *how that happened.*

Preparing for Sammy's morning walk, Laura's forgotten the open door on the veranda. While she dresses in the east wing, Tom waits near the kitchen, listening for Laura's exit from the home. When he's certain she's gone, he enters quietly.

Chapter 3

Leanne

December 15, 2014, AHD Headquarters

With a piercing squint, Leanne increases the font from one-hundred to one-hundred-twenty percent, trying to discern whether the letter is an E or an R. At the age of thirty-nine, Leanne refuses to believe her perfect twenty-twenty vision is failing. For months, she's been in denial, dreading the approaching age her mom started wearing eyeglasses. Lying to herself, she attributes dwindling vision to countless hours of staring at the computer and iPad. *It's just eyestrain* she'd tell friends, refusing to listen when they suggested reading glasses. *Oh, you're so stubborn, Leanne.* However, she realizes she's only delaying the obvious and her eyes are getting worse.

On the Internet, Leanne deliberates designer readers but hates the idea of looking like her colleagues—donning fashionable glasses she never thought stylish, just aging. She remembers her mom's unsightly black-rimmed spectacles despoiling her beauty at forty. And now, she nearing that age she never believed would arrive so fast. She sneers at the colorful assortment on the website. "Polka dots … on the face … now that's ridiculous."

The phone rings and she's happy to relinquish that thought. Quickly, she answers, "Leanne Davis." Adam's husky voice evokes his morning image—sleepy-eyed, bed hair, new facial hair growth outlining his jaw, and his topless, sculpted abdomen exposed like some sexy calendar photo. Noticing the time, she realizes he's just starting his day. She recalls the previous night's heated conversation, and instantly knows why he's calling. Although happy to hear his voice, she's not ready to give him the answer he seeks.

"Hey, babe, can I call you later? It's crazy here today," she says, scrunching her face with the lie. She hates lying to Adam, but she's not ready for this particular conversation. "Let's talk later, okay." But she won't have the answer he seeks, not tonight—maybe never.

Leanne swirls her chair around and deliberates her office of eight years. Lately, an inexplicable restlessness and persistent dialogue about her existence inflict her mind. She never wanted a traditional life; just a successful career. Now she wonders if she's made the right choices. Her nine-year romance with Adam is stronger than ever, but he longs for more commitment. Soon, she will have to make a decision or lose him. Her jaded belief about marriage, a product of her mom and dad's tempestuous nuptials, leaves her fearing matrimony. *Our relationship is so strong and passionate. Why should we change it? Things are fine the way they are.*

Adam is the first man she's allowed in her life. No one needs to assure her he's the right one. She understands him better than he understands himself. Long before an introduction, she'd seen Adam's past. Years ago, the first day of class, she'd sensed his presence behind her. Seconds after the professor called her name; she'd retrogressed and saw Adam scribbling her name in his notebook. There was no need to turn around. She'd felt his gaze on her back. One day, deliberately, she'd turned around, finding his tantalizing brown eyes smiling back. Without a blink, he'd held her gaze. She'd blushed and looked away certain she was aroused and annoyed at once. From that point on, a staring match ensued for days until they grew tired of the game.

She'd catch Adam's eyes across a room. Their eyes would lock until something or someone interrupted. Every feature of Adam's face was memorized during those stares. Dissecting each side, she'd ponder who he favored most—his mom or dad. Thick eyelashes feather his almond-shaped eyes, which always seem to squint. What she'd once thought deliberate, she'd realized was a characteristic, come-hither stare. She'd move to his lip's upward curve—a constant smile without trying. Short, spiky sandy brown hair revealed a slight endearing ear protrusion. The contour of his face she couldn't discern—not quite oval or heart but somewhere in between. She'd assumed his boyish looks will never fade and serve him well as he ages.

One day in class, Adam sat beside her, leaned over, and whispered, *"Aren't you tired of this?"* The moment she'd heard his voice, she'd lost the game, but she hadn't relented so easily, and neither had Adam, who continued to pursue her for several days around the university campus. She'd feared once he discovered her gift, he'd flee in fear. To Adam, Leanne was a mystery and perhaps the source of his attraction.

She'd grown tired of Adam's relentless chase and finally surrendered. He'd become her best friend, and months later, although determined to maintain a platonic relationship, he'd become her lover. Now, she wonders why she'd pushed him away so long. Years later, he'd uproot his life in Chicago and move with her to Charleston. She's often wondered if she'd put her selfish needs before his. She smiles, remembering the night she told him about his childhood—memories no one could possibly know but him. She'd detected Adam's initial unease, which waned with time. She was surprised at how easily he accepted her gift and will never forget his casual response. *"Well, I guess I'm an open book. It will be impossible keeping a secret from you*

... You realize that right? How will I ever surprise you?" He'd joked. But with those words, she'd known he'd recognized the dilemma. That night, Leanne handed him a Moldavite crystal and insisted, *"If you ever want to keep me out of your head just wear this."* She realizes he seldom does.

Leanne swivels her chair around. Her feline green eyes dilate a deeper emerald—capturing fleeting shadows in the corner. Since her first day at AHD, she's seen apparitions throughout the office. In such a historic home, she's bound to encounter past lives. She recalls her first experience inside an old Tudor home in Oaks Park Community, where she'd thought she'd seen a ghost. The moment she'd stepped from her mother's car, the home alarmed her. She'd held tight to her mother's arm, never leaving her side. Inside, an overwhelming energy tugged at her senses. When her friend summoned her to play, she'd resisted with a frown, but her mother coaxed, *"Leanne, stop being silly; go play with your friend,"* and pushed her away.

With trepidation, she'd moved toward strange vibes on the upper floor, while her friend stared curiously at her hesitancy. Inside the room, two shadows flitted about. Frightened, she'd backed away, wondering if her friend saw them as well. She'd stiffened when the image veered in her direction, stifling a scream as the essence passed through her. Weakness ensued, then darkness. Hours later, she'd waken feverish, tingling, and weak in the hospital. Her horrified parents stood over her, and the doctor, surprised by her quick recovery, released her the next morning.

A year later, as her gift grew stronger, Leanne realized the images weren't ghosts, but realms, or portals to past lives. Months later, she'd found the courage to revisit the old Tudor home. Till this day, she retains an aversion of old items, especially old homes, which insult her senses daily. But with time, she's learned to block images with mental chants.

Living in a historical city like Charleston is challenging and near impossible to escape its history. Leanne recalls eight years ago, an instant foreboding as she'd stood at the window of her family's small apartment in Chicago, peering at thick fog floating over Michigan Lake. The phone rang. Marion and Daniel Alcott's voices sailed through the phone presaging change. The Alcotts, relatives on her father's side, have been a constant in her life as well as her father's, supporting him financially as a striving writer.

During her final semester of graduate school, Leanne was stunned to find her student loan balance zero—every dollar borrowed repaid before graduating. Once again, the Alcotts had performed a charitable deed. Leanne's never questioned their generosity but feels forever indebted. She was conflicted when the Alcott's offered her the Website and Blog Coordinator position. She'd felt apprehensive, elated, and of course, obligated. Considering her limited choices, she'd graciously accepted the position.

On contemplation, Charleston's tragic and violent history left her more than fearful. She'd worried past lives would overload her senses. With the Revolutionary, Civil, and the Anglo-Cherokee War, there's bound to be remnants of tragic death everywhere. Not to mention the many hurricanes and the earthquake of 1886, which killed thousands of poor souls and most notorious, Charleston's infamous slave trade. Past essences in historic homes and old fixtures horrified her. No home renovation can scour history's bloodied soil. However, she'd rationalized; all states retain remnants of past lives. Chicago, one of the oldest cities in America and her hometown, certainly has its history.

Before the Alcott's offer, Leanne longed for a change. She'd never considered her father's hometown a place to start a career, but she'd never find a career as promising as AHD. She'd mulled the proposition over and rationalized her fears. Confidently, she'd informed Daniel and Marion she'd take the job, only if they'd find a recently built condo or townhouse. She still hears Marion's complaint.

"In downtown Charleston ... that will be near impossible! Besides, the historic townhouses are simply gorgeous. Sweetie, don't you want a home with character?"

Leanne had compromised. *"A townhouse is okay, but only if the furnishing is new, straight from the factory,"* she'd pleaded.

The Alcotts went out of their way to find Leanne the perfect dwelling. They'd bought contemporary furniture, no old pieces, only items straight from the factory. Nonetheless, Leanne will never escape the home's history or the property on which it stands. It too is imbued with past lives. Accepting her fate, she's managed to control her senses with time.

Swiveling around to her computer, she makes the font larger, realizing soon, she'll need to shed her pride and visit an optometrist. Outside Leanne's office, rapid, clicking heels approach. She recognizes Tara's walk and heads to the door. *On second thought,* she halts with her hand on the knob, sensing Tara's anxiousness about the new Dream Home location. "It can wait," Leanne muttered.

Just as the phone rings, she spins on her heels and contemplates letting the call go to voicemail, but instead, she picks up. "Leanne Davis."

"Hi, honey."

Her father's raspy voice is unsettling. *I should have let it go to voicemail.* She hasn't spoken to him all year and dreads talking to him now. "Dad, what a surprise." Conversation with her father never comes easy.

"How's work going honey? I've meant to call sooner."

"Well, you finally called. How's Chicago? It must be freezing," she says, staring out the window at swaying Palmettos tousled by Charleston's warm breeze.

"It's cold, windy, the typical Chicago weather, sweetie."

Leanne's stomach twists in knots. Her father's sobriquets seem disingenuous. She wonders why she's never told him to stop. His terms of endearment aren't welcome. Trying to dispel building irritation she pulls a long raven tendril, and mouths a silent scream, but it doesn't silence her anger. "Have you spoken to mom?"

"I've tried, but she won't give me the time-of-day," he says with palpable tension in his voice.

Good for mom. Why would she speak to a lying cheat? After so many years, she still hears her mom's Greek fury, words neither she nor her father understood—*"Bástardos, kolos, város sti gi, Áchristos, stin kólasi mazí sas..."* There was no need to understand the words; she'd expressed them clearly with vigorous gestures. As a child, Leanne would often run to her room and turn the music up loud to block their emotions. But she never could. Their rage left a permanent stain on her mind.

"Well, what did you expect? Mom may never get over the hurt. Maybe you should stop trying to make amends."

"Honey, it's been years since we divorced. You'd think she'd be over the pain by now."

"Seriously, what man just disappears with another woman, abandoning his wife and daughter? Do you expect either of us to let you back into our lives so easily?" Aware of her swelling voice, she tries to temper her anger. On the other end of the phone, a deafening police siren approaches. The blare grows nearer, dwindling on her father's end, but growing closer to AHD. *He's in Charleston!*

"Okay, sweetie—"

"Stop calling me sweetie, dad. You'll never earn that right."

"Okay, Leanne. I see you're still angry. I was hoping we could talk ... Perhaps I need to give you more time."

"You had time years ago. You never made an effort; you were too scared of my abilities and that I'd see through your lies. How do you think I felt with all your affairs etched in my head? I couldn't escape them. You've never been able to hide anything from me. I sensed all of your lies when I was young."

"Yes … Leanne your gift is astounding. I admit I was disturbed by your abilities. I left because as a child, you would never understand what you were seeing—"

Leanne bangs the phone on the receiver, unwilling to listen to more of her father's apologies. She'd heard too many as a child. She recalls many lies he'd furnished so easily to mom. She'll never forget the night he walked into the tiny Chicago kitchen. Images of her father with another woman minutes before he came home swelled through her mind. Sauntering into the kitchen with his lover's essence he'd lied blatantly. *"Honey, sorry I'm late. I met with friends over a few drinks … Time got away from me."*

His dishonesty made her recoil. Any time he came near, she'd run in the opposite direction. One day, tired of his lies, she'd screamed, *"I saw the other woman, dad … "* She'd lowered her voice so her mom wouldn't overhear. *"I experienced your moments with the other women."*

Dumbfounded and embarrassed, her father grasped for the first time Leanne's gift of retrocognition. Every action he'd made was open to interpretation by his clairvoyant child. Adult affairs she couldn't understand at such a young age. Uncertain how to handle her; he'd left without any explanation or warning.

I won't be like mom, dependent and helpless on a man, she bristled. Leanne takes several deep breaths to center her mind. She won't allow intrusive thoughts of her father today. Recalling the deafening siren on the phone, she wonders why he's in Charleston.

The iPad beeps, announcing another fan's comment on AHD Dream Home blog site. Eager to forget her father, she escapes into the sweepstake world, noticing several comments since her last post, asking AHD's fans which room is their favorite in the 2015 Dream Home.

Waitingpatiently56: *Leanne thanks for providing updates on the home's décor. Laura did a fantastic job on the interior design this year. This is definitely my style, and I'm ready to move in. I can't wait to wake up in that canopy bed and take a bath in that gorgeous master bathroom. I wasn't sure about the colors of the chairs, but now I love them after virtually touring the house a third and fourth time. So when can I move in?*

TinaB82: *Hi Y'all! My best place in the home is the kitchen. I can't wait to start cooking on that incredible gas range and having breakfast with my family around that gorgeous island. Love the outdoor kitchen. I'd love to cook up a mess of Texan-style barbecue ribs and roasted corn on the cob on that outdoor grill. I just wish the home wasn't in Maine. Too cold! Where oh where will the next home be? I'm hoping Texas this year, close to home, so I don't have to travel far when I win. Good luck Y'all!*

Househappy22: *I've already moved into the 2015 home, and I'm making plans for the holidays sitting around the fireplace in that glorious great room with family and friends. Come join me, everyone!*

Leanne's heart aches, wondering how fans feel when they turn on their computers and find they're not the winner. Over the years, she's seen them bounce back from disappointment and move on to the next Dream Home. Beep …

Amc32: *My wife and I recently suffered a great misfortune. When I lost my job, we also lost our home of ten years. Family was kind enough to take us in. It would be a blessing if we won the Dream Home this year. We're desperately praying.*

Other bloggers must feel horrible reading other's misfortune. I wonder if they feel unworthy of the home. Another beep and a comment appear in response to the last post.

> **Decorlover**: *Do dreams and wishes really come true? Amc32 hang in there! Perhaps your prayers will be answered, if not this year, maybe next year.*

"Aww; there are compassionate people in this world," Leanne mumbles. Beep ...

> **Southernbelle90**: *Gracious me, although I love the architecture of the home, Laura's designs didn't hit the mark this year. Some themes are a repeat of previous sweepstake homes. I'm a Southern Belle and would love to see more feminine themes in the décor, too masculine for me this year.*

> **Waitingpatiently56:** *Hi Southernbelle90. I believe Laura did an excellent job of melding masculine and feminine styles into the home. That canopy bed with the gorgeous chandelier is definitely feminine. Look at some of the other features in that bathroom—now that's a woman's cave :-)*

Leanne laughs and muses over the phrase, *woman's cave*, and makes a note on a pad—*Use woman cave for Dream Home 2016*. She scans more comments, noticing names of regular fans. Not one has won a Dream Home. She's always curious when she meets the winners for the first time and always asks if they followed the blog site. Not one ever said yes. She realizes fans consist mainly of home enthusiast searching for interior design ideas for their own home. And they're happy given a chance to win, even if their dream never comes true.

Suddenly, a long continuous beep sound from the MAC and the screen flashes brightly then dims. The beep stops and AHD's blog site appears in bigger bolder fonts. "What's going on?" The computer has never flashed like that before. Instantly, she's aware of the follower Mountainhigh899. The letters oscillate and then stop. "Impossible" she mumbles. *Letters don't flash in and out like that without help from a software program, and not on our blog site.* "Hmmm … Why is this post the only one flashing," she mumbles. For a while, she's had reservations about Mountainhigh899, whose next comment is in response to Househappy22.

> **Mountainhigh899**: *It's a mistake getting too comfortable in your new home. Keep your doors and windows locked.*

"What a creep. What's suddenly made you so angry?" Leanne mumbles. She's been following this blogger closely for a year. Over time, his comments went from upbeat to bizarre, and now ominous. Something's not right with Mountainhigh899.

Chapter 4

A Taxi Ride

December 20, 2014

"Eighteen Pinckney Street, please," Tara says as she slides inside the taxi's back seat. Her cell phone whooshes, delivering a text message to Laura and Leanne, explaining she's on her way.

"Cru Café?" The taxi driver asks with a familiar accent.

"Yes, thank you. I bet you didn't need the address," Tara says, with a polite smile, noticing the attractive driver through the rearview mirror. "You probably know most of Charleston's restaurants."

"Yep, I can navigate Charleston with my eyes closed," he states with a chuckle.

Suddenly, Tara recalls hearing that dialect in New York. "Nice accent. Have you been in the States long?"

"Oh, thank you," he says, with a quick glance in the mirror. "I've lived in America twelve years altogether—ten in New York and two in Charleston."

"Well, you can't tell by your accent. I would've guessed a shorter time."

"No, Miss … This is my home for a long time."

"I can't place your dialect. Are you from France?"

The driver glances at Tara with a flash of perfect white-piano teeth and smiling brown eyes. "Well, in Haiti, where I'm from, we speak both French and Creole. Have you heard of Creole?"

That's it, she thought. Of course, she'd heard Creole many times in New York. She perceived subtle differences between French and Creole. One sounds more refined and the other a little choppier, but she hates to relegate one language more sophisticated and the other unrefined. It's the same as saying one is better than the other, and she refuses to place labels on anything or anyone. From her understanding, the dialect is a melding of French colonists and African slaves. Two beautiful languages fashioned into one. "Do you speak both?"

"Well, I grew up in a household where both Creole and French were spoken. My father was born in France, and my mom in Haiti. She speaks Creole. So, I switch between the two often."

Aww, you're a half-breed as well, she thought. "Where in New York did you live?"

"In Tarrytown in Westchester, do you know it?"

"Yes. I'm also from New York." She's visited Tarrytown on many occasions and remembers the expensive homes in Westchester County and wonders how he could afford such a wealthy zip code. *Okay, Tara, don't rush to judgment.* After years of meeting various people from her job, she's learned you can't judge a person the first encounter and refuses to draw conclusions about this man.

Quizzically, the driver peers at her from the rearview mirror. "Did you live in Harlem?" He asks.

Tara exhales annoyance. "Did you ask that because I'm African-American?" She replies hastily. It's ironic she refused to judge him, but he's already assessed her status simply on color. She's not surprised by her sharp bite but regrets her tone. "Sorry, I didn't mean to snap, but I hate stereotyped assumptions. No, my family lived on the Upper East Side of Manhattan."

"A city girl … Your family must do well financially to live in Manhattan?"

"And so must yours to live in Tarrytown." Tara wonders why she's so snippy with this man. She's never responded so rudely to a stranger before. *"Yes, Manhattan is expensive," she says in a friendlier tone, ignoring the family money bit.*

When the taxi stops at the light, the driver's eyes linger in the mirror. Tara shifts uncomfortably and peers out the window at Market Hall's Greek-revival style on Meeting Street, standing like a Roman temple. *Did he take the long route to Pinckney Street? From her townhouse, the ride is a straight drive on Longitude Lane.* A little perturbed, she starts to challenge his directions when halted by another question.

"Why did you move to Charleston?"

Again, she catches his eyes in the mirror. Inexplicably, agitation subsides. "Charleston is my family's hometown." Urged by his steady gaze she continues, "They moved back. I came to visit and fell in love with the place," she says in a singsong voice.

"Yes, Charleston is different from New York—more peaceful, nicer people, not so stressful."

"Yes … That's one reason I'm drawn to the city."

The driver stops for a pedestrian crossing the street, and a silent pause ensues. Tara retrieves her cell phone, believing he's finished with questions. When the cab moves again, he resumes the conversation.

"I thought you were from the Caribbean. You resemble women from the island with your amber complexion and wavy hair."

She's heard that before and hates explaining her origins. Although reluctant to respond she's inexplicably compelled to answer. "No, I was born in New York." Changing the topic quickly Tara asks, "So, what brought you to Charleston?" Her question echoes with a lingering pause, and she believes he hadn't heard. She opens her mouth to speak when he replies.

"Law School ..."

She senses a shift in his mood, and wonders why he took so long to respond. "Really ... A law student—"

"No, I drive taxis for a living," he replies bitingly. "Do you think all Haitians are taxi drivers?"

"N-No, I ..." Looking in the rearview mirror Tara notices him smiling.

He winks. "I apologize; I'm just busting your chops. You were so curt with my Harlem comment, I thought I'd get you back," he explains with a big grin.

Tara's lips curl and her brows arch. "Touché!" she says, feeling better about her earlier sharp remark and suddenly drawn to his playfulness.

"Yes, I'm a law student, Miss. This taxi belongs to a friend who lets me drive on occasion to make extra money while in school."

"Which school are you attending?"

"Charleston School of Law over on Mary Street ... Have you heard of it?"

"Yes ... Excellent school. My dad is a visiting professor. He teaches business law when he's not busy running his practice. Have you taken Professor McPherson's classes?"

"Dr. James McPherson?" He asks in a higher pitch.

His excited tone causes Tara's brows to lift. She shakes her head affirmatively, "Yes."

More enthusiastic, the driver glances back, and studies her face. "You're kidding? You're Dr. McPherson's daughter? He's been my professor for two semesters."

"Wow, what a coincidence." Tara has always been curious what impact her father makes on his students, though she's never had the opportunity to see his lectures, she admires his passion for the legal profession. "So how're my dad's lectures?"

"Dr. McPherson has been a great inspiration. I thought Business Law was going to be another boring lecture on torts, contracts, and theories. But your father is sharp; he keeps it interesting."

Happy her dad has a fan, she wonders what he would say about this man as a student. "What type of law will you practice?"

"Environmental law … I've advocated environmental protection for years."

"That's wonderful. We need more socially responsible advocates to prevent conglomerates from destroying our planet."

"That's my goal … What do you do for a living?"

Tara wonders if he'll approve of AHD's ethics. The company is doing everything to give back to the community. And all the sweepstake homes are environmentally friendly. She considers the Alcott's many charitable causes, and she's certain he'd approve. "I'm Managing Director at AHD."

"AHD … What's that?"

"Oh, Alcott Home and Design …" Tara glances at her watch, realizing she's twenty minutes late. Cru Café is probably packed with the weekend brunch crowd. Reservation only, the owners are undoubtedly rushing patrons through the door as fast as they can. She hopes the girls have ordered already.

"Don't worry; we're almost there," he says, catching Tara's worried expression. He speeds down Hayne Street, veers onto Church Street, and makes a sharp turn at the next light. Unassumingly, Cru Café sits in a small, lemon-chiffon, eighteenth-century home.

Before Tara retrieves the fare from her purse, the car door opens. "You didn't have to do that," she says, admiring his manners.

"No, I don't mind. You're such a lovely lady, and I enjoyed our conversation. My name is Ellison. Do you mind if I ask for your number?"

In the back seat, she'd only seen his face. Surprisingly, she's impressed by his sinewy physique. Tara muses—*good-looking, ambitious, law school; he's my dad's student, why not?* "My name is Tara." Handing him the fare with a business card, their fingertips flick, rousing a familiar sensation in her gut.

In the front seat, Ellison pulls a sheet of paper from a notebook and starts writing. "I'm going to call you. So, don't forget my name … Ellison." He folds the paper, tears it in half, and hands her the piece with his name and number.

Tara takes the paper and smiles warmly. "Okay, Ellison." *How can I forget someone who looks so good?* She suspects he took the longer route to Cru on purpose … She knows he did.

Chapter 5

The Girls

December 20, 2014, Cru Café

Tara rushes inside the cozy restaurant and spies Laura and Leanne at their usual table in the back, toward the window, across from the fireplace. Saturday brunch, once a month at Cru Café, has become the norm for the girls. They'd sit and talk about everything while relaxing and enjoying a meal.

"Tara, we got your text. So, we went ahead and ordered a bottle of wine. I thought you might like Peirano Estate," Laura says with a devilish grin and a sip of Merlot.

Tara hadn't disclosed her recent discovery to either Laura or Leanne. "How'd you know I like Peirano Estate?" She asks leaning over and kissing Laura and Leanne on the cheeks.

"Oh ... Just a hunch ... I thought you might enjoy Peirano's Merlot," Laura says realizing her slip.

"Hmmm ... well, you thought right. I'm so sorry I'm late. This weather is driving me crazy. I must have changed ten times before finding the right outfit," Tara says with a deep exhale.

"Sweetie, it's okay," Laura says, pouring her harried friend a glass of wine. "I had the same problem. When in doubt, a simple dress will do. And so does what you're wearing. You look hot!

And I don't mean temperature wise," she says with a chuckle. "Well, you know what I mean," she explains with a wink.

Leanne peers around the menu. "Oh my God, Tara, when do those legs end," she says inspecting her outfit. "Those skinny pants are made for you. You're stunning!"

"Well, I tried my best," Tara says with a gracious smile, appreciating her dearest friend's opinions. She cherishes their easygoing friendship, unlike her catty friends in New York. Somehow in their presence, she's calmer and more carefree.

"Look at you two," Tara says, dissecting her friend's attire. Both have a unique sense of fashion and are always so well dressed. "You look so stylish," Tara praised. She loves Laura's feminine ways. The consummate-Southern Belle, dressed in a purple sheath dress and fetching knee-length boots, she looks impeccable with simple diamond stud earrings that make her bluish-green eyes sparkle. Laura's strawberry blonde hair falls in loose waves, giving her a girlish charm. Possessing the skin of a thirty-year-old, Tara still can't believe Laura is forty-five. Her Southern charm draws people to her anywhere she goes. Like her profession, she makes an ordinary person seem special in her presence.

Leanne, forever composed, sits back in the dark leather booth with that cool Chicago mentality. Like Laura, she loves the qualities Leanne brings to their friendship. She's the strong one who bonds them. Tara figures she developed a thick-skin earlier than most; growing up in an unfavorable environment, Leanne had to be strong not only for herself but also for her mother after her parents' divorce. Intellectually, Leanne seems mature beyond her years, as if she was born with wisdom older than her time on this planet. At thirty-nine, she's easily mistaken for twenty-something. With her hair pulled back in a sleek ponytail, her high cheekbones and green eyes are more prominent. Her Greek and Irish lineages are apparent with her olive complexion and raven hair. Dressed in a black miniskirt, a simple gray sweater set, and ankle boots, Leanne's style is always city chic.

Tara scoots beside Leanne just as the waitress ambles toward their table. She's been craving Cru's Chicken Club Sandwich all week, but before she parts her lips, Laura takes the words right out of her mouth.

"She'll have the Chicken Club Sandwich on Sourdough Bread with Butternut Squash Soup."

"Laura, you did it again," Tara states in awe.

"Oh, Tara, I'm sorry. Didn't you say you've been craving this all week? Do you want something else?"

Tara, doubting herself, doesn't remember ever telling Laura about her cravings. "No, I'll keep the order," Tara says with a curious frown at the waitress.

Pursing her lips, Laura mentally chides her lack of self-restraint. Tara hadn't verbalized what she wanted; she'd caught her thoughts once again. Laura continues giving her order. "I will have the Grilled-Portobello Wrap and Spinach Salad."

With arched brows, Tara wonders how Laura always senses her thoughts. *Can she read minds?* And she laughs inwardly at that idea.

Peering at her two friends, Leanne shakes her head with a grin. "Laura knows too much for her own sake," she says with a look of disapproval and a light tap of Laura's foot under the table.

Laura throws Leanne an unmistakable glare as she taps back in response. But she's taken aback by Leanne's glasses. "Well, shut my mouth! Honey, I'm so glad you finally let go of that pride. They're becoming my dear."

Conscious of her new spectacles, Leanne touches the rim and replies, "Well, I got tired of squinting at my iPad."

"You look so chic, Leanne," Tara states. "They give you a smart-chic style that says, yes, I'm beautiful and smart, *don't-effing-mess-with-me* look."

A wicked laugh escapes Laura's mouth. "You're right, Tara. I couldn't have said it better."

"Okay, girls, thanks for trying to appease me," although Leanne agrees after seeing her reflection in the mirror this morning. She likes the way they define her angular face and high cheekbones, but more importantly, she can read the menu. Leanne hands the menu to the waitress, who's waited patiently since the girl's discovery of her eyeglasses. "I'll take the Garlic Marinated Chicken Club Sandwich as well."

Taking another sip of wine, Laura peers around the table with glee—basking in the comfort of wine and her two dear friends. "So darlings, are you done with your Christmas shopping yet?"

Engrossed in thoughts of Adam, Leanne remembers the difficulty she's having finding him a gift. "No, I have one more," then she segues into an entirely different line of thought—jumping right into what's been on her mind for weeks. "Girls, I don't know what to do about Adam."

Leanne's declaration surprises Tara. She turns, facing Leanne and asks, "What do you mean?"

"Well, he's pressuring me to make a decision soon. I'm not sure I'm ready for marriage."

Laura perceived Leanne's turmoil earlier, but with Tara's presence, she can't mention Leanne's clairvoyance and crafts her words carefully. "Honey, Adam's nine years with you should be enough proof he loves you."

Tara's seen Leanne and Adam together countless times, and her instincts about them as a couple are always strong. Leanne's sudden doubt puzzles her. "What exactly is holding you back?"

"Me," she states pointblank, "and inevitably winding up miserable like my parents. I saw my mom and dad go from cordial and loving to hostile and unhappy people. Their divorce was nasty and bitter, and we ended up hurt."

Stunned, Tara jerks her head back. "Come on ... Your parent's marriage is no indication of yours with Adam. I'm amazed you feel this way. You and Adam are so right for each other."

Sensing Leanne's pain across the table, Laura is aware of her animosity toward her father. "I realize it was painful watching your parents go through a divorce, but you can't let their failed marriage haunt you. You and Adam are special. You're meant to be together. Pardon me for saying this, but you're not your parents. They probably should never have married."

"Well, mom got pregnant before they married. I believe they would have married other people if she hadn't gotten knocked-up," Leanne says while studying the short nail on her pinky.

Tara realizes Leanne only bites her nails when she's stressed. Now aware of the seriousness of her concerns, she rubs her shoulder. Obviously, there's more to her family than she perceived. "Leanne, if your mother hadn't gotten pregnant, you wouldn't be here. Well, if only for your birth, thank heavens for their union. They did one thing right, they had you. Besides, Laura and I need you to keep us in line."

Laura senses another concern of Leanne's and adeptly crafts her words. "Leanne, your parents were together only because of the pregnancy. But honey, you and Adam are best friends and truly like each other. Love is important, but if you don't like the man, the relationship won't work. You're meant to be, sweetie. From what I understand of Adam, he's accepting of your uniqueness." Laura hopes Tara doesn't pick up on her last statement, as she taps Leanne's foot under the table. She sips more wine as if parched by her little speech. Grasping Laura's meaning Leanne throws her a smile of acknowledgment.

Unaware of the moment between her two friends, Tara thinks they're just *more words of wisdom from Laura*; and admires her ability to provide helpful advice when needed. "Laura's right, Leanne. The first time I saw you and Adam together, my guts told me he's the one. And my guts are always right."

With her two friend's assurances, concern softens in Leanne's eyes. "Girls, you have good judgment, and I respect your opinions. I need to stop dodging Adam and be truthful with him. But ladies, in five years if I'm in divorce court; I'll never let you live this conversation down." Leanne smirks, pushing her glasses up her nose.

Amazed at Leanne's acceptance of the eyeglasses, and uncharacteristic vulnerability, Tara, and Laura wear disbelief on their faces. This is not their Leanne, who's always cool, calm, and confident.

Clicking the goblet with her fingernails, Laura changes the topic to Tara's intuition. "Is your gut giving you any clues about the Tahoe location, Tara?"

"Hmmm … No, not yet; but I think Lake Tahoe is a beautiful place." Tara remembers the ominous twitch in her left eye and the dreaded number thirteen and concludes they're too simple to be any real intuitive warnings. "Of all the locations Cody has chosen, this one poses more risk. Think about it girls. The Sierra Nevada Mountains sits on not one fault line, but three. Now, earthquakes are alarming, not to mention the wildfires and snowstorms. I spoke with Cody earlier, and he joked about the Donner Party, which is a chilling piece of history. I was a little concerned these facts might taint our fans perception of the area. Well, nothing we can do about history, but will our fans appreciate a million-dollar home in a potential hazard zone?"

"Tara, many people live in California and move there every day. They purchase homes fully aware they're sitting on fault lines. We need to examine the history of the location; when was the last earthquake in the region? Also, the Martis Camp community has never been touched by a major earthquake or wildfire. Okay, so, there are tremors now and then, and who's to say a major earthquake won't happen. The beauty of the area is the mountains, the lake, and the ski resorts. I believe our fans will appreciate the resort environment and its amenities."

Tara nods her head in agreement. "True."

"If we worried about natural disasters we'd never build homes, especially given tidal floods, nor'easters, sinkholes, and tornadoes occurring lately. AHD has always constructed homes to withstand Mother Nature."

"You're right, Leanne; I'm just concerned about giving our winners the best possible environment."

Laura shakes her head in wonder. "Goodness gracious, we're talking business on our day off. This is not good. Let's get back to being women for a day." Quickly, she peers around the restaurant. "Where's that waiter? I'm famished." Swiftly, she diverts her thoughts to Christmas. "Tara, are Nyla and James around for the holiday?"

"Lately, my parents are never around. I can't keep track of them since mom's retirement. I believe they're spending Christmas in Australia this year. They've decided to enjoy their senior years traveling the seven continents."

"What an ideal way to grow old," Laura murmured, remembering her plans to tour the world with Daniel. "Are they okay with you spending the holidays with us the last two years?"

"Ha! Are you kidding? You know the answer to that, Laura. They love you and Leanne. They're just grateful I have you two to celebrate the holidays. Besides, Nyla is tired of planning large holiday meals every year. At their age, it's time they relax and have their needs catered to for once. You know ... " Tara says in thought, "I'm amazed ... "

"Amazed by what, sweetie?"

"Amazed at how their marriage has grown stronger after so many years. You would think they'd be tired of each other by now."

Leanne notices the fond expression on Tara's face and purposely bumps her shoulder. A vision of Tara and her parents invade her mind, with sensations of love and a familial bond so strong, she's never known. "I wish I'd had your parents, Tara."

"Oh, Leanne, stop it. Your parents are amazing." As a mother, Laura can't tolerate criticism of parenting skills. "Parenting is not an innate ability. It's an acquired skill and no one's perfect. Sweetie, your parents, did their best given the circumstances. You're a remarkable woman because of them. And you're an incredible businesswoman because of your family, Tara."

Tara realizes Laura is a loving mom to Callie, but she's sure it's not always been easy. "Laura, I've never heard you talk about your parents."

"Hmmm ... Why would I? There's nothing special to tell. They're just your typical Southern Anglo-Saxon family with old-fashion values. And they expected nothing more of me than to marry and bear children," Laura says with a grin. "They never dreamed I'd have both a successful career and marriage. But, I love and respect their values and never saw fit to dispute them."

Really Laura ... typical ... There's nothing typical about the Gowans; Leanne thought and throws a shrewd glance at Laura. Anyone who's lived in Charleston long enough, have heard about the clairvoyant Gowan women. But Leanne understands Laura's inability to speak about her family's reputation in Charleston—not just yet.

Laura eyes Leanne, acknowledging her thoughts.

Tara takes another sip of wine, amazed she's already finished one glass. Merrily, she refills the glass to the rim. Wine suppresses her inhibitions and emotions flow as she sits appreciative of her friends. "I can't get over how our friendship developed. Laura with your in-law's ties to my father's family and Leanne your dad's relations to the Alcotts, we're predestined."

"Predestined—that's the correct word for it. I'd often wondered if we'd be good friends if Daniel hadn't brought us together. Tara, I remember when your dad introduced you the first time. There was an immediate connection. I felt I'd known you my entire life," Laura says.

"Me too, Laura. Our first conversation was so effortless; I felt I'd been speaking to you for years."

Laura's lips curl a big smirk. "I had my doubts, you know, you being a city gal and all. I was surprised we hit it off so well."

"Well, darling," Tara says, feigning a Southern drawl, "I believe I have some Southern charm given I'm the product of two Charlestonians."

"Excellent, Tara, your accent is perfect. Perhaps there's a smidgen of Southern Belle in you after all," Laura says with a fond chuckle.

Tara peers at Leanne and ponders the Davis' ties to the Alcotts. She'd heard they're first or second cousins but she's unsure. "Leanne, how's your family connected to the Alcotts again?"

"Well, dad's a close relative. Daniel's aunt, my father's mom, married into the Davis family so, I believe that makes us first cousins."

"How did your parents end up in Chicago?"

Leanne had discovered everything about her father through precognition. She'd never asked the how or why her parents settled in Chicago, she saw with her own eyes her father's past. "My father was tired of small Southern towns and moved away to pursue a writing career."

"Hmmm ..." Laura simpers.

"What are you thinking Laura?" Tara asks.

"Oh ..." she says with puckered lips and tapping one finger at a time on the table, "... just something Daniel used to say. He always referred to the Davis' as the artistic, bohemian side of the family. He'd say, 'The Alcotts are all business and the Davis all talent,'" Laura says with mimicry.

"Yep, dad's bohemian. He's also got an artistic temperament. He would lock himself up for days-at-a-time writing, and forget mom and I existed. Artists ... I run the other way if a man tells me he's a writer."

Squinting and chewing on her bottom lip, Laura senses Leanne's qualm with her father runs deeper than her revelation.

Tara's confounded. She's always seen Leanne as an artist, no matter how much she fights being like her father. She's read many of her articles on AHD's website and magazine and believes Leanne is way too gifted to be writing about architecture and home design. "Perhaps you're such a talented writer because of your dad. I think you squander your talents on blogging. You should consider writing novels?"

"I did … But I don't have the patience to write for days as my father does. I like what I'm doing. It's much more interesting connecting with people."

Laura, fixing her face in a small silver compact, sighs and says, "Such a waste of talent, honey. You could be a celebrated author, telling incredible stories with that mind of yours. My hunch tells me one day you will write an astonishing novel."

Leanne smiles; realizing Laura has read her thoughts. She ponders the countless unfinished novels saved on her laptop—novels she thought she'd finish one day. Laura winks at Leanne again, acknowledging her thoughts once more.

Tara recalls the first time she met Leanne, and how easily the conversation went. Just as it had with Laura, the conversation came easily, as if they'd been talking all their lives. "Well, we were lucky to bring you into the AHD family. I remember the first time we spoke. You were so open and honest. I had an immediate connection with both you and Laura—"

"Yes," Laura interjects, "Leanne, you're younger than me, but you always remind me of the big sister I've never had. So mature and wise beyond your years. Wow, we're three peas in a pod," Laura says with an eye roll and grin. "My lord, we're quite the admiration club aren't we," she continues with her distinctive soul-piercing laugh.

"Hmmm … It's just strange. I felt as if I'd seen you two before we met," Tara says, squinting across the table at Laura.

"Well, Tara, you know what they say; at first glance, real soulmates have instant recognition. Maybe the three of us are meant to be friends."

"I guess you're right… What other reason can there be?" Tara ponders why she's never experienced this with men in her life. Obviously, they weren't the one. Suddenly, she remembers the odd sensation as her finger brushed Ellison's. *Hmmm …* Running her fingers through her hair, and peering out the window, she mulls over her last conversation with Nyla and her persistent worries about her settling down with the right man.

Laura hears Tara's thoughts but waits for her to speak. She senses Tara's doubt and her need to voice her concerns.

"Speaking of soulmates, Nyla worries I'll never marry and have children. It's so frustrating trying to assure her I'm okay being single and independent. Honestly, I think she's just worried she'll never get the chance to be a grandmother," Tara chuckles dubiously and takes a sip of wine. "I'm okay if I never find 'Mr. Right,' or bear children."

Laura places her hands over her mouth, stopping an urge to dispute Tara's statement. She senses her doubt. "You're honestly okay with never finding a husband and experiencing childbirth? You'd make a great mother. Don't you want that experience?"

"I don't know, Laura."

"Well, don't let AHD consume your life. There's more to living than just work. Besides, time won't wait for you to make up your mind." Laura realizes she's hit a nerve but continues. "However, it's never too late to find Mr. Right."

Tara pauses; deliberating Laura's question. "Well, all I know right now, at this stage of my life, I'm not ready. You remember why I broke up with Steve last year. He wanted a family, and I didn't."

"Ha!" Laura scoffs. "I know what Steve wanted, sweetie. He wanted a traditional wife at home, pregnant with his child, and meals prepared for him after work—what we call in Charleston, barefoot and pregnant."

"Yep … And that's just not me," Tara says with one arched brow. "I'm honestly okay with being alone right now. I've been dating, it seems, all my life. I need some time to myself."

"Honey, don't stay out of the dating scene too long. You're gorgeous and have so much to offer a man. I suspect you will have another sweetheart in your life soon. I'm not too worried about that," Laura says with a wink. Laura's motherly instincts take over, and she supplies more words of wisdom. "You realize your parents want what's best for you. So, cut them some slack." She recognizes Tara's needs for affirmation and suspects deep down she wants a family but fears the loss of her career and autonomy. "By the way, who was the gorgeous hunk helping you from the taxi?" Laura asks with an astute grin.

"Oh … That was odd. He's one of my dad's students over at Charleston Law. The moment I stepped into his taxi, there was a peculiar feeling. I felt like I knew him. I couldn't stop talking to him. Generally, I would have put my earpiece on, but there was this pull to continue talking … It was strange."

"What did we just say about soulmates, that instant recognition? I hope you got his number."

"For heaven's sake, Laura … Yes, I got his number," Tara says with a playful eye roll.

"I'd follow up with him; those intuitions are usually right."

Again, Tara thinks, Laura's managed to read her mind.

Quietly, Leanne listens to her friends, but at the same time, studies a childlike apparition blurring in and out as it melds through waiters entering and exiting the kitchen door. It moves toward their table, sits behind Laura, and stares into the unlit fireplace. Leanne doesn't remember seeing this image, but she's seen many others in the restaurant. Laura shifts and follows Leanne's gaze. Her dilated pupils are alarming, but Laura dare not ask what she sees, because she too senses strong vibes behind her.

* * *

An hour later, after four glasses of wine, good food, and lips the color of blueberries, Tara exclaims whimsically, "I love you guys!"

"Tara, you're plain tipsy! We love you too sweetie." Laura says, recognizing Tara's show of affection when she drinks too much, signaling it's time for her to stop.

"Okay, four glasses is enough for you," Leanne says and moves the wine bottle away.

"I was just getting started," Tara jests. "I admit, I can't keep up with you two, but I'm allowed to have fun every once in a while. She holds the glass aloft and toasts the air, "Cheers!"

Laura peers at the waitress, hearing her thoughts. *If they don't leave soon, I'm going to have to ask them to go. No ... I can't do that they're such good customers, besides they tip well.* Glancing toward the entrance, Laura notices the long line of customers waiting for tables. "Girls, our time is up," she says motioning to the waitress. "Please put this on my tab."

Concerned about Tara's state, Laura decides to drive Tara and Leanne home. "Girls, my car is around the corner. Wait here." Pulling the SUV in front of Cru, she sees three men checking out Tara and Leanne. "See what I mean, Tara. Men are everywhere."

* * *

Thirty minutes after dropping the girls off, Laura arrives at the Alcott estate. She stops, presses the controls, and impatiently waits as the gate opens. Finally, driving through, she feels she's leaving the world onto her own island as she continues up the private tree-lined road. The approaching home makes her smile, sensing Daniel's presence around the entire estate. Half a mile later, she arrives at the four-door garage. Inside the home, Sammie's barking alarms her. Quickly, she opens the mudroom door. Sammie rushes straight to the car, barking and growling fiercely at the home's interior.

"Sammie, come here, boy." With teeth bared and a vicious growl, Sammie stares inside the house. "Sammie!" Laura screams with a stamp of her foot.

Sammie approaches, then pause, his sight fixed on the mudroom. "What's wrong, boy?" Sammie has never behaved this way. Laura senses something's wrong, *but what?*

Chapter 6

Silver Wrappings with Blue Velvet

December 24, 2014, Alcott Estate

"*She'll love it, Laura,*" whispers gossamer lips.

"Yes, she will, Daniel," Laura murmured, feeling a spectral energy surrounding her. *Was it really him?* Tears wet her cheeks, and she wipes her eyes quickly not wanting to spoil the girl's holiday cheer. Laughter and chatter spill from the kitchen. Laura glances beyond the family room toward the girls preparing Christmas Eve dinner around the kitchen island. Grateful for their presence, she's savoring every moment and dreading New Year's Day when they leave. Laura recalls how empty the home felt when the holiday ended last year and wishes time could freeze. *Carpe Diem* slips into her mind, and she heeds its meaning.

For a moment, Laura admires the great Balsam Fir and then continues wrapping Callie's gift. At the back of the tree, a small silver gift with a blue velvet ribbon catches her attention. *Blue velvet, it can only be for me. Hmmm ... No gift tag, that's not like the girls.* She picks up the package and notices a small card hidden beneath the bow. Laura Alcott is scribbled in an unfamiliar penmanship. A sharp twinge spreads across her palm. She drops the gift to the floor and swiftly pushes it under the tree. *What was that?* Curiously, she ponders the mysterious vibes it radiates, but only for a second as she continues wrapping Callie's present.

A loud creak splinters and crackles above, causing her to jump. Turning toward the kitchen, she notices the girls are sitting as they had before. She laughs at her jitteriness and resumes with final touches to Callie's gift, admiring the lovely purple box embossed with crystals and sensing the soothing vibrations from the items within. Again, a creak pops louder than the first. Laura rises from the floor and stares at the ceiling. This time, the creak originated from the far corner of the room—upstairs in the master suite.

She places Callie's gift under the tree, and cautiously enters the stairwell. She wonders if she should bring one of the girls with her, but her misgivings are embarrassing. "Laura, I swear, sometimes you worry me," she mumbles. Buoyed by a surge of sensibility, she makes her way up the stairs and into the room.

At the threshold, she reaches inside the room, turning on the light. On the floor next to the bed lays a book. *That's odd … How did it get there?* Picking it up, she returns the book to its usual place on the nightstand. Suddenly, Laura feels eyes at her back. Alarmed, she jerks her head around and stares into the hallway, expecting the source of her angst to appear. She stands frozen in place. The ephemeral sensation subsides but leaves her worried. Bringing her focus back to the bedroom, she scans every corner. *The master closet* she thought with alarm. With hesitant steps, she heads toward the vast dark space, dreading the deep recesses of its interior.

With caution, she enters the room and slides the dimmer to its brightest level. Nervously, she glances around the room, afraid someone is lurking behind the expansive wardrobe. Separating items of clothing, looking below for feet, probing for eyes peering back, searching for a human form; she examines every suspicious shadow until objects become distinguishable. Walking toward the far end of the room, she distresses over the little alcove off to the right. A dressing area surrounded by mirrors and walls of deep dark glass cabinets, big enough for a person to hide. Before entering, she lights the chandelier, illuminating a wall of mirrors. Summoning her courage, she enters, circles the room, and inspects every cabinet—relieved to dispel her suspicions. But there's still the master bath.

Heading toward the bathroom, again she performs an inspection, finding nothing out of the ordinary. "Well, Laura, what did you expect to find?" She mumbles, laughing at her silliness. But her instincts are screaming something's not right. For days, she's felt another presence. Rather real or imagined, the sensation has left her anxious. Every so often, floorboards creak as if under someone's weight. Goosebumps crawl up her skin. "Stop it, Laura. You're just scaring yourself silly."

She exits the master suite, glances down the hallway, and up the staircase, debating whether to check the third floor. Down the hall, Sammie sits staring at her. He turns his gaze inside the room and back, signaling Laura to inspect. His stillness is chilling.

"Come here, boy."

Like a stuffed toy, he doesn't budge.

"Sammie?"

He remains unmoving. Softly, Laura walks toward him ready to investigate the room he guards obstinately. With a low growl, he jumps from his frozen state, taking off at a rapid speed down the stairs. Sammie's sudden action is startling. Laura clutches her chest with a deep breath to calm her racing heart. She's never seen Sammie run so fast, especially not down the stairs. *Something's spooked him.* She reaches for the dimmer inside the room. Standing frozen as Sammie had a moment ago; she scans every corner and listens for noise.

She steps toward the bed, clutches the bedpost, pauses a minute, and then performs the same examination she'd performed only minutes before in the master suite. No sound, no movement, "Nothing." Turning the light off, she walks quietly trying to detect any unusual noise.

Tom

"Damn dog," Tom mumbles listening as Laura makes her way toward the room. Sammie found and followed him to the guestroom, growling as he stood in the dark corner. Trapped, there was no choice but to hide. Just as Laura calls Sammie, he stops growling but sits guarding the room. Tom, ready to strike, picks up a tall candelabrum but changes his mind as she approaches. He scuttles under the large bed, holding his breath, tensing every muscle, ready to strike if he has to. Nervous sweat trickles down his face, and he hopes the dog won't give him away.

Finally, Sammie scampers down the hall when Laura approaches. *Chicken,* he thought with a sigh of relief. He watches Laura's feet from under the bed and holds his breath as she stands in the doorway surveying the room. Nervous beads of sweat gloss his forehead, dripping from his chin to the wooden floor. He stiffens when her feet approach the bed and he hopes she doesn't look underneath. A silent sigh of relief escapes when finally she moves toward the bath and closet beyond. Just as a drop of sweat falls into his eyes, the light dims, and Laura walks out of the room.

A few minutes later, her voice sounds in the kitchen. Quietly, he races to the third floor and into the attic—where he'll wait until they're all asleep. He has to leave the house before Christmas morning—before they open the silver gift.

Down the stairs and into the kitchen, Laura feels more secure in the girl's presence. Sammie has found a spot next to Leanne's feet and stares up as she enters the room, detecting her nervousness. Over the gas range, Callie stirs a hearty soup while Leanne and Tara sit around the kitchen island sipping wine and chopping vegetables for the salad. Laura takes a seat at the counter, pours herself a glass of Merlot, and takes a sip to calm her nerves.

Although Callie didn't hear Laura enter the kitchen, she sensed her presence before she spoke.

"A few minutes ago, I thought I heard something in the house."

Listening to the familiar cadence of her mother's voice, Callie detects fear. She turns away from the stove; aware of concern etched on Laura's beautifully maturing face. "What did you hear, mom?"

"Well, for the last week, things have been happening."

"Things? What things?"

"Sounds, occurrences … I keep hearing creaking floors. And doors I swear I closed, I'm finding open. Oddly enough, food is missing from the refrigerator. I thought perhaps the maids were helping themselves, but they knew nothing about it. I felt terrible interrogating them, but who else can it be?"

Laura is the most levelheaded person Tara knows. When she's troubled the girls take it seriously.

Swiftly, Callie joins the girls around the island and asks, "Why didn't you tell me, mom?"

"I wanted to rule everything out before I mentioned anything. This estate has been around a long time. Maybe the floors are settling, or maybe I'm so exhausted I forgot to close the doors. After all, I'm getting older. Maybe this is what happens at forty-five … forgetfulness."

"Mom, what about the missing food, there's no way you ate something and forgot."

Tara doesn't believe any of what Laura is saying. She senses she's concealing her fear for their sake. "Laura, your mind is too sharp, and you're too young to be forgetful. I doubt you're losing your memory. Gut instincts are usually right. You shouldn't ignore them."

Leanne is aware of the conversation around her, but her eyes are transfixed at the far end of the island. Conscious of Laura's fear, she scans the perimeter of the kitchen and the family room beyond. Suddenly, she's filled with a new fear of her own. "Tara, I've meant to tell you about the odd fan Mountainhigh899. He's back and creepier than ever."

"Who is Mountainhigh899?" Laura asks.

"Oh, he's a regular on AHD's blog site. Lately, his comments are a little menacing which worries me."

Tara takes a small bite from a piece of cheese and deliberates Leanne's statement. "We should block him or her from the site. We don't want our fans threatened by this creep."

Leanne sighs. "I had the same idea, but it's better keeping an eye on him or her."

Tara wonders why but begins to understand Leanne's logic. "Yes, you might be right, but you can still allow his comments to come through; just don't make them visible to the public."

"I've already thought of making him or her invisible, but if they're a threat censoring their comments might upset them."

"Good, then maybe he'll go away. It's our prerogative to choose and restrict posts on the website."

Leanne has her doubts, but leaves it alone for a while, not wanting to cause Laura any more anxiety.

Suddenly, the room is quiet with their silent fears. A presence Leanne can't explain puzzles her as she stares at an area across from Laura. Laura hears Leanne's thoughts and glances across the island, wondering what she sees. Taking a quaff of wine,

Laura abandons the query. Jumping from the chair with a snap of her fingers, she states in commanding fashion, "Okay ladies, it's Christmas Eve. Let's enjoy the night before it's over," she says, trying to conceal her growing concern.

Taking slow bites from the cheese, Tara recalls the man at the gate a few days ago. But with mounting apprehension in the room, she snaps the image from her mind. With that thought, Callie, Laura, and Leanne's heart jump as if in sync.

* * *

An hour later, the girls, stuffed from dinner, sit around the Christmas tree contentedly, listening to Tara's favorite Nat King Cole Christmas classic—The Christmas Song. Tara tries to carry a tune as she sings along but her voice cracks on "Jack Frost nipping at your nose ... *Lah-lah-la* ... *Hmmm-hmmm-hmmm* ..." The girls laugh, and Tara continues to hum the song.

Callie, like her mom, is the perfect host catering to her friend's needs. "More pie, anyone?"

Tara glances at Callie's little figure and down at her own full belly. "Honey, eat all you want. Your twenty-two-year-old body has a faster metabolism than my thirty-eight-year-old one. I'm trying to keep my mouth closed this holiday season. But, I'll watch you enjoy every morsel."

"Tara, you're so thin. One more piece ... Come on it's Christmas."

Tara shakes her head. "No," and continues to hum to the music.

Callie peeks over at Laura and Leanne's eager eyes. No words are necessary. Turning toward the kitchen, she comes back with the entire pie dish. After another glass of wine, Tara's willpower vanishes, and in delight, she consumes the remaining chocolate-pecan pie.

Laura catches sight of the vexing gift under the tree. Eager to dispel the mystery she asks, "Are we ready to open gifts?"

Before she has a chance to question the mysterious gift, Callie reaches for a large square-shaped box wrapped in exquisite abstract artwork with gold ribbons running from corner to corner.

"Merry Christmas, Mom," Callie exclaims, placing the gift on her lap.

"Thanks, sweetie … Wow … Look at this wrapping. It's too gorgeous to destroy," she says while kissing Callie on the cheek. She pauses staring at her daughter, her spitting image at twenty-two.

Callie watches her mother's careful effort to preserve the wrappings as she always does. Taking her time, Laura cuts the tape and pulls the ribbons free with careful hands. Callie wonders if she saves the wrappings for some other occasion. Tonight, she won't rush her, but patiently waits as she unwraps her gift.

"Honey, where did you get this?"

Once again, seeing the painting for the third time rouses Callie's emotions. She notices the bluish-green pool in Laura's eyes. "A year ago, I found an old picture of you and dad in the big trunk in the attic. An artist friend agreed to replicate the photo into a painting. I had it framed in your favorite teak wood."

Laura's silence is telling. Her emotional state exposed with an inability to mouth her words. The painting suffuses her with images of that day—memories with Daniel sitting by the pond in the backyard. She was twenty-nine, and Callie was four-years-old when the picture was taken. "I remember this day so clearly. You were playing with Daniel's camera and accidentally snapped this photo. Do you remember?"

Of course, she did. Callie recalls the day in the attic a year ago and how the memory entered her mind at the precise time she lifted the photo out of the old trunk. Sensations of being four again and running around the backyard as Laura and Daniel watched her appeared so real she held onto the picture for a long time. She memorized every vivid detail of her father's features.

"I remember dad laughing at me because the camera was too big for my hands."

Laura's eyes shimmer; a watery pool ready to spill. With her mother's tears, Callie realizes she made the right choice.

Trying to disguise her emotions, Tara turns away from mother and daughter toward the tree. The emotional scene evokes distant memories of her father and grandfather's phone conversation years ago in New York. Tara senses Daniel's loss is still heartrending for Laura and Callie, especially during the holidays.

Under the tree, Tara searches and spies a burnt-orange wrapping tied with a leather tan string. She recognized the wrappings from her favorite handbag store and suspects the gift is for her. Ripping the wrappings to threads, she screams, "Yes!"

With watery eyes, Laura is a paradox, laughing and crying at the same time. "I thought you might like the bag."

"Laura, this is way too expensive."

"Never," Laura insists. "For my best friends, there's nothing too expensive. Now there's enough room to carry everything, even your laptop. I'm tired of you carrying all those bags, dear friend."

Tara loves the smell of new leather and takes a deep breath as if savoring her favorite dish.

Pulling herself from the painting, Callie discovers a crystal-embossed, purple box—a gift to her from Laura. She has an obsession with jewelry. And every Christmas Laura buys her something for her collection. Inside, she finds a white gold diamond, two-strand, drop Amethyst necklace.

"This is gorgeous!"

"There's more," Laura says. "There're two satchels in the box."

Callie opens the velvet drawstring pouch. A stunning blue Lapis-Lazuli pendant falls out. With her mouth agape, Callie stares mesmerized at the jewel's brilliance.

While Callie admires her necklace, Leanne screams in excitement. "Yes, just what I wanted!"

Startled, Tara jumps with a swift turn of her head. "Leanne, you just woke the dead with that scream."

Leanne, taking the statement literally; glanced for a second at the figure sitting next to Laura and Callie.

Tara stares at the box in Leanne's hand and realizes what the excitement is about. "Okay, who bought her the iPad?"

Laura smirks at Tara's expression. She knows Tara's views on technology and senses her thoughts before she opens her mouth. "I did. You know Leanne; she's got to have the latest and the greatest technology."

"But she already has one."

"But it's basically obsolete," Leanne explains, knowing how much Tara despises the yearly advances companies make in technology. Giddy with excitement, Leanne starts to disassemble gadgets that came with the iPad. "This is much more advanced than the one I bought two years ago."

Tara shakes her head and laughs, understanding all too well her friend's fascination with technology. But she can't help teasing her about her obsession. She's aware Leanne dislikes old objects; craving novelty, especially technology. "I don't get why companies update technology every year. It's a ploy to keep you techies buying," Tara says with a silly face and a wink.

"Okay, ladies, this is our limit for Christmas Eve. We can open the other gifts Christmas morning like we planned, so, no peeking in boxes. However, I'm curious who the silver present with the blue velvet ribbon is from?" Laura waits for a response, but she's greeted with silence. "Come on … One of you had to put it there."

Flummoxed, the girls stare suspiciously at the gift, not a clue between them.

"How did it get under the tree if it wasn't from one of you?" Laura asks, more perturbed than before.

Tara, noticing the bow; suspects it can only be someone who knows Laura's love for blue velvet. "Did anyone from the office leave it here?"

"No one's been in the house except you three and the maids."

Callie and Leanne, sensing powerful vibes from the silver gift, sit stiffly peering in its direction.

"Mom, do you think the gift is from one of the maids?"

"Maybe, but in all the years I've had maids, not one has given me a gift."

Ready to dispel the mystery, Leanne sighs impatiently. "Okay, this is an exception to our rule. The only way to find out who the gift is from is to open it."

Given the odd occurrences in the home, Laura fears the gift's contents. "No, girls, let's wait till morning." With a loud yawn, Laura glances at her wristwatch. "Wow, it's late, and I'm exhausted. I think I'll turn in for the night."

"Me too, Laura," Leanne says with an ensuing yawn.

Tara and Callie continue to stare at the gift, pondering its contents as it sits unrevealed. Laura and Leanne head to their rooms with thoughts of the unopen gift on their minds and a ballooning sense of fear. At the top of the stairs, they yell over the banister, "Goodnight, girls," to Callie and Tara not ready for Christmas Eve to end.

"Goodnight," rings in unison from the first floor.

Leanne makes her way down the long hallway to the guest room Sammie guarded earlier. "Goodnight, Laura, and thanks for my iPad," she says with glee, hugging the box to her chest.

"Leanne, you're worse than a child." Laura throws her a kiss and enters the master suite with the mysterious gift pervading her thoughts. Moments later, she lies in bed with Sammie at her feet, his head straight up staring at the door. Laura ponders the evening—the creaking floors, the ever-present sensation of eyes watching her, Leanne's news of Mountainhigh899, and the mysterious gift. She lies wide-awake listening for any unusual noise until she dozes off.

Tom

In the attic, Tom waits for Callie and Tara to turn in for the night. Earlier, the close call with Laura rattled his nerves, trapping him on the second floor as he tried to leave the house. Staring at his watch, Tom notices it's almost four o'clock in the morning. *What if they don't go to bed?* A few minutes later, the sound of closing doors and peace falls over the home.

He leaves the attic, stepping cautiously onto the second-floor landing, hoping no one exits their room. The door to the master suite stands partially open. Dropping to the floor, he crawls on his hands and knees past the door. Down the stairs and into the kitchen he's greeted again by Sammie making low menacing growls with teeth bared—ready to attack. Unafraid of the little dog, Tom inches toward the back door, keeping his gaze on Sammie's face. Finally, on the veranda, he pulls the door closed without a sound, but on the other side, Sammie's low growls turn into loud, continuous barks.

Chapter 7

Christmas Morning

December 25, 2014

"God, what is it now?" Laura peers at the clock. "3:52 am," she grumbles. Gruffly throwing the covers back, she scurries downstairs. *What's gotten Sammie riled up?* She's surprised his incessant barks haven't wakened the girls. Turning on the kitchen light, and squinting at Sammie prancing to and fro and growling at the back door, she murmurs, "Calm down, Sammie ... What's gotten into you?" Sammie stops, sits on his haunch, and barks loudly at the door. "What? You wanna go out?" Slowly, opening the door and peering into the black backyard, she scans the veranda east to west. Curiously, Sammie peers from the other side of the door, his loud growl now a low grumble.

"Okay, scaredy cat ... are you going out?" With a tilted head and dangling tongue, Sammie stares into the darkness. "Okay, well, you had your chance," she states and closes the door. Sammie glances around her leg expectantly. "Are you expecting guest?" Laura asks, noticing Sammie's head peeking up. He remains on his haunch, staring at the door. "What's wrong with you lately?" Laura mumbles and heads toward the coffee pot.

"Well, I can't just go back to sleep now, Sammie." And she decides to prepare coffee for herself and the girls.

She eyes Sammie agitatedly, pondering his strange behavior. She recalls his sitting at the foot of her bed—head propped up guarding the door. *Maybe the girl's presence in the house has him riled.* Startled by footsteps, Laura jerks her head around as Tara enters the kitchen with a massive head of curls obscuring her face. Like a zombie, Tara heads straight to the gurgling coffee pot, leans on the counter, and inhales the fumes. "Did you sleep at all?" Tara asks with a loud yawn.

"Not really," Laura grumbles. "I had a hard time falling asleep, and then Sammie woke me up. He's freaking me out … And with all the stuff happening in the house, I'm downright spooked!"

Laura's fretful voice widens Tara's narrow eyes with concern. *She's more frightened than she was a few hours ago,* Tara thought. If only she could put her at ease. "Laura, you need a surveillance system. Have you ever considered installing one?"

Remembering her negligible effort and interest in the modern surveillance she'd seen two years ago, she wishes she'd been more concerned about her safety. "Yeah, I did briefly after Daniel's death. The sheer size of the house and being alone frightened me, but I got over the fear after a while. Now this … "

"Laura, do you realize how ridiculous that sounds. This estate is wide-open to criminals."

"Tara, they'll never get through the gate without the code."

Tara disagrees inwardly, reflecting on the ponderous gate. *It opens and closes so slowly, someone could indeed walk in if they tried. With the backyard open to the waterways, anyone with a boat can make their way to the property.* However, she doesn't want to spook Laura any more than she is already. "Well, anyway, you need surveillance around the home." Laura's lax attitude is bothersome. At the moment, Tara wishes she can shake some sense into her. She understands Laura's reservations about selling the home. Although leery of broaching the subject, she believes Laura may reconsider selling given recent events. "I realize how much you love this estate and the difficult decision of putting it on the market, but, Laura, you'll feel more secure in a smaller place."

Laura sits silently alarmed by Tara's thoughts of the waterway access to her backyard. The brazenness of someone just walking right onto the estate makes her shiver. She sensed Tara's annoyance about the surveillance and realizes she's just concern for her safety. Tara's thoughts fill Laura's mind before they reached Tara's lips. She waits patiently for her to finish speaking. Sensing her final word, Laura replies, "Tara, I've thought about putting the house on the market many times … I'm still uncertain. My instincts tell me not to."

"Well, Laura, I'm all about the gut," she states with an uncontrollable yawn. The coffee maker beeps four times and Tara whispers, "Finally." She pulls two large mugs from the cabinet and considers the steaming black liquid, mixing with the contrasting whiteness of the cups.

With a couple of sips, Tara's more awake, but caffeine is only a temporary fix for her lack of sleep. Pensively sitting at the island with their cup of coffee, Laura and Tara stare out the window as charcoal skies fade midnight-blue over Charleston's harbor. Dawn's inky light reveals the elegant Ravenel Bridge, Patriots Point, and the Southeastern end of the Battery. The sinister mood of the night slowly disperses with the view.

Tara peers through unruly curls, beyond the kitchen, and into the family room—eyes fixed on the mysterious gift with a troubled grimace. "Have you thought about that gift anymore?"

Laura shakes her head. "All night … "

"You should cut the suspense and open it."

"I thought we should wait for Callie and Leanne."

"They won't mind. We have other gifts to open."

Laura doesn't need much convincing. Just as curious to uncover the mystery, she heads toward the family room, retrieves the package, and brings it to the kitchen.

Intense chills races down Tara's spine. Instantly, she senses a threat.

Laura unravels the blue velvet bow and peels the silver wrappings cautiously. A brown box emerges. She pauses and peeks at Tara, who appears troubled. She recognizes that expression from somewhere. It scares her more than the box she's holding. Inside, she discovers an AHD keychain and an envelope. "Strange ... This keychain was given to our Dream Home winners."

"Open the envelope!" Tara urges.

With shaky hands, Laura tears it open and finds a note in bold-typewritten print. YOU BROKE YOUR PROMISE.

Alarmed, they stare at each other with quizzical expressions.

"Wha—what the ... What does that mean? What promise?" Laura can't fathom who would leave such a note. "And how did this get under the tree or in the house?"

"I have a bad feeling about this, Laura. Should we call the police?"

"I don't believe there's enough evidence of a threat. The police won't believe the note is anything other than a joke ..." Suddenly, Laura reflects on the sounds in the house the last couple of days. "You think someone has been in the house? All those sounds I heard can't be a coincidence. And Sammie's odd behavior the last couple of days—now this all makes sense."

With stronger chills, Tara stares at the note. "We're going to the police. And you're getting surveillance as soon as possible."

Tom

Heading toward East Bay Street, Tom delivers another package to Tara McPherson's home. He will make two more deliveries before he checks into a hotel. A baleful grin slits his face. At any moment, Laura Alcott's security will be ripped away in her own home. Now she'll fathom fear as her secure world changes in an instant.

Pulling into Tara's private driveway, Tom exits swiftly toward the side of the townhouse. He checks several ground floor windows. With no success, he rushes to the backyard and onto a covered patio. A basement window catches his attention, but like the others, it's locked securely. Stepping backward and staring above, he notices a screened-in porch, and over the porch sits a small window slightly ajar. He considers leaving the package at the front door, but he's determined to strike fear in their hearts.

Directly behind him, he studies the long branches of an oak tree that lean over the top of the porch. Without thought, he scuttles onto the first branch, climbing until he's over the rooftop. Pausing, he looks down and studies the skylights below. Dangling from the branch, he takes a deep breath and drops with a loud bang on top of the porch, barely missing the skylight. The small window sits right at his waist. Noticing the size of the opening, he realizes his body might not fit. *It'll be a tight squeeze.* Undeterred, he lifts the window high and pops his head inside a large glass enclosed shower. He deliberates how to position his body, and then enters feet first. For several minutes, he struggles. Scrapping his arms, he manages to wedge his entire body through, dropping into the stoned tiled shower.

He makes his way out of the bath, down the hallway, and into Tara's bedroom. He places the package in the center of the bed—a spot she'll notice instantly. He exits the room and heads downstairs. Before he leaves the house, he draws all the shades on the first floor. *This will chill her blood*; he thought. Then he exits through the back door.

Chapter 8

A New Year

January 3, 2015

Tara hates leaving her friends after the holiday, but especially this year. After finding the ominous gift, leaving Laura alone was difficult. No matter how she and Leanne tried to stay, Laura protested, saying she didn't need a babysitter. *"After all, Callie's here; I won't be alone,"* she'd said. However, Tara sensed Laura hid her fear behind a false mask of courage.

When Tara enters her townhouse foyer, an instant chill runs down her left arm—an acute foreboding that only strikes her back, never her arm. Warily, she places her bags on the floor and advances inside the home. Beyond the living room, shades are drawn on every window as if done intentionally. When she's away, she always leaves them down. In the middle of the room, her body lights with greater chills. Fearfully, she circles the room, searching her possessions for anything missing, out of place, or that doesn't belong. Easing her cell phone from her handbag, she continues into the kitchen and grabs a knife from the counter. Cautiously, she checks the main floor but finds nothing unusual.

Tara's heart races as she ascends the stairs with a firm grip on the knife. Opening the bedroom door, her heart leaps to her throat at the sight of the ominous silver gift in the middle of her bed. She refuses to take another step and instantly dials Laura's number.

"Tara?"

"Laura, someone's been in my house, and they left the silver gift."

"Did you open it?"

"No, I'm afraid."

"Tara, open it."

Hesitantly, she steps toward the bed, picks up the gift, and rips the wrappings to threads. Again, the brown box emerges with the AHD's keychain and an ominous message—YOU BROKE YOUR PROMISE, is more fearful that the first note. Tara runs down the stairs, out of the house, straight to her car.

"Tara?"

"I left the house, Laura."

"Have you heard from Leanne? I'm getting worried."

Quickly, Tara starts the car and backs out of the driveway. "I'm heading to Leanne's now."

Leanne

Driving faster than normal, Leanne's eager to spend time with Adam and ready to give him the long-awaited answer. Pulling into the driveway, through the side alley leading to the garage, the townhouse appears desolate—no lights on anywhere. She notices the patio door is ajar and wonders if *Adam forgot to close it.* Exiting the car, she enters the house through the open door, alarmed by silence. The TV or music is always playing when Adam's home.

"Adam? Adam, are you here?" There's no reply. Concerned, she cautiously begins inspecting every room. *Anyone or anything could have walked right in.* She pulls a can of pepper spray from her handbag, turns on all the lights, and walks through the home, making sure windows and doors are locked. Certain no one's inside; she heads to her office. The answering machine blinks green. She hits play, and Adam's voice comes through distant and solemn. His voice echoes frustration. Concerned, she picks up the phone, ready to dial his number when beside a stack of mail; blue velvet and silver catch her attention.

Grabbing her purse and keys she races from the house, certain whoever left the package left the patio door open. *But how did they get in? Did Adam forget to lock the door?* She races to the car, puts the car in reverse, backs out of the driveway and immediately brakes, avoiding a collision with Tara's bumper.

Chapter 9

Unease

The girls leave the precinct feeling no more secure than when they first arrived. Searching for her car keys, Laura suppresses an urge to scream, recalling the apathetic policeman, who sat expressionless behind his desk. "I knew this would be a wasted trip."

Leanne remains calm, certain an emotional outburst won't help, although she wanted to throw a chair at the stone-faced officer to elicit emotion. "We needed to report the break-in, Laura. Now there's an official police record, and if this person resurfaces, the police will take it more seriously next time."

Tara walks behind the girls toward the car; trying to still chills ripping through her body. "You're right, Leanne, but regardless, some protection should be offered. For God's sake, the person broke into our private space. Do we have to be battered and bleeding for them to send security? Girls, we can't wait for the police to help," Tara says, wincing from electrical currents surging through her body like a radiating missile over every inch of her skin. All she wants is to dive into a cold pool of water.

Trying to disguise her discomfort, she sits still as a statue in the back seat.

"Girls, it's up to us now," Laura says, sensing Tara's discomfort. "We need to stick together until we figure out what's going on. Since my home has more space than yours, I think you two should move in until we figure this out. Neither of us should be alone at this point. Leanne, where's Adam?"Laura asks.

"I messed up," Leanne says in a tearful whisper. "I'm sorry guys. I screwed up this time. I think he left for good."

Tara shakes her head. "That's ridiculous. Adam would never leave you; he loves you too much."

"Well, he did. He's gone back to Chicago for the holiday. I think he's finally had enough of my nonsense. He left a message earlier saying he'd call, but I don't know when or if he's returning." Finally realizing how much she wants and needs him in her life she says, "I just don't want to lose him."

"Leanne, you're not going to lose Adam. He probably just needs time to think. Believe me, that man's not letting you go that easily, sweetie. You'll see. Okay, ladies. I'm taking you home to pack. You're moving in with me."

With no better alternative, the girls don't protest as Laura drives away from the police precinct. Silence fills the car as she turns onto Broad Street straight to Leanne's townhouse.

January 5, 2015, Alcott Estate

Two days later, Laura sits in her office examining the new surveillance. The entire house, all thirty rooms, have cameras installed at every major entrance—back door, side door, hallway, window—every entrance in the estate. Laura wonders why she hadn't done this earlier. Although the girls feel more secure, they're still on edge anticipating the next note, phone call, or physical encounter with their stalker.

Cody

At the entrance, Cody stomps thick powdery snow off his boots and pants before entering the Constellation Hotel at Northstar in Tahoe. He walks toward the fireplace in the lobby, stopping to warm his hands before heading to his suite.

"Mr. Darling," called the desk clerk. "You received a package today by UPS."

"Thank you," Cody says, and wonders who the package is from. He heads to his suite on the fifth floor, and shakes the box, trying to determine its contents. Inside the small kitchen, he looks for a knife to cut the thick brown UPS packaging. A tiny gift wrapped in silver with a blue velvet bow falls out. He searches the envelope deeper, hoping to find a card or note from the sender. *Maybe it's from the staff.* They're the only ones privy to my whereabouts. He unties the bow and unwraps the silver wrapping to find the brown box, keychain, and note it contains. Perplexed, he empties the contents on the desk hoping to uncover another clue to its sender ... *Nothing.*

He studies the keychain, remembering this particular one was discontinued last year. For eleven years, AHD gave this chain to previous winners before redesigning the new 2014 keychain. No one could have access to these—only the winner and the staff. He reads the note: You Broke Your Promise.

Why would a winner send this or anyone at AHD ... But no one else has access to this chain. He ponders the note and emerges from thought even more perplexed. He reaches for the phone to call Tara but stops when he realizes it's midnight on the East Coast. Again, he deliberates the note and jeers at the cryptic message. Too tired to ponder its meaning any further, he places it on the desk and heads for the shower.

Chapter 10

The Shushing

January 10, 2015, McPherson Home

Nyla knows her daughter will visit today. She saw this moment long before Tara was born. For thirty-eight years she's been waiting for this day. With the onset of the girl's troubles, she realizes Tara will have no choice but to embrace her gift of precognition. To soothe her anxiousness she's prepared Tara's favorite treat. The aroma of blueberry cobbler fills the home, and if the bittersweet treat doesn't assuage her worries, a chilled bottle of red wine is on the dining room table.

When Nyla was pregnant with Tara, her dreams and vision were so vivid, she feared for her unborn daughter. With each touch of her swollen belly she saw the exact date and time of Tara's troubles, and most disconcerting, there's nothing she can do to change her fate. Nonetheless, she will help her daughter develop her talent when the time comes. Today is that day.

"Hello, honey," Nyla says without turning around.

"Mom, how'd you know it was me? I swear you have eyes on the back of your head," Tara says in amazement.

Nyla turns around and proceeds to the dining table with the blueberry cobbler. "Honey, can you bring the bowls and spoons on the counter?"

With one raised eyebrow, Tara collects the utensils and follows Nyla to the dining table. "Were you expecting me? You only make blueberry cobbler when I visit."

"Come; let's talk."

Placing the bowl and spoons on the table, she studies Nyla's deliberate actions. *Had she's planned this moment?* "Mom, you're freaking me out."

Nyla has to help her daughter relax. The conversation about to take place is a crucial one. "Sit, honey, let's eat."

Tara surveys the table and her mother's deliberate actions—cobbler and red wine—something's up, besides the annoying chills radiating up and down her spine. "Okay, mom, since you knew I was coming, tell me why I'm here?"

Without turning around, Nyla suspects a creeping frown across Tara's forehead, and her warm hazel eyes deepening a darker shade of brown. She slices into the cobbler, filling Tara's bowl with a huge chunk and a topping of whipped cream. She sighs and wipes her hands on a napkin. Taking a seat at the table, she finally acknowledges Tara's face—a face, which reminds her so much of her own at thirty-eight. "Well, honey, things are happening to your body causing you great distress. Tara, these are sensations I've also experienced. In fact, every woman in our family experiences similar forebodings," Nyla says with a steady gaze. "It's your gift, Tara."

"Gift, this is not a gift when my entire body radiates like a missile ready to explode."

Nyla cups her mouth to contain a grin and muted laugh, understanding all too well Tara's frustrations. "You will feel this way until you release your fear. Right now you're blocking your energy because you're frightened. Just let it happen, and your body will feel normal."

"How do I do that? And what happens when I'm unblocked?"

"Eat your cobbler, dear," Nyla says, trying to find the right words. "In my time, our gift was called the gift of foresight; some call it precognition or premonitions. However, today, people choose to call it intuition, gut instincts, or sixth sense. Remember I told you when you were younger to listen to your intuition because you're extremely intuitive, and this runs on the female side of our family."

Impatiently, Tara waits for Nyla to make her point. "Uh huh … I remember."

Nyla senses Tara's growing agitation. "Tara, bear with me. There's a lot I need to tell you today, okay?"

"I'm sorry. I just want to be rid of these chills!"

"You will, but you need to understand a few things first."

"Such as …"

With care, Nyla chooses a crucial time in Tara's life. "I've been aware of your gift since your childhood, but I couldn't tell you until this point. Do you remember ever experiencing visions as a child?"

Tara twists her lips and says, "No."

Nyla knows she's blocked her childhood vision, but she was hoping Tara remembered some of their conversations. "You've forgotten a great deal, Tara. We had this talk on your seventh birthday, but it's slipped your memory. Do you remember Janie?"

Tara glances at her mother, pondering the name. "Janie … No, should I?"

Nyla squint her eyes. "Think a little harder, Tara … Do you remember your play dates after school?"

Tara shakes her head; afraid there's something she should remember, but can't.

Nyla pauses and wonders how to proceed. "When you were seven-years-old, you had your first vision. One day after school, during a play date with Janie, you sat staring at her with an odd expression. Later when her parents picked her up, you told her mom Janie is sick. That same evening, you said you didn't want Janie to leave. I'd asked you where she's going, and you'd said to heaven."

"What! Wow, I should remember something so grim, but I have no recollection."

All those years ago, Nyla knew Tara was experiencing the first signs of clairvoyance. "Tara there's no way you could have known your friend was sick. Janie was diagnosed with leukemia and died several months later. Your instincts were exceptional as a child. After Janie, you started noticing other things about people and would make remarks that absolutely frightened me about our next door neighbor." Nyla sees doubt in Tara's arched brow. She's stiller than Nyla ever remembered. "Tara?"

"I'm listening."

Nyla realizes how shocking this must be, but Tara has to remember the past. "For some reason, as you got older, you stopped listening to your instincts." Nyla pauses, staring harder, for some sign of remembrance in Tara's face, but her expression is blank. "Do you remember the name of your imaginary friends?"

A nervous laugh bursts from Tara's mouth. "Imaginary friend … You and dad must have thought I was crazy."

"No, we realized children have imaginary friends, but yours coincided with your first vision. Your mind grew more receptive to your environment." Contemplating her words, Nyla takes a spoon of cobbler. Her next revelation will surprise her daughter. "Tara, listen to what I'm about to say. This will give you some clue how strong your gift was as a child. Your imaginary friend's names were Laura and Leanne." Nyla waits for a response but receives only a wide-eyed stare. "You used to tell me about Laura's interests in decorations, and her favorite color and texture—blue velvet. You also described both Laura and Leanne's hair and eye color precisely. I worried when you told me about Leanne's fright when she spotted a ghost. Every day, details of your friends became clearer. Some of the things you told us, you'd never understand at that age. You even talked about the Pink Lady."

"No way …"

"Yes, you did, Tara. You described in exact detail the pink house with sweeping piazzas on the waterfront. I'd often wondered if the house you foresaw was AHD's headquarter. You were experiencing visions of your future."

"Laura and Leanne, imaginary friends," Tara mumbles.

"Some days I had a terrible time pulling you away from your playtime. For hours, you would rearrange furniture, pretending to decorate the room with Laura. You even asked me to buy Leanne a new earpiece for her iPad." Nyla's loud guffaw echoes through the room. "Tara, you realize in 1983 how strange I must have appeared, walking into a toy store inquiring about the iPad. Little did I realize the iPad hadn't been created yet? Hmmm … If I'd been wise, I should've invested in Apple when I had the chance," she says with a snicker.

Laughing with Nyla, Tara almost chokes on a piece of cobbler. Nyla rushes to the refrigerator for a bottle of water. "Tara, I'd forgotten about your imaginary friends until the night of the Alcott's dinner, almost twenty-two years later." Handing Tara the water, Nyla continued with her story. "There they were, Laura and Leanne, as you described at seven-years-of-age. I realized you'd seen the future all those years ago."

"How could I have forgotten?"

"I believe something happened. I think you witnessed something sinister because one day you just stopped playing. Your premonitions stopped altogether. Whatever your vision revealed scared you so much you blocked them, and then the chills started. Chills are a sure sign in the family of blocked premonitions." Nyla realizes Tara's gift has been hibernating all these years, but she also knows with a little help, her memories will come back.

"Have you ever wondered how I sense your thoughts?"

Tara peers carefully at her perspicacious mother. "I used to think your ability was peculiar, but I believe all mothers are somehow intuitively linked to their children."

"No, Tara. My abilities are not as simple as that. My intuitions are as powerful as yours. I possess the family gift as well. You were curious how I sensed your presence earlier ... Well, I've seen this moment here with you at this same table before your birth," she says staring at the shiny, cherry wood table, and smiling and rubbing a spot she'd scratched with a carving knife years ago. "My visions are so exact, I can see the date, place, and time in my premonitions. You will understand the importance of this meeting when we're finished today. Your childhood visions are happening already. Your senses are growing stronger because the people you love are in danger. The chills will only get worse until you learn to release your fear."

Does she know about the silver gift? Downing the bottle of water she tries to squelch the chills running along her spine. "I'll do anything to get rid of these things. Can you show me how?"

Tara's growing desperation, tells Nyla she's ready to receive her visions, and harness her gift. "I will in a moment sweetie, but there's more to tell." While Nyla finished the cobbler, the image of the silver package with the blue velvet bow resides in her mind. She dislikes her powerlessness over the girls' predicament. If she could change their fate, she would. However, changing destiny can never happen without dire consequences. If Tara can see her vision, and stop Tom before he sets the chain of events in motion, then, and only then, will their fate change. This is Tara's chance to become who she's meant to be. "Tara, do you dream about things that make absolutely no sense?"

"Sometimes; for several weeks dreams have become obscure."

"These dreams are your second sight. You're receiving snap-shots of some future event. Honey, you need to start keeping a journal. The more you record your dreams, the clearer the message will become. Most women in our family recorded their premonitions and were able to see the exact day and time events will happen. This requires enormous mental energy, Tara. So, you need to learn how to clear your mind of all noises. You won't heed the message if you're fearful. Before you can make any progress, you'll have to remember your childhood vision. Right now, there's a wall blocking your abilities."

Nyla stands and approaches Tara, lightly placing her index fingers on her temples. "You need to silence the mental chat-ter masking your gift and quiet this mind," she says, pucker-ing her lips. Nyla makes a shushing sound, explaining how her mom—Shelley Crum—silenced noise by shushing her soul.

"Shushing the soul?" *What a strange expression.* "Is this prac-ticed by all women in the family?"

"Shushing has been called many names over the years—chants, mantras, and more, but your grandmother coined the phrase shushing-of-the-soul. Many women in the family use mental chanting to open their minds, or block visions." In a deeper tone, Nyla warns, "You must be careful with this gift. You can misinterpret the meanings of your dreams and visions. Honey, I have to stress, do not act on your premonitions until you shush your mind completely ... Okay?"

Tara senses the urgency in Nyla's voice and reassures her she won't act rashly.

"Tara, I believe you already possess the ability to sense dan-ger—the chills running through your body, but you need to hone your gift. You need to capture the when, where, and how of each visions. And again, these elements will appear only when you release your fear."

Nyla recognizes Tara's conflicting view about her gift. But she will soon understand clairvoyance is not a curse, but a blessing she'll reap happiness from. "Tara, this is not about gloom and doom, your gift will open you to many spiritual benefits. You're part of a whole and can connect to the universe. And if you use your gift correctly, your spiritual life will be delightful."

Still trying to grasp the shushing, Tara asks, "How do I shush my soul?"

Nyla releases her hand from Tara's temples. "Come with me."

In the backyard, Nyla leads Tara to the old carriage house, a place she'd renovated years ago into a studio on the second-floor to practice yoga and meditation, but Tara had no idea about shushing. The studio has been off-limits to both her and dad until now. Climbing the stairs to Nyla's private loft, a little alcove with a triangular window made from crystal emerges. "Wow ... Beautiful." A small sitting area with several large floor pillows lay in front of the bejeweled window. In the corner of the room, a small waterfall babbles tranquility. Various crystals and gems are scattered about the pillows.

"Sit, honey," Nyla says, assuming a crossed-legged position on a large pillow adjacent to Tara.

"What are the crystals for?"

"They help facilitate meditation and shushing. Nyla picks up a beautiful jagged Amethysts crystal and places the stone in Tara's hand. "This will help you quiet your mind." Tara rolls the stone around her palm as if done many times.

"Shushing may take a while depending on the strength of your gift. You might feel the effects today or it could take several days of practice." Nyla takes Tara's hand and folds it around the crystal. "You ready?"

Tara nods and waits for Nyla's directives.

"I'm going to guide you to a calmer mind. Listen to my words and just follow. Close your eyes and listen to every sound in the room. Then limit sounds to the babbling water until it's the only sound you hear."

In the distance, Saint Michael's ringing bells make it difficult for Tara to focus. The moment she closed her eyes every sound amplified—barking dogs, passing cars, pinging on the rooftop, and whistling wind around the carriage house. It takes several minutes before the babbling water is the only sound she hears.

"Okay, now, listen to your heart and breath." Nyla studies Tara's face, sensing slowing breathes. "Take a deep inhalation and hold until I tell you to release it. Feel your heartbeat and the jagged crystal in your palm. Your heart beats slows, slower and slower ..." Nyla takes Tara through the ritual several times before she's entranced.

When Tara finally breathes, she finds herself in a surreal place, surrounded by heat, and acidic smoke strangling her throat. Overpowering fumes trigger deep, hacking coughs. *I can't breathe! I'm choking!* Her heart races, a dull faint comes over her. In the dark, a piercing scream sounds. Tara wakes disoriented and choking from phantom smoke—unaware she's been in a trance for ten minutes.

Noticing Tara's shaken state, Nyla takes Tara's hand and squeezes reassuringly. "What did you see?"

"Oh my, God, I still feel it," Tara says shaking off the dizziness. Remembering the incalescent atmosphere, Tara rubs her arm and face. "Nyla, my skin warmed from the heat, and I thought I'd pass out from the smoke. It was so real," she says, brushing her arms briskly. "I sensed a fire and heard someone scream."

Nyla recalls the fire she saw in her vision thirty-eight years ago, but she can't tell Tara. She has to remember the vision on her own.

"The smoke, it was so real," Tara continued in disbelief.

Hmmm ... Nyla ponders; *she's more advanced than I believed.* "That was a snapshot, honey. You need to see the full movie in your head. The more shushing you practice, the more you will capture. You have to see it entirely."

Since she woke from the trance, the electric currents have subsided. Tara breathes deep and stretches her legs to discard remnants of dizziness and pins and needles numbing her legs. Then she notices a tan, leather-bound journal in Nyla's lap. "What are you holding?"

While Tara was in a trance, Nyla collected the book containing their ancestry. "I've been trying to find the right moment to show you this. There's something you need to understand about your heritage."

"You've already told me our family history—"

"Yes, but not our blood-ties to the Alcotts and Gowans."

"The Alcotts and Gowans?" Haze from the trance clouds her mind. It takes a second to register Nyla's words. "I'm related to the Alcotts ... Laura's husband's family?"

"Yes, and your father's a distant cousin of Daniel."

"So, I'm related to Laura?"

"In more than one way; Laura is a direct descendant of the Gowan family. In the 1800s, Daniel's great-great-great grandfather, Zachary Alcott, married Melissa Gowan. The Gowan women are remarkably clairvoyant. With the Alcott-Gowan union, every female offspring in the Alcott family inherited the Gowan gift. You claimed the gift from your father's side as well as mine."

"Yours? But you're not an Alcott."

"Tara, I have their bloodline."

Tara stares at warm, hazel eyes which comforted her during childhood and ponders the secrets they've sheltered all these years. "But, your maiden name is Crum. How are they connected to the Alcotts?"

Nyla pauses with a troubled expression and ponders what she's about to disclose.

Tara waits without interrupting; realizing the burden of secrecy Nyla has carried for so long, and the enormous relief of finally unveiling the truth.

Nyla adjusts her body on the pillow and speaks as if she's telling a well-rehearsed story. "William Alcott, Daniel's great-great-grandfather, and the son of Melissa Gowan had an illegitimate child with one of the Alcott servants—Susan Cox. The birth was shrouded in secrecy. William Alcott forbade Susan from telling anyone. For years, others assumed the child was conceived from a servant in the Alcott household. Susan Cox gave her son her surname, to hide his true father. Tara, my bloodline to the Alcotts stems from Nathan Cox. All Nathan's daughters were born with clairvoyant abilities, and the gift continues to his last descendant ... You."

Astonished, Tara sits unmoving, grasping every word. "So, this makes you a relative of dad?"

"Yes ... At first, I was appalled, but after researching our lineage, I realized I'm so far removed from James, our shared bloodline doesn't make a difference. I'm not even a distant cousin, but just a family branch that fell from the tree. Nonetheless, my bloodline stems from the Alcotts." Nyla relinquishes her hold on the book and hands it to Tara.

Still lingering on Nyla's connection to the Alcotts, Tara shakes her head in confusion.

"Honey, I am giving this book to you. Study your family tree ... This is your heritage."

Tara glances over the cover, and runs her hand over a symbol she sees every day at AHD—the circle enclosing a square and triangle is embossed on the leather jacket. Opening the book, she's confronted with rows of branches containing names and dates spanning from 1798 to the present. Her eyes fall on the Davis surname. "Leanne's family ... No way!"

"Yes, you're related to both Laura and Leanne. Daniel's grandaunt, Sharon Alcott, married Allen Davis, thus starting another branch of the Alcott Family."

A sudden realization pokes at Tara's mind. "So, if all the Alcott and Gowan women are gifted that means Laura and Leanne are also clairvoyant."

Nyla hoped Tara would understand, and shakes her head with a discerning grin. "From what I've kenned their gifts are as powerful as yours."

"Why do you believe that?"

"Tara, I could be wrong, but my instincts are always right." Nyla stares at Tara as she searches the pages in awe. It's now Tara's turn to take action. "I've told you a lot today. I don't expect you to grasp everything yet. I had to reveal your bloodline because you need to understand the strength of your gift. I also want you to talk to Laura and Leanne. It's time you three acknowledge your gift and your blood-ties."

Pulling at a strand of hair, the curl releases with words from her mouth. "Is dad aware of your kinship?"

"Your father has known for as long as I have."

"How did you find out?"

Nyla recalled the phone call from Marion Alcott thirty-years ago asking her to meet at the Alcott estate. In awe, she'd sat in the massive Alcott living room, comforted and reassured by Marion as she'd explained the history of her ancestry. "Marion was cleaning out the attic in the Alcott estate and came across a letter from William Alcott to Susan Cox; the testament hidden away all those years. The last will and testament explained William had conceived a child—Nathan Cox with Susan Cox—and he bequeaths a portion of his estate and homes to Nathan and his progeny. All my life I assumed my relatives were Alcott servants. I was amazed to find William took this secret to his grave. With the help of Daniel's mother and your father I completed the family tree."

Tara imagines the shock and surprise Nyla must have felt discovering her shared bloodline with her husband. For a few moments they say nothing, and the waterfall in the corner appear louder than before. Curious about the last will and testament, Tara asks, "Did Nathan Cox or his family ever receive the land?"

"Yes. Nathan Cox was raised by the Gowan sisters as one of their own. An agreement was made between the Alcott family and Gowan sisters, which stipulated Nathan and his progeny's financial welfare. From what I've seen, the arrangement was honored. And Nathan and his ancestors were taken care of extremely well."

"I'm curious, so what happened to the land Nathan Cox inherited?"

"You're sitting on one of his properties. The others include the townhouse you're living in, as well as other properties scattered about Charleston."

Aww ... Tara pondered. Now understanding why the townhouse is rent free. "So the townhouse is my property?"

"Yes ... Daniel's parents are the executor of the family foundation. When your dad and I moved back to Charleston, she made sure we got this property and more. So, when your grandfather passed away, we not only inherited the McPherson estate but also part of the Alcott estate. Tara, your dad's family, and the Alcotts are the reason you and your friends are together at AHD. As you know, the Alcotts own the company and, of course, the Pink Lady. AHD is yours, Laura's, and Leanne's."

In disbelief, Tara mumbles inaudibly, "Laura and Leanne ... Family? I can't believe it." Searching through the book, Tara examines five mazes of Alcott generations. The labyrinths of branches are so complex; she wonders how Nyla acquired all the years of history. The long, diverging limbs of Alcott, Davis, and McPherson's converge at the bottom of the family tree, bringing together four distinct descendants—Laura, Leanne, Tara, and a single branch extending from Laura to Callie. Tara glances at Nyla. "Callie?"

"Yes, Tara, I perceive Callie will be the most gifted of the group."

It was late evening when Tara arrived at the Alcott estate. The excruciating currents have all but left her body. She understands the chills will return if she doesn't practice shushing. Stopping at the gate, she punches in the passcode. It still opens as slow as molasses, but she's happy the estate finally has surveillance cameras. She waits as the lock clicks into place then continues down the Alcott's private road. Since leaving Nyla, the winds have picked up force. Along the private road, the trees sway from strong winds. Tara spies the ominous, purple skies sitting behind the estate, and perceives the storm it foretells.

With the tan leather-bound book, Tara heads straight to the east wing, and into a large suite, wondering how to tell Laura and Leanne what she's learned. *Will this change the dynamics of our friendship?* She hopes not. No matter what happens, she needs to notify them soon, because whatever trouble is coming is going to cause heartache for all.

Desperate to unblock her vision, Tara puts the book in the desk drawer and readies her mind for more shushing. She moves to the reading annex off the suite, sits with crossed legs, holding the crystal in her hand. The pace of her heart slows to a steady beat, and once again, she travels to an unfamiliar place.

> *Illusory walls fluctuate with the home's vague interior. Snow glows through a large triangular wall of windows. Smoke surrounds a blurry figure, and a piercing scream emanates from outside the home ... Tara!*

"Tara?" Laura calls from the hallway.

Lost in a trance, Tara believes Laura's voice is the voice in her vision.

Chapter 11

Touch

January 10, 2015, Alcott Estate

With nightfall, lightning sparkles around the estate and winds sweep crevices, playing a creaky chorus. Toward the back of the main floor, in the old guest wing, thunderous booms and crackling logs serenade Leanne hiding beneath the covers. One touch of surrounding objects and she'll venture to a past she doesn't care to visit.

Today, copious visions overwhelmed her senses. One tiny touch of an object thrust her into past lives. Peering about the room, she searches for the misplaced Moldavite ring. "Of all nights ... where is it?" Most days, she doesn't need amulets or stones to protect her. She welcomes her visions, but not after the soul-sapping day. She feels some force is guiding her to images missed on previous occasions.

On many visits, she'd seen Laura's husband and previous Alcott generations roaming about as if ghosts. She'd realized they're merely harmless vestiges of the past, however, on Christmas Eve, she questioned Daniel's essence. Most visions don't stare back as Daniel's had, watching Laura and Callie all night. She's certain it was his spirit. *Thank goodness for alcohol,* a necessary elixir imbibed to dull her senses on Christmas Eve.

Now Leanne wonders if she'd chosen the right room. *Of all the spaces in the home, why is this one haunting her?* She'd deliberately chosen the renovated guest wing because it felt calmer, unlike hot spots in other rooms. At first, the suite was soothing, until her foot's direct contact with the floor threw her into a past life she'd never seen before. She wasn't scared, only drained. Now, hours later, she dreads the trek across the room to the bathroom. Hesitant to place her bare feet on the floor, she slips inside thick fuzzy slippers. With a single glide of her covered foot, she's thrown into a past life inside this room. Her essence is that of William Alcott.

> *He sits wheezing with difficulty, trying to finish a letter to Susan. Illness oozes from his pores—tainting the air a bitter odor. The penmanship blurs as he reads over the letter. With shaky hands, he seals and stamps the letter with an Alcott Crest. He secures it in a leather pouch and stows it inside the desk. Too weak to stand, pale, veiny hands grasp the edge of the bureau. With a slow turn, and a few steps on frail legs, he peers down at his feet, and the floor rises swiftly to his face. The door swings open. A female essence moves through Leanne. The woman screams for help and kneels to the floor, lifting William's head.*

Leanne wakes with warmth radiating through her feet. She looks at the spot William Alcott collapsed many years ago. Quickly, she races to the bathroom and hums chants until she's back in bed. Flat on her back, William Alcott's sickness imbues her body. She dozes off in a weak state, and dreams invade her mind.

Seated on a wooden chair in front of the crackling fireplace, warm tears stream down Susan Cox's youthful brown skin. She swallows painful sobs so other servants can't hear and gazes at her exposed round belly, aware the pregnancy will be obvious to others soon. She rubs her belly as if stroking the child it holds. She'll never reveal the child's real father—a bastard to be rejected by both the black and white community. She makes her way to the bath and immerses her weary body in soothing water. Rivulets roll down her face, dotting the bath as she recalls Williams scolding words when he learned she's pregnant with his child. She understands if others find out she'll be sold from the only home she's known in Charleston. Susan sinks her head under water, testing her courage to end it all, but she can't. Coming up for air, she gasps and shakes her head. She can't bear to hurt the child.

Leanne wakes, gasping for air, her pillow soaked with Susan's tears and her mind replete with her sadness. Every emotion Susan held melded with her consciousness. Weak and listless, Leanne quickly falls into a deep sleep. She dreams of a baby boy named Nathan Cox.

Busy about their day, the Alcott family has no idea of the birth taking place in the servant's quarters. Surrounded by her two sisters, Melissa Gowan stands over Susan Cox, fearful they'll lose both mother and child. Covered in blood and sweat in the sweltering back room, Melissa screams, "Breathe, Susan! Don't give up," as she delivers her baby. "This child must be born Susan." The first time Melissa touched Susan's belly, she kenned the child's importance to future generations. Melissa knew she'd help Susan bring this infant into the world.

Melissa foresaw the progeny of Susan Cox's baby—Tara McPherson, and the two powerful Alcott women together. She saw the powers of the three: past, present, and future brought together. Now standing over Susan Cox, Melissa sees Leanne's image, witnessing the birth as if her essence were in the room. She recognizes Leanne's importance in telling the history of this family and this child.

"Come on, Susan ... breathe." A weakened Susan gives one final push and then falls unconscious from the pain. Holding the baby, her grandchild, Melissa cleans him off and wraps him in a cotton blanket while gloating at the innocent child conceived from her son William. Melissa places the child in her sister's care where Nathan Cox will be hidden and protected from harm. Melissa turns her gaze to meet Leanne's as if she were physically there.

Intrigued by Melissa Gowan's power, Leanne holds fast to her dream, but the connection severs. *Did Melissa bring her to that moment to witness Nathan Cox's birth? How had she seen her posthumously?* Her ability to foresee her and the girls all those years ago is astonishing. Melissa and Tara are kindred souls. *Is that why Melissa could see so far into the future?*

Leanne wonders what happen to the young servant girl, Susan Cox, all those years ago. Did she get to hold her baby boy, or was there an implicit agreement between her and Melissa Gowan? Leanne rolls her head toward the nightstand and notices it's seven in the morning. She rolls her weak body out of bed, wondering how she'll make it through the day. Throwing on her robe; she drags to the kitchen, hoping caffeine will revive her energy.

Chapter 12

Out of the Bag

January 14, 2015, AHD Headquarter

The sun sits at high noon above AHD headquarters, casting three-dimensional shadows across the Pink Lady's facade. Inside AHD's conference room, the girls sit quietly around a conference table, waiting for Cody's update by Skype. An eighty-inch screen hangs from the ceiling, displaying Cody in Tahoe's Constellation at Northstar's conference room. Dressed in a gray turtleneck and jeans; his flawless brown skin is tinged a subtle plum possibly from Tahoe's chill. Cody's charismatic personality always commands attention, but not today as the girls sit wordlessly, consumed with other matters.

Laura sits observantly watching Tara's tight clutch on a leather-bound book, and sensing concerns about their bloodline. As soon as the meeting is over, she intends to ease her worries.

Also aware of Tara's ancestral knowledge, Leanne is anxious for the meeting to end.

Pondering the girls' distant expressions, Cody asks, "Ladies, why so quiet this morning?"

Glancing at Leanne and Tara, Laura responds, "Cody, we just have a lot on our minds today."

Cody's unconvinced, sensing a different energy around his friends. "Come on, ladies; snap out of it. I assure you there's good news about the project. Tara, what happened with all the questions? You're making me nervous girl. It's not like you to be without questions," he says with a chuckle.

Pulled from her reverie, Tara smiles apologetically and feigns interest, but her clairvoyance friends consume her thoughts. "Cody, tell us something good."

"Welcome back, Ms. McPherson." With a signature chin rub, Cody peers quizzically at the screen. "You sure ladies ... If you need more time to get your thoughts together, we can meet another day."

Tara sits straight in the chair and says with spurious words, "Cody, you had my attention the entire time."

"Sure did," Laura says, bolstering Tara's lie.

And Leanne nods her head in accord.

Clearing his throat, Cody delivers his update. "All right ladies," he says with a squint. "Tara, as soon as I received your email, I spoke with the developers and builders. They're thrilled to take on the new project, and all the details are under consideration."

Recalling setbacks and issues from the previous year Tara asks, "No opposition to the lot selection or size of the home?"

"Nope, not a one this year ... Tara, by the way, thanks for referring Michael Anders as your choice of architects. He's a fantastic guy, and his work is going to blow your mind. His industrial-mountain home is the style we're aspiring to build. As soon as we draw up the blueprint, I'll send it via email."

Confused, Tara tries to remember when she'd chosen Michael Anders as the preferred candidate. She remembers emailing Cody the architect list, but she doesn't remember recommending Michael. Reflecting on December fifteenth, Tara recalls how unreal it felt sending the email to Cody. *Ah!* Now she remembers. She'd highlighted a name. It must have been Michael. Why she'd chosen him, she's uncertain, but nonetheless, she trusts Cody's professional judgment and squelches her questioning mind. "Thanks, Cody. I'm excited to see Michael's design."

Finally, Tara loosens her hold on the book, clears her throat. "Cody, the team and I wonder if the design will consider the three fault lines beneath the Martis Camp community."

"That's our first consideration, Tara. The engineers will use steel beams to prevent the house from collapsing during an earthquake and to withstand heavy snowfalls in the region. We will also include sloping roofs with triple-exposed beams to allow runoff from torrential downpours. Don't worry, ladies. We've thought of everything, even material to withstand wildfires. Many of the homes in the region already use these techniques."

Just as Tara says, "Great," a new foreboding tugs her gut and she wonders if her instincts are warning her about the region or something else. Again, Cody's voice trails across the room, pulling Tara back from concern.

"Laura, you and your design team will be out here soon—"

"Yes, Cody," Laura interrupted abruptly. "Tara and Leanne will also accompany me this year."

"Oh?" Cody queries, with narrowed eyes and a rub of his chin. "Is there a reason you three will grace me with your presence this year?"

Laura proceeds to tell Cody about the gift received at Christmas, and their agreement to get out of Charleston for a while.

He'd all but disregarded the package until this moment. "Wow, this is more serious than I thought. I also received the package. Has anyone gone to the police?"

"We did, but without proof of a physical threat, they won't help. So, we're on our own."

"Of course, well, maybe getting out of Charleston is a good idea, but my only concern is how this person found me. You three might not be any safer here in Tahoe."

"That's a good point. But we're safer together than alone," Tara says with growing alarm. "Is it possible to find another hotel or an undisclosed location before we arrive?"

"Tara, I'll start scouting for another place as soon as we're done today. On your end, you need to be discreet and try not to leave a paper trail. I'm still curious how this person found me at the Constellation. I suspect there's a leak at AHD."

"That's a possibility, Cody. I'll look into it later and have a word with the staff," Tara says.

"Well, just be cautious. I think it's a good idea for you three to stay together until we figure something out. Maybe this is all some twisted game. But, just be careful, girls. Anyhow, you three are lucky to have remote access to headquarter from any location. You might enjoy working from Tahoe and get a chance to enjoy the slopes while you're here. Oh, by the way, Laura, you owe me a match."

A smile crosses Laura's face as she remembers the ski-match four years ago in Tahoe between Cody and Daniel. "You bet, darling," she says feistily and clears her throat. "Mr. Darling, anytime you're ready."

Cody chuckles. "I'll take you up on that, Laura. Well, ladies, I'll start searching for other accommodations. I'll see you soon and please keep safe."

"Thanks, Cody; you too," they say in unison. Cody clicks the console in the middle of the conference table. The screen fades to blue.

"Tara, what's that you're holding?" Leanne asks as if she didn't know.

"It's the reason I wanted to speak with you two after the meeting," Tara says, taking a sip of water to soothe her nerves.

Leanne gestures with her hands. "Do you mind," she asks, pointing at the book. Tara releases her hold; sliding it across the table. As soon as Leanne's hand brushes the cover, she stiffens with a frozen glare.

Alarmed, Tara mumbles, "Leanne?"

Leanne sits unblinking.

Laura sits unfazed by Leanne's rigid pose. Instantly, tension releases Leanne's body, and limply, she slumps in the chair.

"Leanne, you okay?" Tara asks.

"Yep … Whew, I'm good," she replies with a deep sigh. She sits straight and opens the book.

"Tara, she's fine," Laura confirms. Laura realizes Tara has planned a big speech about their blood ties but cuts to the chase. "We know, sweetie … We have for some time." She pauses and studies Tara's reaction.

"What!" Tara yelps in surprise.

"We made a promise to Nyla to keep our blood ties a secret until she spoke with you. She had her reasons for not telling you sooner. Leanne and I've been waiting for you to approach us. We figured you needed time to digest the information," Laura states.

"Well, this is a twist I hadn't expected. Do you realize I spent an entire week trying to figure out how to reveal our blood-ties?" Tara explains as she reclined with relief into the chair. "So, you've known all this time we're related?"

They both nod their heads in accord.

"My grandmother spoke about you years ago. We never figured out where the lineage started, which is why I asked to see the book. Lately, I've had visions and dreams about Susan Cox. I figured she might be the beginning of your bloodline."

"Your trance just now, was that what you were sensing from the book?"

Leanne shakes her head and explains, "Tara, I'm what you would call Retrocognitive and Clairsentient. I possess the ability to observe past events through touch, visions, and dreams. My gift is the opposite of yours. You foresee the future, and I see images that happen a second ago or even centuries ago. I can also sense other's physical state."

"Physical state … Like how they're feeling?"

"Yes, to be more exact, I can tell if a person is sick or diseased. And on some occasions, I can sense a person's thoughts or emotions."

Suddenly, everything makes sense—Leanne's dislike of shaking hands and her aversion to antiques. She wonders what Leanne saw years ago when they shook hands for the first time. She recalls the woozy expression and quick release when their hands touched as if she'd touched something hot.

"Tara, you realize how difficult it's been keeping this secret?" Leanne says. "I was itching to tell you, but I couldn't break my promise. Nyla wasn't sure of your gift's strength. She feared if she told us details of the family tree, you might foresee our knowledge through a vision. Our combined gifts are so confusing; we had to hide our talents, until now." Leanne peers at Tara, wondering what she's thinking. "You okay, Tara?"

"Yep ... I'm trying to wrap my mind around what you just said—foreseeing the future and knowing what you know ... Now that's confusing."

A brisk laugh escapes Laura's mouth. "Isn't' it!"

"So, Laura what's your gift?"

"Honey, don't you remember all the times I finished your sentences?"

"Ha! How can I forget? But I never imagined you were clairvoyant."

"Sweetie, I'm Clairsentient and Claircognizant. Like Leanne, I can sense a person's emotional and physical well-being. But I can also read other's thoughts. As a child, I had to learn to keep my mouth shut and let people finish speaking. I was always ruining family and friend's secrets. Once friends started avoiding me, I realized I needed to keep my mouth shut. Tara, my gift has also been a blessing. Clairvoyance has gotten me out of some terrible situations. It's allowed me to sense who's genuine and who's not. And it sure is handy when you're dating," she says with a wink.

Tara glances at her psychic friends and wonders if they've been reading her mind all these years. "So, do you read my mind a lot?"

"I would be lying if I said no," Laura replies with raised brows, "but seldom, Tara. After a while, I realized you're a genuine soul. So, I stopped intruding in that brilliant mind of yours. Besides, you got all that noise rumbling around in your skull. It makes me dizzy, sweetie," Laura says with a grin.

"Yeah … I do over-analyze a lot," she says, feeling mentally exposed. "Well, thanks for staying out of my head, girls." And she wonders how that's possible. *Can they turn their gift on and off that easily?* "Thank goodness you're my family. This is so confusing and unnerving. My family … I still can't believe we're related."

"Tara, believe me, I'm so happy you're family and my best friend. I wouldn't want it any other way. So, to ease your concerns, our friendship will never change."

Tara smiled at her intuitive friend and wonders when she'd sensed her concerns about their relationship. *Had it been the same day Nyla revealed the truth?*

Laura laughs fondly. "Yes, Tara, I sensed your doubt the night you came back from Nyla's."

"You just heard me?"

"Uh huh," Laura mumbles with a shake of her head.

"Wow …"

"Tara, now that you understand our gifts are you comfortable talking about your own?"

Tara had never heard the term Clairsentient until today, but it explains her ability to sense other's health. "Nyla told me when I was younger, I felt other's illness. So, I guess that makes me Clairsentient as well. And as you both already know I'm precognitive, but unlike you two, I've not perfected my gift."

"You will, Tara. I assume foreseeing the future is a lot scarier than seeing the past. I used to freak out seeing apparitions all around me. It was a while before I realized they're only essences of the past and can't harm me. I'm relieved to see only what's occurred. I can't imagine knowing what's about to happen. Now that would freak me out more."

"Leanne, that's why I've blocked my premonitions, all my abilities have been impeded by fear. Whatever I saw as a child must have been terrifying."

"Tara, fear will always be a component of our gifts. You just have to learn to control it. And you will with time," Leanne says.

"Well, I'd better learn soon," Tara says, reflecting on the childhood vision she's yet to recapture. *Childhood ...* "You're going to find this strange, but when I was a child, you two were my imaginary friends."

"Really?" Laura asks in astonishment. "For a child, those were some sharp insights. I wonder what you saw all those years ago. Were we in your vision?"

Picking at her fingernails, Leanne remembers her first meeting with Tara. "The first time I shook your hand, I saw bits and pieces of your first premonition, but a wall blocks most of what you foresaw as a child."

"But you're retrocognitive," Laura says perplexed. "How can you see Tara's vision?"

Tara tries to rationalize Leanne's abilities. "I guess because the premonition came to me as a child—my past—even though I was foreseeing future events." Tara squints as if comprehending something too complicated to dissect. "Past, present, and future converging, our gifts complement each other. Now I understand Nyla's hesitancy. Leanne would have seen my past and glimpsed my vision, and Laura you would sense everything in our mind."

They stare at each other; understanding for the first time, the power of their relationship. On the ceiling, an ethereal glow wavers with the image of the Alcott floor medallion. Oblivious, the girls continue talking as if for the first time, now that the secret is out of the bag.

Chapter 13

Unhinged

February 16, 2015, Charleston

Only blocks from AHD Headquarters at Harborview Inn on Two Vendue Range, Tom sits in his room staring at the laptop. Inadvertently, his eyes catch the date on the bottom right of the computer, February 16, 2015. Two months have passed since he left his home in Vermont. Only concerned with his mission, time is slipping by without measurable impact. Smugly, he ponders fear set in motion at AHD, but he's not done yet.

Four envelopes lay neatly in a row on the desk—three addressed to the Alcott estate and one to the Constellation at Northstar Hotel in Tahoe. Each contains a message more fearful than the first. He takes a razor, slits his index finger, and smears blood on each note. With the message, he places a particular token inside each envelope. *What's a temporary moment of fear? They haven't seen anything yet.* With that thought, a shooting pain sweeps his forehead, blurring his vision. He clutches his head to contain sharp pain, but the intensity is so great he collapses, unconscious, to the floor.

Several minutes pass before he opens his eyes. Next to him, the cell phone glows fuzzy green. After several minutes his vision focuses on numerous text messages from his wife, Ellen. With no words to explain his digressions, he ignores the texts.

Lifting his body from the floor, he heads to the desk and studies four videos inside the Alcott estate displayed on the laptop. While hiding in the attic, he managed to place cameras and microphones in several rooms. In the kitchen, the Dream Team makes plans for the winner's weekend in Maine. Tom recalls his winner's weekend two years ago. Laura Alcott wielded words of inspiration as they sat around the winner's dinner. And the Dream Team sat with sanctimonious expressions as they granted another million-dollar home. Escorted room to room by the Dream Team, his wife had squealed in delight beside him. *"We'd never have a home this beautiful without the help of AHD,"* Ellen exclaimed with tears of joy. At that moment, Tom understood he'd do anything to keep the home.

Descending into a rage, Tom clenches his fist, pummels the desk, and then slings the chair across the floor. Hauling around, forcefully, he throws a cup at the wall. It shatters into several pieces.

A voice booms from the adjacent room. "Quiet in there!"

Tom punches the wall and screams, "Shut the fuck up!" A ring echoes in his head and he clutches his ears uncertain whether it's from his loud scream or the phone. Peering at his mobile, messages from Ellen fade in and out faint green lettering.

> *Tom, I'm worried about you. Are you taking your medication? You know what happens. I don't want you hurting yourself or others. Please, honey, call me or let me know you're okay.*

"Stop telling me to take my medication!" Tom screams at the cell phone. "I very well can't take something that dulls my senses! I'm fighting for us, Ellen!" Frantically, he paces in a circle. "I didn't forget my medication! I stopped taking it!" He laughs. *I fooled you, didn't I.*

Tom's gone days without sleep, but he's more energetic than he's ever been. Restless energy fuels his maniac pacing as he mumbles to the insidious dweller in his head. "My mind needs to be sharp. I can't let AHD build another home." He returns to the laptop and surfs through AHD's website. On the home page, the 2015 Dream Home winners pose in front of their new coastal home in Maine. A young family with a son reminds him of his own. He clicks on AHD's blog site and writes a message to Leanne Davis.

> **Mountainhigh899***: The new winners need to keep their eyes and ears open. Deception is everywhere.*

Running his hands through his hair, Tom stares at the laptop with legs twitching nervously. "Two more weeks … Just two more weeks," he mumbles under his breath. Opening the desk's top drawer, Tom removes a white folder containing a boarding pass and hotel reservation. A sneer mars his face, as he deliberates the cunning he'd exercised with ease. Posing as Laura Alcott's assistant, he used the information found in her files to reserve a seat on the same flight as the team. In his mind, he replays the conversation with the reservationist.

"*How many are joining the team?*"

"*Just one more,*" Tom said businesslike.

"*Should I bill this to the business card on file?*"

"*No, this will be on a separate card.*"

To appear credible, Tom provided AHD's business card, but he hadn't planned to use it. Doing so will only give the team clues to his whereabouts.

"*Will you be staying in the same suite sir? There's an additional bed.*"

"*No. The ladies will be uncomfortable with a man in the suite. If you can find a room on the same floor, I'd be grateful.*"

"Amazing," he murmured, shaking his head in disbelief. *This is too simple*, he thought. Once more, he glances at the boarding pass and reservation for Constellation Northstar Hotel. *My plan is unfolding so easily.* Restlessness builds, and again, feverishly he paces the floor. *They won't build another Dream Home, not while I'm alive.*

Chapter 14

No Home Is Safe

February 22, 2015, Alcott Estate

At midnight, the girls arrive at the Alcott estate from the hectic winner's weekend celebration in Maine. Laura glances through the rearview mirror at Leanne and Tara sleeping awkwardly in their seats. Passing through the wrought iron gate, lanterns light the private road a soft yellow hue as Laura delivers her tired friends safely home.

Unable to sleep, Laura grabs the mail left by Jennie on the credenza and heads toward her office with a cup of chamomile tea. Stepping into the long glass corridor, she's more wary than usual of the dark panel of windows. She rushes into her office, lights a fire, collapses with a sigh onto the sofa, and rummages through assorted junk mail, monthly bills, magazines, and catalogs, pausing at a glossy interior design publication. Lustrous pages of beautiful homes calm her nerves momentarily until three letters stuck between magazine pages fall onto her lap—envelopes addressed in the same shaky penmanship she'd seen on the silver gift.

Laura considers ripping the letters to pieces and throwing them in the fireplace, but destroying the evidence won't solve the girl's problem. With shaky hands, she slits the letter open with a fingernail and a picture taken in front of Leanne's townhouse slips from the envelope. Indignation mars Laura's face. *He was watching and photographing us the entire time! How dare he infringe on our personal lives*! She remembers the day she drove the girls to their homes to retrieve their luggage—the day they moved into the Alcott estate, the day they went to the police station. Laura shivers at the thought of their stalker's proximity. From the angle of the photo, he was only a stones-throw away—the adjacent townhouse.

She yanks the note from the envelope and gasps when her finger touches what appears a bloodstain. Repulsed, the letter falls to the floor. An intense current runs through her hand, the stalker's turpitude invades her mind, his emotions decipherable—turmoil, doubt, and rage. Frenetic voices battle in his mind. He's clearly unstable. She glances down at the message the note proclaims. NO HOME IS SAFE.

Heaven help us! We're in more danger than originally thought. Overcome with fear; she races to wake the girls, but halts abruptly in the corridor, imagining their fear. *No, no, wait until morning. We can't do anything tonight.* Suddenly, aware of the wide expanse of glass, she rushes back to her office toward the French doors, checks the lock, and peers into obscurity beyond the window, imagining their stalker glaring brazenly in the dark. Weak with fright; she swiftly lowers the automated shades and pulls the drapes across the windows.

She continues to the computer, accesses surveillance cameras, and scours every room, window, and entrance. Flicking back and forth between each wing of the estate, she watches the girls sleep until she's certain they're safe.

NO HOME IS SAFE.

The cryptic message sears her mind and rattles her nerves. Laura remains at the computer, watching over the home and her friends. *Thank heavens Callie is traveling.* She couldn't fathom anything happening to her daughter.

* * *

Hours later, a pale light streams through white curtains and morning wakes Laura from her sleep. Painfully curled in the wing-back chair, she unfurls her aching limbs and jumps with a start, noticing Leanne frozen and holding the letter near the fireplace. Once again, the ominous warning pricks Laura's mind. She wonders what Leanne is sensing.

Thirty minutes later, aflame with chilling currents, Tara glares at the photo snapped across from AHD's front gate. The thought of their stalker's imminence is disturbing.

"I believe we have enough proof for the police," Leanne says, gnawing on a fingernail.

"Yes," Laura says, narrowing her eyes and tapping a finger on her mouth, "… but I have a better idea … We have something the police don't," she says with a devilish glint, "… one another … our combined powers." Laura peers at her rattled friends, sensing doubt, and then acceptance.

Tom

Tom watched Laura's every move as she opened the letter in her office. He wondered why she flinched when she touched the note. A startling realization showed in her stillness. Her strange glare sparked his interest. And with fascination, he watched all night as she sat behind the desk, searching the surveillance until sleep overwhelmed him. Fast asleep, he failed to witness Leanne enter the office holding the photo in a trance.

Chapter 15

The Power of Three

February 23, 2015, Alcott Estate

Outside floor to ceiling windows, snow falls on tall pine trees and beyond, vein-like trails come alive on snow-covered mountaintops. Inside, an expansive room appears a mile long with dizzying high ceilings of exposed wooden beams. The sun, rising from the east, cast dark blue, purple, and magenta across the horizon, and beams onto a towering stainless-steel oven hood looming over the kitchen. The immense home rises frighteningly over Tara's diminutive frame, causing fear of exposure. An aura of sadness pervades the air. A peculiar odor emanates around her. Sun rays highlight a spotted black and white magnet securing a note to the fridge. The letter fades in and out, bold then pale. Tara reaches for the note, but the room grows wider and wider, her arms farther and farther away.

There's a sudden confusion of space and time. Instantly, she's standing in an area equally grand. Watercolored rooms melt as she floats by. Her heart races with the speed of movement through a long glass-enclosed foyer. Windows frame scenes of winter and snow suspend in animation on both sides of the corridor. Above, pendants light the way; leading to another massive space sandwiched between two large triangular walls of windows. Overhead, exposed wooden beams and metal trusses seem mile high. The home has an illusory familiarity. Nothing seems real. A slow moving smoke crawls around the foyer. A pungent odor permeates the air causing her eyes to water and sting. The room melts brown, yellow, blue, gray, and orange around her. From somewhere inside, an angry male voice pierces her soul, and again, she's fearful. Smoke traps and claims her breath and sight. A scream rings out.

Tara forces herself to wake. Quickly, she grabs the diary and pencil beside the bed—capturing dream images before they slip away.

* * *

A few hours later in Nyla's tranquil loft, the girls sit in Indian pose, holding hands in a circle, eager to unearth their stalker. Tara glances at her psychic friends in disbelief—a snicker forms on her breath at the oddity of it all.

Nyla glares reprovingly at Tara but recognizes her discomfort. "Tara, you have to take this seriously. I know this is strange, but soon, you will understand why this is important," Nyla says with an emphasis on will.

Frowning at Laura and Leanne, Tara detects a hint of amusement. As soon as her eyes meet theirs, cackles burst across the loft.

"Okay, girls, I'm going to ignore this," Nyla says, placing crystals in the center of the circle. The girl's nervous laughter doesn't faze her. She remembers the oddity of her first group shushing. Nonetheless, Nyla surmises, the girls probably need a good laugh after months of unease.

"Nyla, I'm sorry. This is all so witchy."

"Is that even a word, Laura?" Leanne asks.

"No, it's not, and this is not witchcraft. It's your natural-God-given talents," Nyla replies. You're not casting spells, but getting in touch with your innate abilities. Now, if you want my help, I suggest you get a little more serious."

"Nyla, this shushing is like taking a step back in time. This is modern-day Charleston, not the 1800s."

"Laura, you'd be amazed at what happens in modern-day Charleston. This is a mystical town."

"Okay, girls, it's time you take this serious," Tara says, recognizing Nyla's impatience, but she's also aware Nyla understands their laughter stems from nervousness, not ridicule. "Mom, I'm ready." Tara peers at Laura and Leanne with a question on her face, engendering a response.

"Ready," the girls say.

Nyla assumes her place outside the circle. "Okay, that's better. Girls, we're going to meld your gifts of past, present, and future using the essence-imbued objects of the stalker." Nyla places the blood-smeared notes and keychains in each of their laps and asks them to join hands. "Remember what I showed you. It's just like meditation, girls. The only difference, this time, is fusing your visions. So, take each other's hands and don't let go until I say so. Close your eyes. Quiet your thoughts. Listen to your breath and heartbeat. Open your minds."

The room's serenity silences their minds, and before long they're in their stalkers past, present, and future. Instantly, Leanne is standing at Laura's kitchen door. The stalker's essence is hers.

A breeze pushes at Leanne's back as she enters the open door. A large pair of black Nikes steps inside the kitchen. "Come on, Sammie, let's catch some sun," rings from the family room followed by the whoosh of opening and closing French doors. She rushes inside the home; catching a glimpse of brown boots and white fur as Laura and Sammie turn the corner. A deep growl emanates from her stomach and she tiptoes toward the large stainless steel refrigerator. Quickly, she retrieves two bottles of water, some fruit, cheese, leftover pasta, and stashes them in the heavy satchel hanging from her shoulder.

Footsteps approach somewhere on the second floor and continue down the stairs. She stumbles and slides behind the large, granite island; waiting as the sound grows farther away. She moves forward to sneak a peek. A young woman—presumably the maid—exits the front door. Hesitantly, she scrambles up the stairs to the second floor.

A vacuum cleaner whirs down the corridor. She rushes to the third floor, away from sounds. A myriad of intersecting passages stirs confusion. Footsteps grow close. She freezes. Taking two steps at a time, she rushes upstairs to the next level, and into the attic.

She moves toward an indigo door. Inside old furniture and trunks reside. Quietly, dumping the heavy satchel on floorboards, she unloads miniature cameras and microphones. Crunching gravel sounds. She tiptoes toward the small attic window, as a car moves down the driveway. The woman seen on the main floor drives away. Laura waves good-bye and resumes her walk toward the boathouse with Sammie.

Suddenly, Leanne's standing in another space and time within the Alcott estate.

From a second-floor bedroom, she watches Laura's car back and turn out of the garage, and disappear down the private road. She grabs the miniature cameras and microphones, race to the main floor and attaches the camera to a lamp fixture—aiming it toward the sofa and kitchen beyond. Sammie follows barking and growling viciously. Unperturbed by the tiny dog, laughter springs in the air as she moves into the kitchen and finds another spot to hide the second camera and microphone—above a large art piece next to the cabinets.

Down the long hallway, she searches for Laura's office. Through a glass corridor and behind a barn door she finds the large white space and searches for a discreet spot to hide the third camera. She examines the massive fireplace and then slides the camera between the dark recesses of two stone slabs. Underneath Laura's desk, she places the inconspicuous microphone.

On the desk, she opens the bottom drawer, searches rows of folders, and finds expense reports from Laura's trip to Maine. She folds the paper into her pocket and continues searching through files. A green light winks from the computer—revealing it's still on. Tapping the keyboard, an email pops open exclaiming the next Dream Home site is Lake Tahoe.

Anger surges and a menacing voice taunts, "Fool, print it!" Heeding the voice in her head, she does as it says. Sammie circles her, growling and barking. With one swift kick, Sammie flies backward, scuttles onto his feet, and scampers away fearfully.

Leanne's jolts from her vision, tinged with the stalker's illness. With her hands still linked to Laura and Tara, she's now sensing Laura's vision in a dark space.

Through drawn floor-length beige curtains, sunlight slivers linear across the room. Darkness conceals the area but computer light shadows a man typing with intermittent taps. He shakes his head and types with rapid pecks. Angrily, he jumps from the chair, kicks it to the floor, and mumbles harshly. The laptop highlights his last post on AHD's blog site.

Mountainhigh899! Laura and Leanne snap out of their trance. Meanwhile, Tara's vision is clearer than ever. She travels to a dark room in the future.

The girl's voices fill the space as a man with twitching legs studies three rooms displayed on a laptop—the Alcott kitchen, family room, and Laura's office. The girl's conversation echoes clearly in the kitchen. Lights from Charleston Harbor shine in the distance as they chat around the island.

"… This is the resort at Northstar in Tahoe." Leanne takes the brochure from Laura. "Wow, fantastic, I can't wait. Tara, look at the ski slopes," Leanne says, passing the folder to Tara.

"Laura, have you stayed here before?"

"No. Daniel and I always rented a cabin on the lake. We never stayed at the resort, but I can't wait."

"How far is Martis Camp from Northstar?"

"Cody says about three miles, which is not bad. By car, the drive will take us less than fifteen minutes."

Immersed in the conversation, the man jots information on a pad, then drops the pen and glares at the cell phone. Anger surges. He throws the phone into the top drawer and slams it closed.

His anger frightens Tara from the trance. She opens her eyes to Laura and Leanne's outraged glares. There's no need to repeat what she'd seen. She senses they've already sensed her vision.

Laura's horrified and incensed the stalker hid inside the estate. "He's been listening and watching us for days!"

Does he know we're clairvoyant? "Do you think he knows about our gifts?" Tara asks.

"No, I would have sensed his awareness," Laura says. She shudders with indignation. "What audacity! How dare he just stroll around my property like that! And he kicked poor Sammie, the brute!" Laura screams.

Leanne's foot still vibrates a phantom throb from contact with Sammie's small body. *It was so real.* Leanne flinches at the thought of Sammie's pain and the stalker's callousness, and tries to assuage Laura's anger. "Thank goodness Sammie is okay."

"Ahhh ... Now I know why Sammie ran into the garage and refused to go back inside the house," Laura murmurs ... "He was frightened; our stalker was still in the house." Laura shudders at the man's immediacy. *How long had he been on the estate?*

A dreadful silence slides across the loft. The room's calm no longer tapers their fear. Leanne ponders Tara's vision. "Tara, thank goodness the conversation in your vision hasn't happened yet. We need to be cautious of what we say from now on."

Recalling the conversation in the kitchen, Laura says, "I think we should arrange for another hotel."

"How can we, there aren't any reservations yet. The conversation happens in our future." Leanne understands Laura's anger is preventing her from thinking rationally.

"Laura, we shouldn't change anything. Let him believe we're staying at the Constellation Hotel. We'll find other accommodations. We need to stay a step ahead of him. Let him believe what he's seeing."

"You're right, Tara," Leanne says. "Well, at least, my suspicion about Mountainhigh899 is confirmed."

"Leanne, we still need to see his face," says Laura.

"I was hoping to glimpse his image in a mirror or catch a reflection in a window, but I'm always him—in his body." Leanne pauses for a second; her green eyes squint feline. "I need to view him from a different angle, through someone else's eyes."

Nyla enters the room, studies the girl's faces, perceives they're on the right track, and throws a positive affirmation. "Girls, it will come to you soon." She smiles and heads back down the stairs.

Laura continues pacing around Tara and Leanne in a dizzying circle. "Without his face, our plan is hopeless."

Unknown to the others, Leanne has retrieved the AHD keychain and has entered another trance. Again, she's not watching the stalker, she's him.

Fidgeting with the camera, she keeps her gaze on Tara across the street until AHD's door closes behind her. Placing the camera in the satchel, and rising from the bench, her legs buckle instantly. With an unsteady gait, she walks shakily across the street to AHD's front gate when dizziness assaults her, forcing her to hold the gate for support. Just as she lifts her hand toward the knob, light bounces off the gold wedding band, blinding her sight. She squints and stares up at Tara.

Leanne gasps and drops the keychain to the floor. "Tara, I need your hand."

"What's going on?"

"I need your eyes to capture our stalker's face. The man you saw from the piazza." She takes Tara's hand and the keychain once more. Before long, she's standing in Tara's office.

The room's stifling. She rushes to the piazza, removes her trench coat and scarf, and breathes Charleston Harbor's warm breeze while viewing Ft. Sumter in the distance. Something moves in her periphery and she looks toward the front gate where a strange man stands dazed. Light shines and bounces off his ring, blinding and framing his face. He flinches and gazes upward. He looks familiar. With haste, the man turns and walks away—a continuous wave of chills assault her spine.

Leanne drops Tara's hands and stiffens with chills. "Tara, those things are powerful ... Whew!"

Tara laughs. "I'm glad you know my discomfort."

"They're fierce!" Leanne shudders, blowing air from her mouth to lessen phantom chills. "Now I understand that awful expression you get when they occur," she says wiggling away spectral chills. "Tara, you thought he looked familiar."

"I did, but now I remember so little of his face ... "

"You know, he did look familiar. Something about his eyes—his face is like a word on the tip of my tongue that just won't form. Hopefully, I'll remember where I've seen him before, sooner than later, I hope."

"What did you see?"

"Well, he's tall. My guess is a little over six-feet. He has brown eyes and hair and his face was clearly unshaven. But the feature that stands out the most is his broad lips ... I also detected a small, white scar above his left eyebrow. Oh, and he wore a gold wedding band."

"I'm impressed. How did you get all those details? I couldn't possibly have seen all that from the piazza."

"Tara, it's hard to explain. My view is telescopic—magnified—when I'm in a trance. I also felt a sickness in his body—both mental and physical."

Laura remembers the mental illness she sensed in her office when she touched the blood-smeared photo. "Leanne, I got the same impression from the photos. His mental state is what scares me the most."

"Did you sense a medicinal flavor, Laura?"

"As a matter of fact, I did. It seemed he was coming out of a stupor."

"You're right, Laura. When he watched Tara at the gate, I felt foggy and unbalanced."

"Well, at least we have some idea of what we're up against," Laura says still focused on the cameras in her home and the overwhelming need to get rid of them. "What about the cameras? What should we do?"

Maybe we should give him a show.

"Not on your life, Leanne," Laura retorts.

"You heard that? Well, I'm just kidding," Leanne smirks.

"I certainly hope so," Laura says, resuming her pacing.

"What should we do?" Tara asks.

Biting her nail, Leanne deliberates their next action. Letting the stalker believe they're oblivious to the cameras is the wisest move. "We do nothing ... We keep the cameras. We can't let him know we're on to him."

PART 2

Chapter 16

Tahoe Bound

March 3, 2015, Lake Tahoe

Standing under Reno-Tahoe International Airport's canopy, Tom grows impatient studying countless travelers entering and exiting the airport. With a momentary spark of sanity, he questions his behavior, but the angry dweller in his head prevents clarity from seeping through. Anxious to find AHD's Dream Team, Tom paces the canopy vigorously, spying into cars, taxis, and shuttles as strangers stare warily.

Blowing hot breath into his hands to warm tingling fingers numbed painfully from biting cold, the taunting voice heckles again. *Are you going to stand out here like an idiot and freeze? They're not here, Tom. They tricked you, and you fell for it. How stupid can you be?* He pulls the thin jacket's collar around his neck, aware it's too sheer for Tahoe's brutal temperatures. *No hat, no gloves what were you thinking,* the voice snapped. The biting wind gradually claims his face and finger's mobility. Heedful, he heads back inside, scanning faces as he strolls towards Hertz's car rental.

At the front desk, an elderly man with ruddy cheeks, and embonpoint figure hands Tom keys to his SUV Jeep Wrangler.

Studying a map, Tom tries to determine the quickest route to the hotel when dizziness he hasn't felt since Charleston blurs his vision again. Standing rigid and holding tight to the counter, he waits for the spell to pass, hoping it doesn't return while he's behind the wheel.

The elderly clerk notices Tom's unsteady state. "Sir, can I help you?"

Looking up from the exhausting map, Tom stares at the man's blurry image. "Yes. I need to get to the Village at Northstar."

"Oh, you're heading to the resort ... Beautiful area. We provide shuttles right to the door. Are you interested?" The man, worried about Tom's state, hopes to sway him from driving.

"No, I'll be here for a while and will need access to a car."

"Okay ... Well, it's a long trip to Northstar. And we're expecting more snow this evening. You sure you can handle the roads?"

Tom notices the man's expression and realizes his appearance must be alarming. Steadying and straightening his stance, he replies, "Yes, I prefer driving."

"All right, sir. That's about a forty-two-minute drive, but with the snow, it could take longer," he reveals, peering at Tom with concern. "And we're expecting a heavier snowfall this evening. The roads can be treacherous this time of year. Even folks from these parts have difficulty driving in this weather," he stresses, hoping the caveat will change his mind.

"I'll chance it," Tom says unconcerned.

"AL 'righty," he says, picking up a pen and paper. "I'll write the directions just in case the car's navigation sends you on a longer route, which they do sometimes." He glances at Tom's tight grip on the counter. "Once you punch in the address, the system should guide you straight to the door. However, in case you prefer paper, here are the directions," he says, handing the paper to Tom with a steady gaze.

Tom shivers and blows warm air into his hands, cold still lingering in his body.

The clerk eyes Tom's thin jacket and shakes his head. "I hope you brought a thicker jacket. Temperatures can be harsh around here."

"I've noticed," Tom says, annoyed and impatient to get on the road.

* * *

Inside the jeep, Tom makes his way to Interstate 80, all the while, wondering why the Dream Team wasn't on the flight. He checked up and down the airplane aisles, hoping they only changed seats, not their flight. Confounded, he pounds the dashboard. "I can't believe this!" They have to be at the hotel. I didn't come all this way for nothing," he mumbles, negating the taunting voice in his head. He's certain the Dream Team left for Tahoe. He overheard them on the surveillance system and saw them pack and leave for the airport. He peers at the hotel reservation sticking from his black satchel on the passenger seat, hoping his plan doesn't backfire. A mechanical female voice interrupts his thought:

> "Continue on Interstate 80 West to Interstate 89 toward Sierraville—Lake Tahoe."

Interstate 80's traffic crawls imperceptibly—the view a virtual whiteout. Impatiently, he turns on the radio, switches back and forth between stations, and then settles on the local news broadcasting forty-miles-per-hour winds and two more feet of snow. The traffic report warns of a major accident on Donner Pass, and numerous cars spinning out of control. The newscaster's tone changes, as he happily heralds, "Good news for the ski resorts, a good old fashion blizzard is heading our way." Resignedly, Tom places his head on the headrest, dreading the dangerous drive ahead. The newscaster's joyous exclamation perturbs him, and he switches the radio to the only music station. The haunting words of country western singer, Toby Keith, pours through the speakers—"I just don't wanna know how it ends ..." And Tom wonders how his plan will end.

The winding interstate, covered in fresh snow, carries him through rolling hills. Heavy-eyed, he winds the window down slightly, letting cold air jolt his drowsiness. The snowy scenery reminds him he's driving through a national forest. On both sides of the jeep, tall pine trees drip with thick snow, and billboards signal ski territory ahead. Three billboards down, another sign broadcasts—Lake Tahoe is the 2016 Dream Home Location. Catching sight of AHD's logo, Tom snaps his head around. He's seen that symbol somewhere, long before he won the home, but can't remember where. After fifty minutes, the mechanical female voice guides him once more.

"Turn left onto Highway 267. Continue for 5.5 miles ..."

After five miles, the female voice instructs:

"Turn right onto Northstar Drive."

Snowflakes fall thicker and harder obscuring visibility. Tom follows a white, shuttle bus with Northstar on its side. He's certain the coach will lead him in the right direction. Finally, on Northstar Drive, narrow roads twist and turn. The jeep careens, winding him toward his final destination. Pine trees grow closer and denser on roads narrowing shoulders. Every other mile, red wooden destination signs indicate the approaching village. Behaving like a tourist, he's eager to arrive at the vacation destination ahead. For several more miles, the car angles behind the shuttle until it turns left, on a forked road. A big billboard with a skier on a mountaintop heralds The Village at Northstar. In the town's center, lights shine heavenward, revealing a surreal vision—Sierra Nevada's snow-covered mountains.

* * *

Inside the Constellation at Northstar, the desk clerk greets with an unfamiliar accent. "Welcome to the Constellation. May I help you, sir?"

"Yes. I have reservations. I'm with the AHD group. Have they arrived yet? They're booked for suite twenty-two."

"I'll check," the young man says and stares quizzically at the computer. "No ... I don't see reservations for the AHD group."

"They have to be here. Can you check again," Tom urges. "Perhaps they're registered under Laura Alcott or Tara Mc—"

"Ah, they've canceled their reservation."

They fooled you again, the voice taunts. "Are they booked for later?"

"No. There was a straight cancellation."

"Oh, strange ..." Tom says, ignoring the jeering voice and restraining growing anger. "Well, can I get the key to my room?"

"Your name, sir ..."

"Cavanaugh, Sean Cavanaugh." Using the name of his deceased brother who passed away six months ago, Tom believes their resemblance will go unquestioned.

"Do you have the credit card on file?"

"Yes." Tom pulls out his brother's Visa and passport. "I'm paying with cash if that's okay."

"Well, we still need a credit card to secure the room."

"Sure." Tom hands the clerk the passport and credit card, hoping there's no computerized system revealing his brother's deceased status.

"One minute please ..." The clerk examines the passport picture, with a quick glance at Tom then back at the passport. "You appear a little different here."

"Well, the picture's eight years old. I've recently lost a few pounds."

"Did you bring other ID?" Tom expected this to happen and pulls out two credit cards and gym membership with his brother's photo. For years, people thought Tom and his half-brother were twins. Both had favored their mother and no one ever knew they had different fathers. "Will this do?" Standing stiffly, beads of sweat dot Tom's shirt.

A few seconds later the clerk responds, "Thank you, sir … Here's your key. Do you need any assistance with your bags?"

"No, I can carry them."

"Have a pleasant stay at the Constellation."

Unresponsive, and lost in thought, Tom doesn't hear the clerk wish him a pleasant stay. He proceeds to his room containing immense anger. Inside the small suite, he hurls his bags onto the sofa and heads straight to the telephone. Laura's Southern drawl lilts through the answering machine. Forcefully, Tom slams the phone and swears at pain vibrating through his hand. Unzipping the laptop case, he accesses cameras placed in the Alcott estate, hoping the girls aren't still in Charleston.

Chapter 17

The Slip

March 3, 2015, Charleston, SC. McPherson Home

Meanwhile, back in Charleston, Laura and Leanne study a painting above the McPherson's fireplace with an uncanny resemblance to Nyla and Tara—a young African-American woman with hazel eyes, reddish-brown hair, dressed in a simple ivory dress that belongs to another era. Her eyes sparkle warmly as if pleased with what she sees.

"Is this Nyla?" Leanne asks.

Tara turns and glances at the painting. "No, Anna Cox."

"I've never seen this painting before," Leanne murmured. Moving closer, she runs her finger along the artist's initials—NC. A young man studying his subject fondly flashes in her mind. "I don't remember this painting being here."

"No, you wouldn't. Nyla just hung it recently. She started pulling artwork from the attic after she'd revealed my heritage. The painting is of Nathan Cox's wife, Anna."

"Wow, such a striking likeness to you and Nyla," Laura says.

Tara laughs. "Too much so; at first, I thought the drawing was Nyla. She's storing a considerable amount of artwork in the attic. I haven't seen them all yet. She treats them like a treasure."

"Could be; maybe the paintings hold a story Nyla's not ready to reveal," Leanne says with an inkling of history hidden in the attic.

"Well, I'll let Nyla tell me when she's ready."

Slowly, Laura saunters back to the sofa, grateful the McPherson's provided access to their home while they're out of town. "Girls, do you think our stalker bought our little act?" Laura asks.

"I hope so," Tara says. "There's no reason he wouldn't. We went through all the motions flawlessly. All he viewed on the cameras were three women preparing for a trip. I liked the way you made sure he heard us checking our flight time … Smart move, Laura."

"Well, Tara, I did study acting for a little while," Laura says batting her eyes.

Leanne finishes a text to Adam, turns off her cell phone, and joins the conversation. "I wonder what our stalker is up to now. Do you honestly believe he'd follow us all the way to Tahoe?"

Earlier, Tara had asked herself the same question. "We can't put anything past him. He's broken into our homes, taken pictures of us all over town, and placed cameras in Laura's place. Why wouldn't he get on a plane to Tahoe?"

"He's psychotic, remember the bloodstain. His mental state knows no bounds and that's what scares me the most," Laura says.

Leanne sitting on the edge of the couch, biting her painfully short nails, contemplates their stalker's motive. "Something doesn't make sense. Why is he so angry with us, or what does he believe we've done? There's a missing piece to this puzzle."

Tara clutches the sacred-seven pendant around her neck as if a clue will materialize. "Leanne, I wondered the same thing many times. Until we figure out who he is, we can't determine his motive."

Tara and Leanne's thoughts bounce around Laura's mind incessantly. She wishes she could shut off her mind, silence it for an hour or so. "Well, thank goodness for the McPherson estate. We can stay out of his reach while Cody makes plans for a secure hotel in Tahoe. It'll give us a little more time to figure out his identity. I hope we've thrown him off at least for a while. By the way, Cody has a contact at the Constellation, who'll inform him if anyone inquiries about us."

A wry expression crosses Tara's face. "That would be a stupid move. Why would he be so obvious to inquire about us?"

"Well, Tara, remember, he has no clue we're on to him or know he's in Tahoe. Why wouldn't he ask around?"

Tara tries to put herself in their stalker's mind and hopes he's still somewhere in Charleston.

Cody

March 3, 2015, Tahoe, Constellation at Northstar

Cautiously, Cody enters the Constellation's lobby, makes his way toward reception, and inspects the area for a man fitting the girl's description. He's relieved the team's booked in safer lodging nearby. At the front desk, he spots Scott and approaches with stealth. "Hey, Scott, did anyone inquire about AHD today?"

Scott steps to the far end of the counter with his back to his colleagues. "Yep, around six o'clock this evening a man named Sean Cavanaugh checked into room 22E. He was obviously pissed about AHD's cancellation," he whispers.

"Do you have a description of him?"

"I'd say he's in his mid-forties, brown hair, brown eyes, and thick eyebrows. I noticed a small, white scar along the outline of his left eyebrow. Oh, he's slim built, maybe six-feet-three. Something seems a little off about his eyes. They seemed vacant ... lifeless."

"Hmmm … How long is he booked at the hotel?"

"Three weeks. But there's a note in the system showing a possible extended stay."

"Scott, you've been a great help." Cautiously, Cody slides Scott his business card. "This is my cell number. If anything changes with this guy, give me a call. When he's certain the other clerks aren't looking, he slips Scott a tip. "Thanks, man."

"Anytime, Cody …"

Cody surveys the lobby as he makes his way toward the exit. *The girls were right.* If they hadn't been so insistent about not involving the police, he'd alert them immediately. He glances at his watch, estimating its 11:00 p.m. on the East Coast. With dismay, he dials Laura's cell phone, realizing his news will cause them more distress.

Chapter 18

Wiser This Time

March 4, 2015, Constellation at Northstar

On the laptop, a female enters the Alcott kitchen, but it's not Laura, only Jennie the maid. Since he arrived at the hotel, Tom's been glued to the screen, but there's no sign of the three women. *They're definitely not in Charleston.* Racking his brain all night, he pondered their change of plan. *They must be in Tahoe.* He heard them confirm their reservation at the Constellation and watched them pack and leave. *What now,* he scowls in deliberation. Suddenly, he knows where to uncover their whereabouts. Rebecca, the gullible receptionist who accommodated him a few months ago, will indeed know where they are. *But will she be as obliging this time?*

"Good Morning, AHD."

"Good Morning, Rebecca. I hope you remember me. We spoke a few months back … the architect for the Dream Home. I was expecting Laura Alcott for a breakfast meeting this morning, but she failed to show up, and I can't reach her on her cell. By chance, do you have her hotel number in Tahoe?"

"Can you hold one moment Mr.?"

"Oh, Mr. Goldsmith …"

Rebecca definitely remembers this man. He lied to her months ago when he called inquiring about the team. She felt stupid not verifying his information back in December, and responsible for leaking the team's information. But this time, she's wiser. Tara told her to inform the team of any suspicious calls. So, immediately, she places Mr. Goldsmith on hold and dials Tara's mobile.

"Ms. McPherson?"

"Yes ..."

"This is Rebecca. There's a suspicious call on the other line from a man claiming to be the architect for the Dream Home. He's asking for Laura's hotel information in Tahoe."

"Rebecca, what's the number on the caller ID?"

"It's blocked, but he says his name is Mr. Goldsmith and this morning Laura failed to show for a breakfast meeting."

"Thanks for calling, Rebecca. Tell him nothing and if he ever calls again just hang up."

"Will do Ms. McPherson ..."

Rebecca switches to the other line. "Sir, I don't have any information."

Tom suspects Rebecca is lying but remains cordial. "Thanks for your help, Rebecca," he says, knowing full well she called the team while he was on hold. He suspects she's now aware he's not the architect. His one connection to the team severed, but he'll find another means to their whereabouts.

For a while, he paces the hotel room when it dawns on him he'd printed Tara's email from Laura's computer back in December. He rummages through his bag and finds the folded paper telling Laura the Dream Home's new location, Martis Camp, a place he's sure he'll find the three women.

Cody

March 4, 2015, Constellation at Tahoe

151

In the hotel lobby, seated next to a large column, Cody pretends to read an Alpine Life Magazine, while he awaits Scott's signal. He glances up just as Scott's face explodes and his eyes veer to a tall, thin man exiting the elevator. Sean Cavanaugh walks toward the lobby's fireplace, pauses and surveys hotel guest coming and going. When he looks in his direction, Cody lowers his head and stares at the magazine a few seconds then raises his eyes furtively toward Sean Cavanaugh, catching him exiting the hotel. Cody rushes to the entrance and watches him approach a titanium gray Jeep Wrangler. When the ignition starts, Cody rushes to his SUV.

"Here we go," Cody mumbles a few minutes later, rolling stealthily behind the Wrangler. The jeep turns right onto Highlands View Road and continues Northwest on Route 267. "Bastard, he's heading to Martis Camp," Cody mumbles. After a few miles, they near the gated community. *He's looking for the girls. Thank goodness construction doesn't begin for another month.* "You won't find anything today buddy," he mutters.

A few minutes later, the Jeep Wrangler stops outside Martis Camp's entrance. Cody slows to a halt a few yards back, watching Sean Cavanaugh survey the guarded community. *Is he trying to find a way around the guards?* His bold persistence riles Cody, and he watches in disbelief. "You're not getting in, buddy. Martis Camp is a fortress."

The Jeep Wrangler slowly pulls up to the security hut. For a moment, Sean engages the guard, who points him down the road. Sean waves back and continues on Route 267. Cody drives at a distance until the Jeep Wrangler turns off the road toward a roadside café.

Accelerating, Cody speeds past the restaurant, more convinced than ever the girls are in danger. He taps the cell phone logo on his dashboard and commands, "Call Tony."

"Tony Winston ..."

"Hey, Tony, it's Cody. We're going to need significant security around the Dream Home construction site. Can you handle that?"

Chapter 19

Martis Camp Community

March 5th Village of Northstar

For several days, without success, Tom walked the Village at Northstar hoping to catch a glimpse of AHD's Dream Team. Seated at the Patio Bar and Grill adorned in a baseball cap and sunglasses, he leisurely sips coffee. At the next table, a young family lunches and plans their afternoon. A little girl tries to bite a sandwich much too large for her mouth. Dripping sauce splatters her mittens. Clumsily, she fumbles to wipe it off when one mitten escapes her hands and falls to the floor. Tom watches her futile attempt to retrieve it from the deck. Her short arms dangle, fingers splay and stretch unsuccessfully. The chair begins to rock and topple sideways. Speedily, Tom reacts and holds the stool steady.

The girl's mother glances over with a protective glare which turns appreciative when Tom places the mitten in the child's hand. The woman's initial response reminds him of his wife's reaction whenever his moods would appear—a fierce, protective stance guarding their children even if it meant harm to herself, an expression which causes shame and pain even now. Beneath his shades, regret saddens his eyes. He sighs, rises from his chair, and throws the young girl a smile. With forty minutes to kill before meeting with a Martis Camp's sales agent, he strolls past eager vacationers, spying through shop and restaurant windows for three distinct women.

* * *

Forty minutes later, at Martis Camp Clubhouse, a young woman dressed in cold-weather gear and boots greet him at the entrance, ready to escort him through the community. Nearing the security hut, she pulls an electronic gadget from the glove compartment and points it at the gate.

"Good afternoon, Bill," she greets the guard as the car rolled to the other side.

"Are security guards always on duty?"

"Yes, they come in shifts all day. But when guards aren't at their post, homeowners can open the gate using this little gadget, and if lost we keep a bunch at the clubhouse. The staff is on call for twenty-four hours."

"Well, that's good to know … I like lots of security," Tom says, smiling at the agent. Studying the small gadget on the dashboard, he ponders pilfering it without her notice.

Inside the gate, the car winds narrow roads, as the agent points to various amenities and a large golf course in the center of splendid abodes. Looming Sierra Nevada Mountains in the distance reminds him of mountain views from his Vermont home.

"Several vacant lots are available. How much land are you looking for, and what square footage are you seeking to build Mr. Cavanaugh?"

"Oh, I'm not sure … At least an acre. My two boys are growing bigger every day. So, square footage is important—nothing less than 3000 square feet."

"There're restrictions and zoning laws."

"What type of restrictions?"

"You can find a list in the brochure."

She continues past empty lots and existing homes. Tom sneers at large mountain mansions, not rustic cabins built for seasonal weekend getaways. Homes made for the wealthy who can afford the sizable property's expense, an exorbitant maintenance cost he's paid to keep the Vermont Dream home. He masks distaste with a fixed gaze.

The agent's face brightens as they approach a vacant lot with a signpost displaying AHD's Dream Home and the Alcott logo. A symbol that slipped his memory, he suddenly remembers. *How could I forget?* His last employer managed one of the Alcott Foundation's Charitable Trust. The symbol covered all their paperwork. The day the firm's owner acquired the billion dollar account, he disseminated the news throughout the firm.

"This lot belongs to AHD Dream Home," the agent says.

"Oh … I'm sure the publicity will bring much attention to Martis Camp."

"Well, we're hoping so."

"When will construction start?"

"We were told sometime in April. Soon, the lot will be buzzing with construction and camera crews filming the project."

Feigning ignorance Tom states, "How exciting … won't the noise disturb neighbors?"

"Oh, no, the homes are spaced at some distance. The nearest neighbor is a quarter mile down the road. This area is unpopulated, but soon empty lots will be filled with newly constructed homes."

Perfect, no one will question my presence, he thought. "Is there a map of the community? I would love to study the lot selection closer."

"You bet, as soon as we get back to the clubhouse."

After a circular tour of the secluded community, Tom covets, despises, and envies the gorgeous homes all at once. In the near distance, a woman appears with two boys like a mirage of Ellen and his two sons. Her features blur in and out a figment of Ellen. The sales agent brings the car to a crawl and lowers the window. Ellen's features dissolve into a stranger's.

"Afternoon, Sarah, beautiful day for a cross-country trek."

"Taking the boys out for a little while," the woman replies.

"Have fun, boys."

They smile and wave as the car pulls away.

"Sarah and her family own the home a few miles back. Such lovely boys; you and your family should have no problem fitting into our little community."

"Good to hear …" Tom says. Disturbed by the mirage, he peers through the side view mirror at the woman and her sons with a sudden longing for his family.

* * *

Back at the clubhouse, the agent guides Tom into her office and searches for a sitemap. She throws the electronic gadget into a bin crammed with several of the devices. Tom watches her closely, waiting for the perfect moment to swipe the gadget. As soon as she turns her back, he reaches into the bin and swiftly places the gate opener in his coat pocket. Inadvertently, he notices a board with rental listings above the bin. "Martis Camp allows owners to rent their homes?"

"We most certainly do … Ah! Here's one," the agent says. She places the sitemap inside a large Martis Camp brochure and hands it to Tom with a smile. "However, there're strict guidelines for renting. We don't discourage rentals because most owners use their homes as a vacation destination, but we do have year-rounders. Even so, many homes sit empty for a good part of the year."

Studying the rental listings, Tom discovers a house near the Dream Home lot. "What a great idea. I'd love to rent for several months just to get a feel for the community." He points to the board and asks, "Is this rental still available?"

His sudden interest surprises the agent. She responds in a high pitch, "You bet! Would you like to see the home?"

"No. That won't be necessary. What's the procedure?"

"Well, I'll need to contact the owners first. They're away until October, so the home is free for seven months."

"Perfect."

"Once I get the owner's okay, I'll need some personal information and first, second, and last month rental cost."

"What's the rental cost?"

"Well, monthly they rent for $4000."

Reassessing the funds he just withdrew from his retirement account, he states emphatically, "I can pay as soon as you get confirmation from the owners." Tom writes his contact information on a piece of paper. "I'm staying at the Constellation at Northstar. You can reach me at this number," he says, noticing the agent's astonishment.

Tom considers his luck as he leaves the clubhouse with plans abuzz in his head. *I couldn't have planned it better.*

Back at Northstar, he heads to the village square and sits at a café bordering the skating rink. Tom does a double-take when a tall, thin, African-American woman approaches his table, but up close, she looks nothing like Tara McPherson. He unfolds the sitemap on the table, circles lot number 795—the Dream Home site and lot number 793, the rental location. Well, well, well, we're neighbors, he smirks.

Cody

March 11, 2014, Tahoe, Ritz Carlton

Cody scrolls through his mobile's contacts for Jake Holden, the Private Detective he hired several weeks ago. After following Sean Cavanaugh to Martis Camp, he realized this guy's not going away. He dials Jakes number and he answers right away.

"Jake Holden."

"Hey Jake; you find any more information on Sean Cavanaugh?"

"Cody, we did find a Sean Cavanaugh in Boston given the passport on file at the hotel, but get this, he's not in Tahoe. Sean Cavanaugh was a neurosurgeon at Boston Memorial Hospital. The hospital informed me he died six months ago. Whoever this person is in Tahoe, he's not Sean Cavanaugh."

"You're kidding! How did he obtain Dr. Cavanaugh's passport and credit cards?"

"That's a good question, Cody. My team is on it as we speak. They're contacting Dr. Cavanaugh's family in Boston. Give us a few days to investigate and I'll get back to you the moment I find something."

"Sounds good, Jake. I hope you find something soon. From the looks of it, this guy isn't going away."

"Maybe you should let the hotel know he's using false I.D."

"I'll call now. Thanks, man."

With haste, Cody dials the Constellation's reservation desk.

"Good afternoon; The Constellation at Northstar."

"Hey, Scott, how're you doing? I just received puzzling information about Sean Cavanaugh. He's not who he says he is. He's using false I.D."

"Cody, I was just going to call you. Sean Cavanaugh checked out early this morning. I just noticed his room is vacant."

"What! Just like that?"

"Yep, unfortunately, I wasn't on the desk at the time. I could have gotten more information for you. Sorry, man."

"Damn! Well, so much for that. No worries, Scott. Thanks for your help."

"Anytime, Cody …"

Chapter 20

March 11, 2015, Truckee-Tahoe Airport

The girls step off Alcott's private plane onto Truckee Tahoe Airport's tarmac. A biting wind pushes them through the gate and inside the small terminal. Laura rushes in with a shiver, and quickly pulls a ski parka from her carry on and exclaims, "It's freezing here!"

"Anything below Charleston's balmy eighty degrees is freezing," Tara says, pulling a beige faux fur-lined hat over her head. "Ms. Chicago, the cold is nothing for you."

"Wow, Tara," Leanne says, "you should see yourself in that hat. Your eyes look wolfish surrounded by fur."

"I feel like an animal wearing this thing," Tara says widening her hazel eyes. "Aren't you cold?"

"No. I'm enjoying this after Charleston's hot weather. Kinda makes me homesick for Chicago's winters, but our snow is nothing like this. This is so pristine and powdery. The air smells so pure," Leanne says, smiling at the girls all bundled up and ready to brace the cold.

"Tara, New York has cold winters. You'll acclimate with no problem," says Laura.

"Are you kidding? You don't see snow like this in New York. Besides, the moment it snows, the city plows it away," Tara says, following Laura and Leanne sluggishly toward the baggage carousel.

Retrieving their bags, they head toward the entrance and search for their ride to the hotel. Tara notices the wall of looming snow around the airport. "Wow ... That must be at least ten feet high?"

"You'll get used to it," Laura says laughing at Tara's wide eyes. "After all, we're in ski country and Tahoe's snow can last from October 'til July."

"Well, I guess we can add skiing to our daily schedule," Tara says.

Leanne frowns. "Among other things ..."

Laura turns and bumps into a man standing behind her with a big grin. "Cody!" Laura exclaims. "What are you doing here? We thought someone else would pick us up. What a delightful surprise," Laura says, kissing Cody with a loud smack on the lips.

"Ladies, welcome to Tahoe!"

Tara and Leanne glance at each other, grinning at the fond greeting. They've always pondered Laura and Cody's friendship, but Laura keeps reminding them he's like her brother. *"After all,"* she would say, *"he was one of Daniel's closest friends."* After Daniel's death, Cody and Laura's bond grew deeper; both seeking solace in their time of grief. Tara always believed their friendship would change to something romantic. *They're perfect for each other,* she thought watching them so close together.

"So, Cody, where's this secure hideaway you've chosen?" Tara asks, hoping it's a luxury hotel or resort.

"Well, since it's your first time in Tahoe, my team rented a Ritz-Carlton suite at the Village of Northstar—not too far from Martis Camp. You ladies will have all the amenities of the resort, private access to the mountains, and shopping and dining galore. You're going to love it. Plus Laura, towns are close enough to shop for accessories and furnishings for the Dream Home. Girls, your stay won't be all work."

Heading to The Village at Northstar, the girls sit in awe and alarm of Alpine beauty and winding, dangerous, snow-covered roads. Finally, on Highland Courts Road, the village glistens ahead. Weary from the long trip, they're eager to relax in resort surroundings.

Moments later, a collective scream resounds as they step into the Ritz-Carlton suite, noticing ski slopes ending at the base of huge triangular windows.

"Now this is a treat," Tara says, taking in every inch of the space. In the center of the room, a double-sided fireplace burns warm and bright. A plush sectional and chairs sit on colorful throw rugs, overlaying shiny wooden floors. The room resembles a French Chalet with high walls forming a triangle and a chandelier dangling from the towering tip. Wearily, the girls plop onto the sofa, tired from days of worry.

Minutes later, Laura makes her way upstairs, thrilled to find en-suite bathrooms, canopy beds, fireplaces, and balconies with magnificent mountain views in every room. "Girls, we have our own bathrooms. So, there'll be no fighting in the mornings," Laura exclaims. Instantly feet sound on the stairs as Leanne and Tara rush upstairs to claim their bedrooms.

"I'm never leaving this place!" Tara's voice echoed from her room.

"This has to cost a pretty penny. How much are we paying to stay here?" Leanne yells.

"Leanne, that's not your concern. Think of it as a bonus from the Alcotts," Tara replies. "Plus, travel and hotel accommodations are expensed every year when we take on new projects," Tara says, recalling the exorbitant stipend built into the Alcott Foundation's clause to cover all AHD's Dream Home costs annually. Every year she's in awe of excess funds donated to charitable causes. However, she never questions the Alcott's largesse.

Finding the kitchen, Laura marvels at the stainless steel appliances and gourmet amenities. *It couldn't be more perfect* she thought. On the counter sits a container of gourmet hot chocolate and a courtesy basket filled with scones and other treats. She prepares three cups, hoping to relax the girls. For the first time in days, her mind is silent with just her thoughts. The girl's incessant mental chatter which has accosted her since they moved into the Alcott estate has ceased. For weeks, their constant worries mimicked her own and tripled her anxiety.

"Girls, come here," Leanne summoned upstairs on her balcony. Underneath the veranda, a couple in the throes of passion glistens with misty steam.

With a tray of hot chocolate, Laura makes her way to the balcony and peers below. "We shouldn't be spying on them. That's an invasion of privacy."

"Well, if they didn't want others watching, they'd be in the privacy of their rooms," Leanne says with a sheepish grin.

Tara glances around the balcony, spying a covered corner. "Ladies, look ... we have our own hot tub, but it won't be much fun without male company," she says with a wicked grin.

"What happened to that gorgeous law student, what's his name ... Ellison?"

"Leanne, I can't think about Ellison right now; not with a stalker on our tails. We have too much to do. Besides, he's all the way back on the East Coast."

"He's called you several times, Tara. At least you can return his call, even if you're not interested," Laura says, knowing darn well the man intrigues her.

"I will; just not now," Tara says, lost in the mountain views.

Laura hands Tara and Leanne hot chocolate and steps off the balcony with a shiver "Come back inside, girls, its freezing."

Downstairs around the fireplace, they sit in silence, viewing the wintry scene around Northstar Village and tension free for the first time in months, although, they realize danger's nearby.

"Laura, did Cody find any more information on our stalker?" Leanne asks.

Cody's last phone call about Sean Cavanaugh's visit to Martis Camp will dash momentary calm, but Laura can't keep this from them much longer. "Girls, Cody followed our stalker to Martis Camp."

"What!" Tara screeches. "How did he find the Dream Home location? We haven't disclosed the site to anyone."

"Hmmm," Laura ponders. "Maybe he overheard us at the house. But I don't recall ever speaking about the Tahoe location inside the Alcott estate."

"Laura, he got into your computer," Leanne says, discovering her fingernails again. "Remember my vision back in Charleston. He printed the email from Tara. He also went through your files while he was hiding in the estate and possibly accessed all your information."

"Leanne, now that's plain scary," Laura says recalling personal documents in her computer and desk. "Well, Cody hired a security firm to oversee the project until the home's completed. So, we'll have guards 24/7. He couldn't get to us if he tried," Laura says, concealing her fear. "Anyway, girls, let's get off this topic. I can't believe we're finally in Lake Tahoe! We can work, hit the slopes, and do the resort thing … just have some fun for a change. We only live once."

"And if we're lucky, we'll make it back home alive," Tara says.

"Tara, stop being so morbid; just relax and enjoy the surroundings." Suppressing thoughts of their stalker, Laura considers the meeting with Cody and the new architect tomorrow evening. "Tara, how much do you know about Michael Anders, our new architect?"

"Well, to be honest, not much, Laura. In December, when I sent Cody the list of candidates, I had no idea I'd highlighted Michael's name. But I've visited his company's website. Mr. Anders has a fantastic reputation for building environmentally friendly homes in the region."

"So, you've never met him?"

"No. We've spoken a few times over the years. I haven't had a chance to meet him in person. But, I did check out his Internet profile. He's an attractive man."

"Girls, do you want to come to dinner tomorrow?"

"No, Laura. This is your meeting. You can fill us in later. Hmmm ... Michael is quite the looker. You might even enjoy your evening," Tara says with a wink.

"This is all professional, not a blind date, Tara." Laura laughs and pulls her sketch pad from the portfolio. "Well, I'm anxious to finish my drawings. Cody set up a great workspace, why don't you guys check it out. I believe it's near the sitting area off the dining room."

Behind two sliding doors, an office appears with a picturesque view like an Adam Ansel photo. Tara marvels at three large MAC desktops and other tech gadgets, knowing Leanne will be in heaven. She turns and finds her immersed once again in the iPad. With a sigh, Tara saunters toward a desk near the window and claims her space.

On the iPad, Leanne's stares at a menacing comment from Mountainhigh899 on AHD's blog site.

Mountainhigh899 – Ladies you can run, but you can't hide.

She deliberates telling the girls, but hates spoiling their first day in Tahoe. A few moments later, Laura enters the office, detecting Mountainhigh899 in Leanne's thoughts. "We're safe here. He'd have to be ingenious to find us," Laura says with a perceptive stare.

"Or incredibly clairvoyant," Leanne smirked.

"No, if he's clairvoyant one of us would know ... right?" Tara asks. "No, he can't be."

"Well, let's hope so," Laura says, taking a sip of hot chocolate. "I believe we gave him the slip last week. Tara, I appreciate Nyla and James' help."

At the mention of her mom, Tara remembers her promise. "Girls, I'm worried about my premonitions. What if I don't see the full vision in time? I'm only seeing bits and pieces, which makes absolutely no sense to me."

Leanne recalls the smoke-filled room in Tara's vision and the overwhelming breathlessness and dizziness. She's just as eager as Tara to see the full vision. "Tara, it will come soon. I'm sure it will."

Tara sighs and throws her hands in the air. "Well, if we're going to defeat this guy, I need to shush more."

Tara searches around the condo and comes upon a media room with cushiony leather chairs and sofas situated in front of a large screen. When she turns off the light, snow glows through the window, illuminating the room. "Perfect!" In front of the window, she assumes an Indian pose and grasps the crystals around her neck. Several minutes later, she's inside a hallway.

> *Noxious fumes assault her nose as she follows a tall, slender male down a slate-tiled hallway into a bedroom overlooking a snow-covered patio and pine trees. He heads upstairs, dispensing liquid from a can. In the long foyer, chains rattle as he pulls them through sliding doors, locking them securely in place. Snow floats like cotton balls around the outdoor patio, blanketing a dining space. She follows him through the foyer towards a kitchen with a long granite island and a towering stainless-steel hood. In the great room, a blurred figure strapped to a chair sits terrified. Angrily, he approaches and drags the chair forcefully toward the center of the room.*

Chapter 21

Kindred Souls

March 12, 2015, Cottonwood Restaurant

Michael Anders, a distinguished looking man in his mid-forties, dressed in a blue turtleneck sweater, jeans, and boots addresses his staff at Anders and King Architecture, LLC. As Senior Partner and owner of the firm, he swiftly briefs employees on the AHD project, answers a few questions, and then rushes to meet Cody Darling and Laura Alcott for a business dinner.

In historic downtown Truckee on Donner Pass Road, shops and restaurants buzz with locals and tourists. Michael turns off Donner Pass onto Brockway, and then straight up Rue Hilltop Road to one of Truckee's most popular eats—Cottonwood Restaurant. He'd chosen the spot because of breathtaking views of the Sierra Nevada Mountains. The restaurant feels like a rustic Tahoe cabin with whimsically decorated walls of wooden skis, sleds, and votive-candle chandeliers surrounding white linen-covered tables. Michael wants Cody and Laura to taste Tahoe's finest while discussing the sweepstake home's design.

He enters the restaurant and finds Cody and Laura seated near the terrace. A bewildering glow outlines Laura as he approaches the table. His eyes lock with hers when she looks in his direction.

"Enjoying the view?"

Surprised by Michael's entrance, Cody swiftly stands and shakes his hand. "Awesome spot, Michael; with these views, I could sit here all day."

"I thought you might like it."

"Michael, this is Laura Alcott."

"Hi Laura; we've only spoken once on the phone, but I feel like I already know you. Are you enjoying your stay in Tahoe?"

Michael's presence intrigues Laura. Tongue-tied for the first time in her life, she forces words from her mouth. "I—oh—I love Tahoe. I've spent many winters skiing in the area, but this is the first time I'm here for business."

Captivated by Laura's accent, he stares longer than customary at her bluish-green eyes. "Well, I hope you'll find some time for fun and relaxation while you're here."

"I hope so too," she says, with hands still clenched in Michael's firm handshake. An uncanny familiarity ensues when Laura releases her grip. The moment he entered the restaurant, she sensed a change in the air. *There's something special about Michael.* She can't put her finger on his unusual energy, but she's drawn to it. She studies his attractive features and his athletic physique—the body of an outdoorsman. His skin's slightly tanned with a roughness she's seen on many outdoor sports enthusiasts. The blue turtleneck sweater draws attention to his grayish blue eyes. But she can't determine his nationality—a hint of American-Indian mixed perhaps with Irish or Scottish ancestry.

He possesses the casual self-assurance of wealthy Southern men she's met over the years. Surprisingly, his self-possession reminds her of Daniel. Lost in the peaceful vibe emanating from Michael, she smiles bashfully when he catches her eyes.

Michael slides his chair into the table next to Laura and waves to the waiter. "Let's order some wine."

"Wine sounds splendid," Laura says; needing a glass to taper her new emotions.

"Do you have a preference ... red or white? He asks looking at Laura then Cody.

"Pinot Grigio," Laura answers.

"That's fine," Cody replies.

The waiter approaches. "A bottle of your best Pinot Grigio," Michael requested and the waiter shakes his head and leaves to retrieve their finest.

"So, where should we start?" Michael asks.

"Well, Michael, business first, and the pleasure of good company afterward," Laura says, sensing his intentions.

Michael searches Laura's eyes, detecting something extraordinary behind their bluish-green tint. "You took the exact words out of my mouth."

"She does that quite often, Michael. You better get used to it," Cody says, winking at Laura.

"Ah!" Michael utters, studying Laura closely. "You have a touch of clairvoyance."

Taken aback, Laura asks, "Do you believe in such things, Michael?"

"I do. Many people have a six sense that goes undetected. My grandfather was American Indian, and they believed in spiritual gifts—the third eye. I think people waste their talents, or never fully develop them. Laura, you might be one of those people."

"You might be right, Michael," Laura says with a sly grin. She peers back and forth between Cody and this remarkable man. *Why didn't the statement faze Cody? And why can't I read their thoughts?*

Possessing a unique talent for reading body language; Michael notices Laura's unblinking eyes and subtle shift in the seat when he mentioned clairvoyance. He's stumbled on some truth. The waiter appears with a bottle of locally-sourced Pinot Grigio, fills each of their glasses, and leaves the bottle in the center of the table.

"Okay, you two, let's get down to business," Michael says retrieving the iPad from his portfolio case and placing it on the table. "Laura, Cody and I met a few weeks ago. This is what we've come up with," he says and slides the iPad toward her. An interactive three-dimensional blueprint showcasing the skeleton of the home's exterior and interior swirls revealing every detail of the floor plan. "Cody, your addition worked nicely. Our engineer believes extending the porch is a sound decision."

"I'm glad to hear that … Sound and aesthetic," Cody says while rubbing his chin.

Michael glances at Laura's elegant hands, admiring mauve-colored fingernails as she maneuvers the iPad. "Laura, tell me what you think. Oh …" he says, reaching toward the floor. "… I brought a portfolio of homes I've designed in the region."

"Wow, this is fantastic, guys. The home is beautiful even unfurnished. Technology, how did we work without it," Laura mumbles, lost in the three-dimensional blueprint.

"Cody and I decided on an industrial mountain style. The industrial aspect comes from the exposed metal beams running throughout the home and other metal accents. And of course, the exposed wooden trusses give the home a mountain style upstairs and downstairs." Michael moves his chair closer to Laura, points to and explains other design features on the iPad.

With a slight bump of shoulders, emotions are aroused. Laura's face warms, and she hopes her color won't betray her attraction. She senses alluring undertones and moves closer to decipher the sensation.

"Laura, with all the metal accents in the home, we'll need your expertise to make the space warm and inviting."

"I understand what you mean ... Metal can be tricky to work with. Wow ... But those windows surrounding the space are magnificent. So, we're working with several different materials here, not only wood and metal but also glass and stone. I created some ideas in my sketches I believe will work well. I'm thinking bold accent colors to brighten the space. I've been in Tahoe during the spring and winter seasons, and I'm always fascinated by nature's colors. I believe using some of the red, yellow, and orange colors from native plants will connect the home to its environment. Don't you think?"

"You're hired!" Michael exclaims with a look of awe and excitement. "Bringing the environment indoors is a concept I teach my staff all the time. My designs consist of natural elements to create environmentally friendly homes. You're good Laura. I can't wait to see what you come up with."

Michael's excitement reminds Laura of her own when she starts a new design process. She's going to enjoy working with Michael for several months. Another feature of the home catches her attention. "What a bold fireplace ... It's the best feature in the great room. I believe decorating the room with small pieces will highlight the architectural beauty."

What a gorgeous woman.

Finally, Michael's thoughts penetrate her mind. She casts her eyes down, stumbles, but keeps talking. "I-uh, so, Michael, it appears the kitchen, dining, and the great room runs in one long line. The West wing is essentially one big space—no walls."

"Yes, the west wing is an open concept ... so there has to be a seamless melding of space," Michael says.

Laura's eyes meet his again. "I was just going to say the same."

Peeking from his wineglass, Cody's not only noticed the immediate attraction between Laura and Michael but also their design affinity. *They will work well together.* "Laura, you got the eyes for this particular design."

"Cody, give me a big budget, and I can work wonders, sweetie."

"Well, you gotta talk to Tara about finance. She's the business guru," Cody says with a chuckle. "Michael, you'll love Laura's interior design for the Vermont Mountain Home. It's absolutely stunning."

"In fact, I did view your designs online. I love all the homes you've designed," Michael says, rapt with her eyes.

"Why thank you, Michael, I love designing those spaces, and it's so hard letting go when I'm done," Laura says, swimming in his soothing essence.

"Well, I guess we have that in common, Laura. I love designing homes, and you love decorating them. A perfect complement, wouldn't you say?"

"Yes, we're quite the complement."

In more than one way, I hope.

With Michael's thought, she stutters. "I—well—um meant as architects and interior designers ... I like to refer to the two as hard and soft engineers. You build the skeleton, and I design the internal spaces," Laura says with a nervous laugh as Michael's eyes dissect every inch of her face. *Stop Laura. What's wrong with you? This is work, not a date* she chides. The foreign essence invades her senses making it hard to concentrate. *A moth lured to a flame,* she thinks, but this flame is a calm, peaceful light.

She tries to hide her attraction and again catches his eyes. "This might sound cheesy, but I always compare homes to the human body, the skeleton is the architecture, and the internal organs are the interior design," she says, steadying her voice. *How obtuse can you be, Laura? You're acting like a schoolgirl.*

"Good analogy," Cody says. "The only difference is one is the divine creation of the heavens, and the other is the earthly design of man."

"I think I'll use both of those in my company's promo," Michael says with a disconcerting grin that reminds Laura so much of Daniel.

"I wouldn't; the comparison is too rudimentary," Laura says, realizing her analogy might be unoriginal. She suspects their words are merely polite accolades.

"It might be, but it's still a damn good analogy. There's no other comparison," Michael states with a winsome smile.

Though not surprised by their physical attraction, Cody's amazed at their mesmerized expressions—as if they can't believe their captivation. "Laura, the construction doesn't start until April. You'll have plenty of time to design around our blueprint, before the home's completion in September. So, take the diagram back to your suite, think it over, and we'll sit down again to discuss what you come up with later."

"Cody, as you know, I need to feel the room's ambiance. So, some of my design ideas won't come until I've stepped into the completed structure." Laura stares in astonishment at glossy photos of mountain homes in Michael's portfolio. "These are beautiful, Michael." Laura pauses at a luxurious Mountain Home overlooking Donner Lake. "Wow ... I would love to look inside this one. Do you think we can get the owner's permission?"

"When do you want to see it?"

"As soon as possible ... "

"Well, how about tomorrow?"

"You can get the owner's permission that fast?"

Michael grins. "Well, you're looking at the owner."

A little more intrigued; Laura sighs in exhilaration. She remembers how Daniel's presence always soothed her, and the similarities in Michael's presence are striking. "Cody, have you seen Michael's home?"

"Have I? Michael's architecture blew my mind. He couldn't get the camera crew or me out of his home the first time." Cody glances at Michael; recalling the first visit when he and the camera crew usurped his time. They roamed the home all-day then made themselves useless in front of Michael's television watching football all night. The next morning, finding themselves passed out on Michael's sofa from too much beer, they issued apologetic words. A casual acquaintance soon felt like an old friendship. "Michael's work solidified my decision on Lake Tahoe. You're going to love his lakeside home." With a deliberative squint, he states, "Actually, Michael's interior designs might inspire ideas for the Dream Home. They both contain similar architectural features."

"Fantastic idea, Cody ..." Laura's voice trails as she continues examining Michael's photos. She wonders if he lives in the home year-round. "Michael, were you born in Lake Tahoe?"

Michael waves his hand towards the waiter; trying to get his attention. "No, Seattle. I fell in love with the Tahoe region during college semester breaks. After grad school, I came back, got married, and never left."

Laura hadn't noticed a wedding band or entertained the idea of marriage. "Oh, is your wife from the region?"

"Yes, well she was. She passed away a few years ago."

"Oh ... I'm sorry, Michael."

The waiter approaches with the menu. "Let me know when you're ready to order."

"Can you give us a few minutes, please," Michael says, never looking at the waiter, eyes fixed on Laura's face as the waiter smiles and walks away. "How about you, Laura; were you born in Charleston?"

"Yes, and I can't imagine living anywhere else. I've been many places, but I prefer my hometown."

"What about your husband?"

Laura catches Michael's eyes, and for an instant, they peered beyond her face and back as if something caught his attention. "Daniel was a Southerner; born and raised in Charleston." Laura pauses, remembering Daniel's passion for skiing, which she always thought unusual for someone raised in the South. "He loved Tahoe; this used to be our winter retreat until he passed two years ago."

"Oh, seems we have something else in common."

Cody sits quietly watching the two with a realization—they're kindred souls. The similarities, not so obvious earlier, grow more apparent with the approaching evening.

Meanwhile, Michael senses a spiritual presence around Laura. A male presence he believes is her husband and a female named Melissa. Laura peers up quickly from the portfolio, hearing Daniel's name in Michael's mind, but the rest of his thought is imperceptible.

A few minutes later, Laura's intoxicated with Michael's essence. *Or is it the wine?* Laura thought. Since Daniel's death, she hasn't been attracted to another man, but she's been strangely drawn to Michael since he stepped into the restaurant. Laura frowns at Cody smirking behind his wineglass. She recognizes the sly squint in his hazel eyes—scrutinizing her and Michael.

Cody throws Laura a mischievous look, teasing her like an annoying brother. He laughs inwardly at her obvious embarrassment. However, Cody's thrilled she's relishing in another man's presence. From the moment he'd met Michael Anders, he'd found similarities to Daniel. His appeal is obvious. Cody's hoped Laura would find happiness again. Losing Daniel was hard on them both. Since his passing, an unexpected bonding occurred between them—a security and comfort he couldn't explain. Although there've been moments, they've traversed friendship and intimacy, Cody would never take advantage of Laura's vulnerable state or endanger their friendship with a momentary lapse of willpower. Peering at Michael, he couldn't think of anyone better, and throws Laura a nod and a wink of approval—causing her to almost choke on her wine.

After an hour of business talk and several glasses of wine, they decide to order dinner. Cody orders a pecan and sage crusted USA catfish, grain-mustard-Creole-burre Blanc, herbed rice, and vegetable dish. Michael talks Laura into trying the seafood stew with shellfish, prawns, scallops and Andouille sausage in a saffron-tomato broth over linguini topped with Asiago cheese.

"Sounds luscious, Michael," Laura says.

And so are you, Michael thought.

Laura bites her lip to conceal arousal. *What's wrong with me?* This is unexpected, she thought, gluing her eyes on the view beyond the window, certain the moment she looks into Michael's eyes she'll lose all composure.

Minutes later, the three savor their dishes with senses fully alive from wine, food, and awe-inspiring views as they witness the town below light like the heavenly constellation. From a distance, they appear old friends, not business acquaintances meeting over a business deal for the first time.

Chapter 22

The Fire Pit

March 14, 2015, Ritz-Carlton

> *Three figures sit in the middle of an illusive room, bound to chairs as smoke crawls around a corner. Tara moves toward them and their faces clarify fearfully. Laura sits unconscious and bleeding from the head while a tearful Leanne yells "murderer" at their assailant. Tara touches her body, and instantly, she's bound to the chair. Furiously and swiftly, a man moves toward Leanne. The floors vibrate with his steps. In the distance, a frantic voice screams.*

Tara wakes with a deep, loud wheeze, grasping for air. Her heart races and her mind burns with Laura and Leanne strapped to chairs and their assailant's murderous intent. She grabs the pen on the nightstand, captures every dream detail in the journal, and shudders as she writes BLOOD ... streaming down Laura's face and Leanne's swelling tears and piercing scream of "MURDERER." *They can't see this! I need to keep them out of my head ... At least, until I see the entire dream ... But how?* Suddenly, she remembers what Nyla told her. *"If you want to keep others out of your mind, wear the Moldavite stone necklace. The stone protects and blocks others from reading your thoughts.*"

Unease gnaws at her gut. Unable to calm her mind, Tara flings the covers off and stares at snowy mountains outside her window—the peaceful haven a drastic contrast to her fearful mind. Desperate to dispel anxiety, she springs from the bed, rushes to the chest, rummages for the Moldavite stone, and places it in her robe. Quickly, she dresses in workout gear and stashes post-workout clothes in her gym bag. Just as she reaches the door, she remembers the Moldavite necklace in her robe. Like a shield, she places the stone around her neck and quietly exits the suite.

At six in the morning, snow swirls on chilling winds. Artificial light bounces off snow-covered grounds and cast faux-daylight through the village and mountains in the distance. Gondolas and ski lifts swing askew, waiting to whisk skiers to various slopes. Skipping the cold village square, Tara rushes through the tubular glass atrium leading to the gym. Her legs freeze in a scissor stance as her eyes gloss with a vision.

A slender male approaches from the opposite end of the atrium. "It's him." Fearfully, she turns about-face, finding an exit to the village square. She glances back at a familiar face that stared at her from AHD's gate, now peering at her through the glass atrium.

Tara's vision ends as abruptly as it appeared. She stands in the middle of the tubular space searching one end to the other. Picking up her pace, and assuming a run, she exits to opposite end. Her mind echoes, *he's here.*

An hour later, in the sauna, steam and endorphins from the forty-minute run relax tense muscles but does nothing to assuage the alarming dream and vision in the atrium. Thick steam obscures benches across the way. Thoughts of the stalker seated and watching chills her hot skin. Draping the towel around her body she rushes from the sauna to the dressing room, throws on dry clothes, and exits the gym.

Bypassing the atrium, Tara makes her way through Northstar village. The hamlet stirs with early risers ready to hit the slopes. In the distance, the smell of coffee pulls her behind skiers heading toward Mountain Blue Café. She misses The Bakehouse Bakery Coffee, but this will have to do.

Minutes later, with her coffee, Tara strolls through the village square, perusing countless shops, restaurants, bars, movie theaters, and the skating rink in the village center. Northstar appears like a small town, secluded from reality. With her next step, dawn turns to dusk.

> *Nightfall lightens Northstar's sparkling evening bustle. A tall man's posterior towers her anterior view. She trails his long, slow, strides through the square toward a small group seated around flaming smoke.*

The vision disperses, and Tara gasps, finding herself standing over a fire pit. A disturbing sensation emanates from the area. Vibes grow stronger as she winds the circular space. Tara takes a seat in one of several Adirondack chairs stationed around the pit. Moving from chair to chair, and searching anxiously for the source of warning, the next chair slides her into the future.

> *Fire crackles and smoke plumes around the crowd. Beside her, Laura and Leanne chat with a young couple about their day on the slopes. Disturbing energy pulls Tara's attention direct across the fire pit. A man dressed in a ski jacket and low-hung baseball cap sits unmoving. Night shadows his features but his prominent broad lips and jaw standout. He sneers, aware of her discovery.*

Cautiously, Tara tugs Laura's arm. "He's here, but don't let him know you're on to him. He's in the baseball cap across the fire pit." His essence fills Laura with fear. She whispers to Leanne, "Let's go, sweetie. He's here." Leanne, sensing his anger sits frozen, unable to move. Laura pulls on her arm, smiles, and says goodnight to the young couple. Calmly, they walk toward Manzanita Restaurant's entrance. Tara peers back, catching his glare. Inside, they circle through the restaurant, into the arcade, finding a back door to the opposite end of the village square. Vigilantly, they enter the hotel, but across the *lobby, their stalker enters.*

"Miss, you okay?"

A male voice pulls Tara from her trance. Dazed, she glances at the young man holding skis. Embarrassed, she realizes how odd she must appear. "Thanks, I'm all right … just daydreaming," Tara says with a forced smile. Rising from the chair, she heads toward the hotel.

Back in her room, she ponders the Moldavite necklace. After the village square visions, she realizes concealing her premonition puts the girls in danger. She places the stone on the nightstand, stares at her face in the mirror, sighs, and murmurs, "You have to tell them about the dream."

In the kitchen, Laura and Leanne sit at the dining table, glancing over a Village at Northstar map. "We need to stay clear of the fire pit and the atrium," Tara says proceeding to the refrigerator. "I had another dream and several visions this morning. I saw the figures in the middle of that room." She pauses registering the girl's impassive miens. Tara frown disquiet and states, "The images are the three of us tied to chairs."

Lifted brows steal Leanne and Laura's blank expressions.

"And what else?" Leanne asks.

"That's it, that's all I got." Tara dreads revealing Laura bleeding and Leanne's tearful murderous scream.

Laura sighs. "Tara, it's okay. Leanne captured your vision when you came in this morning, and I heard your thoughts a few minutes ago. I'm not afraid. If your visions continue, we can elude this man. No matter how bloody or scary, we need to know, sweetie."

"What if I don't see his next move?"

"I'm sure you will. You just need to keep doing what Nyla said. And if the full vision fails to materialize, we'll figure something out," Laura said.

"Tara, were you wearing a Moldavite stone?" Leanne asks.

"You saw the necklace?"

"Yep ..."

"Well, I didn't want you two to know about my dream."

"Tara, you can't interfere with us seeing your visions. We need to read each other's minds. Our gift is our most powerful weapon against this guy."

"Okay, okay ... it was a stupid move. I removed the necklace."

"Tara, the Moldavite hinders your vision?"

"Nyla said the stone will prevent others from reading my thoughts."

"She's right but it also hinders your visions. You need to learn more about the crystals and stones you use. I believe Nyla meant you should use the stone as protection against others, not us. Besides, it will block, not promote your gift."

"Okay, guys, I'm ignorant of crystals."

"Keep wearing the sacred-seven-stones. It'll strengthen your visions," Leanne says with a chuckle.

"I apologize, girls," Tara says, opening the refrigerator, retrieving a bottle of water, and swiftly changing the topic. "So, Laura, aren't you seeing Michael's lake home today?"

Since Cottonwood, Laura's thought of nothing else. "Aren't you girls coming? I think you'll enjoy his company and his home."

Playfully, Leanne nudges Tara with her elbow. "Doesn't Michael want you to himself? We'll be third wheels," she says puckering and kissing the air.

"Leanne, stop it right now. I'm not looking to start an affair with Mr. Anders."

"Michael, you mean? Isn't he hot?" Tara teases. She perceived Laura's cheery mood the night she returned from Cottonwood and knew she'd found a new love interest in Michael. "From what I understand, you two have much in common."

"Okay, I'm not discussing Michael any further. You two are coming with me, and no arguments."

Chapter 23

A Shaman in Our Midst

March 14, 2015, Michael Anders Home

When the girls leave for Donner Lake, the sun dips low in the western skies. The entire trip, Tara admires indigo skies smeared with tangerine ribbons slicing twilight. With nightfall, sadness always invades Tara's mind, a melancholia she can't grasp. Perhaps darkness, the denouement of light is the trigger, but tonight, like most evenings, she'll transcend sadness with her friend's company.

They arrive at Michael Ander's mountain mansion in awe of its beauty, size, and resort ambiance. Architectural shapes mimic mountain peaks made of glass, steel, stone, and wood. Internal spaces display magnificent views of nature through towering windows as Donner Lake follows room to room. The home furnishings—chic, minimalistic, with a masculine touch complements nature.

On the back patio, Donner Lake laps on rocky paths tapering Tara's sadness. Absorbed in the spa-like space featuring a fire pit, outdoor dining, and a hot tub, she speculates all homes in the area boast resort themes.

Upstairs, Leanne peers through a long telescope placed strategically at the window. She aims heavenward at the sky, mountains, the surrounding lake community, and then into Donner Lake's dark waters. A long pier runs from the backyard to a sundeck. East of the pier, Leanne spies a group eating around a fire pit. Again, she pivots toward celestial constellations, pondering stars divination.

Stepping away from the telescope, Leanne moves onto the third-floor deck and peers below at the rocky edge ... *a mountain castle.* The home's large windows take in the rustic scenery, making it part of the environment it mirrors.

Earlier, when Michael toured them through the home, Leanne felt a strange vibe on the second floor. Now, compelled to uncover the source, she wanders toward a door the aura originates. On entering the inexplicable space, an unfamiliar energy grips her senses. On the walls hang crystals, dried herbs, and unfamiliar tools. A large feather headdress framed in glass hangs in the center of the room. *Perhaps it's a family heirloom.*

Along the adjacent wall, an Indian cloth and various colorful feathers extend from one corner to the next. Some items are antiques, some family heirlooms. She runs her fingers along beautiful feathers, sensing Michael's essence transcending spiritual plains. His energy is peaceful. When her finger touches the center of the feather, she's slung to another sphere. Alarmingly, her body grows weightless. Various colored lights speed beyond her consciousness. Afraid of the light's destination, Leanne yanks her finger from the feather.

Never before has she experienced such tranquility. *Perhaps the feathers are used to connect with the spiritual world.* Intrigued by the headdress, Leanne runs her fingers along the glass encasement, witnessing Michael's relative's powers to heal people and nurture the land. An elderly man places the headdress on a young Michael Anders. In the room's center, peace and resolve emanate from a turquoise-beaded rope displayed on a glass top table. Leanne reaches out to touch it, but stops, averse to intruding on Michael's privacy. But the necklace's energy is overwhelming, forcing Leanne's hands along the gems. An image of Michael's wife, Asia, wearing the turquoise about her neck as Michael communicates with her posthumously appears. He makes peace with Asia's death and promises her he'll move on with his life.

Leanne covets Michael's tranquility. His heritage is healing, nurturing, and benevolent. The room's energy is so powerful; she forces herself out of the room. On top of the staircase she's mesmerized by a puzzling light prism on the dining room wall—an unusual glow she assumes from Donner Lake. Slowly, she makes her way downstairs, halting with Michael and Laura's voices around the corner.

* * *

On the couch, Laura sits next to Michael, enthralled by the longest fireplace she's ever seen, a focal point that sweeps the entire wall. "Michael, this must have cost a fortune. I'm impressed."

"Well, money means nothing when it's your sanctuary. I wanted a home connected to nature."

"Well, you captured the environment exquisitely. The house is basically floating on Donner Lake. And the massive windows seize those awe-inspiring mountains." Above the fireplace, Laura notices a photo of Michael holding hands with a beautiful raven-haired woman with an enchanting smile. Dressed in snow gear and snowshoes, they pose on a snowy trail. "Is she your wife?"

"Yes … Asia."

"She was beautiful."

"Yes, she was. That's one of my favorite photos. Asia loved the mountains and all snow sports. This photo was taken on

Donner Trail one of our regular treks." Michael eyes the picture with a smile.

"I imagine you both skied a lot."

"That's putting it mildly," he says with a grin. "We did everything—snowshoeing, snowboarding, alpine, and cross-country." A wistful pause ensues, as he replaces the picture on the mantle. "Asia was the daring one. She was always on the slopes either snowboarding or skiing."

"So, she was athletic?"

"Well, she was more extreme. She was a triathlete."

"How did she die?"

"Doing what she loved."

Michael's resolve is apparent. He's moved on without his wife, *but how* Laura wonders. Living without Daniel has been excruciating.

Michael notices Laura's eyes darken. "It's okay. I've made peace with Asia's death. She had an undiagnosed heart condition. One day during a training session, her heart simply gave out. It was her time to go."

"Michael, I'm so sorry. The heartbreak of unexpected loss is devastating."

"Laura, if you don't mind … how did Daniel die?"

"His death was sudden as well. During a hurricane, his car went off the road. He was killed instantly. I was in denial for months. I swear, Michael; I still sense Daniel's presence in our home."

He's still there. Should I tell her Daniel's been protecting and watching her since his death? No, the time isn't right.

The moment those thoughts entered Michael's mind; Laura received the confirmation she's wanted for two years. She swallows emotions threatening to appear.

Leanne enters the room, sensing a slew of emotions. Not wanting to surprise them, she clears her throat. "Ahemmm … Michael, you have a beautiful home. I believe it's bigger than the

Alcott estate," Leanne exclaims, afraid she's broken the amorous mood.

Laura sweeps hair behind her ear and peers around with a strange expression Leanne's never seen on her face before. "You might be right, Leanne. Michael, what's the square footage?"

Pulled from deep thought Michael stirs a cinnamon stick around hot spiced cider, and looks up with a pensive squint. "It's fifteen thousand square feet."

"Nice. The Alcott estate is just a fraction bigger at twenty-thousand square feet."

"A fraction?" He chuckles. "Wow, that's a big home. You're living by yourself?"

"I am, but not by choice. Occasionally my daughter drops in when she gets time from the University," Laura explains. She ponders Michael's countenance. He's sensing her precarious situation—the widow, longing for her family. "I've considered selling the estate, but it's Alcott's history and should be passed on to future generations. I believe Daniel would want that."

"Laura, I agree with you. You'll regret selling the estate later," Leanne says.

"I know I will. Besides, Callie's fit-to-be-tied when I mention it. She wouldn't stand for it." Suddenly, Laura realizes Tara is missing. "Where did Tara disappear to?"

Michael had last seen her on the back patio and glances over his shoulder pass the dining room, where she stands staring at the lake. "She's on the patio."

"It's freezing! Tara, come inside," Laura called.

Tara walks in, skin glowing from the cold. "Michael, I'm in love with your home. I never thought a mountain house could be this spectacular."

Michael, sensing sadness and a chill in Tara's body, hands her a cup of cider. "Well, this is the style I build around the area. But each home is unique with different shapes and sizes. The Dream Home will contain similar features, just on a smaller scale."

"Cody was right about your home. My mind is spinning with ideas. Apparently, our budget won't accommodate this grandeur, but I believe some of the ideas will work well," Laura says.

Leanne deliberates Michael's strong vibes, sensations from the room above, and sips the potent cider. Besides Michael's undeniable attraction to Laura, other benevolent vibes surround him. *He's truly at peace.* She's never sensed total serenity. An earlier inkling pricks at her mind. *He's aware of our gifts.*

"Tara, I can't help noticing your sacred-seven pendant. The stones are lovely."

"Oh," Tara murmurs, touching the gems. "It's a gift from my father."

"Do you wear the stones for a particular reason?"

She glances at the girls briefly then back at Michael. "Not really ... I understand the stones soothe the soul."

"They also strengthen your talents," he explains.

Laura peers at Michael, detecting an unspoken thought. *The stones will enhance your visions.*

"Michael, do you practice Shamanism?"

"Leanne! What an unusual question to ask," says Laura, although she suspects the same.

Impressed by her keen perception, Michael states, "And you must be clairvoyant as well, Leanne." Michael notices the change in their faces and reassures them. "Don't worry ladies. I felt each of your gifts earlier. Laura, I sensed your talents the moment I met you in the restaurant, and I sensed Leanne and Tara's gift when you walked into my home."

Laura reflects on the night at Cottonwood, and her suspicions had been right all along. She recalls how difficult it was sensing his thoughts and decided her attraction blocked her gift.

"So, Michael, are you a Shaman," Leanne pressed on.

With thoughtful gray eyes, Michael says, "Leanne, I prefer not to use Shaman. My family frowns at that label. We prefer spiritualist or healer," he explains diplomatically. "People have a stereotypical idea of Shamans chanting around a fire and communicating with spirits," he chuckles. "Some of my ancestors were medicine men or herbalist, as I prefer to call them. However, many people still use the word shaman. But it's so difficult to dispel stereotypical beliefs ingrained in American culture. Basically, my gift is a natural gift just like yours."

"Michael, I didn't mean to insult your culture. I'm one of those ill-advised Americans, who assumed shaman the correct terminology. I apologize for my ignorance."

"Don't worry; many people make the same mistake. You'll find in some American-Indian communities, the term is relevant, but not in my family."

"Is your heritage purely American-Indian?" Laura asks.

"No, Laura. The Anders name is Swedish, from my father's side. My mother is American-Indian."

"Interesting combination; I'd never have guessed your Swedish blood."

"Both my parents were architects back in Seattle where they met, married, and started their own design firm. My parents' passion for architecture is the reason I chose the field."

"So, Michael," Leanne starts, wondering what talents Michael possess, "What do spiritualists do?"

"Well, ladies, like you, I'm blessed with the ability to feel others emotions, but I'm not as gifted as you three. As a spiritualist, I see spirits of people and feel vibrations of inanimate objects. You might also call me a naturalist. I can sense ecological vibrations, which inspired my passion for environmentally friendly homes. I'm lucky to channel my unique gift into my career. Spiritualist run on my mother's side of the family, but that was years ago. Fortunately, I inherited some of their talents." Michael carefully crafts his next revelation to the girls.

Leanne notices a slight change in Michael's face.

"Ladies, when you walked through the door tonight, I sensed a powerful presence around you."

Instantly, Leanne recognizes who Michael speaks of. Since her vision of Nathan Cox's birth, she's sensed it too. "Do you know who it is?" She asks, testing his abilities.

"I sense a female named Melissa, but I can't capture her surname. I believe its Goodwin or Godwin—"

"Gowan," Leanne interjects. "She's our ancestor."

"So, you're all related. Ah! Now I understand why her presence is so strong. Ladies, I also sensed you're in danger. Do you want to tell me about it? I understand if you don't."

"Girls, he can help us," Laura encouraged.

After witnessing Michael's talents on the second floor, Leanne has no doubt he'll be useful. "Michael, I visited your meditation room upstairs. I believe your gift will help us find our stalker."

"Well, Mr. Anders, if the girls are okay, then so am I," Tara says.

"I'm glad you approve. So, Leanne, you discovered my ancestral room?"

Leanne's lips crescent ruefully. "I hope you don't find my curiosity intrusive."

"No, not at all, the room is where I practice my art and pay homage to my ancestors. I've kept a few artifacts from my mom and grandfather. It's a family tradition to pass these items on."

"They're fascinating," says Leanne.

Now assured of Michael's abilities, Laura deliberates where to start. "Michael, has Cody mentioned our problem?"

"No … nothing."

"Well, it all happened out of the blue back in December. We've been stalked for several months. We don't know who he is, but we've foreseen some physical characteristics."

"He's here in Tahoe?"

"Yes. This morning, Tara had another vision of him in the village. The sacred-seven stones are used to strengthen Tara's gift. But, she's only recaptured a small portion of what she saw as a child."

"So, Tara, you're Precognitive—"

"And Clairsentient," Tara interjects.

"I'm Clairsentient-Retrocognitive," says Leanne.

"And I'm Clairsentient as well," Laura reveals.

"Hmmm, past, present, and future; what a gift," Michael mumbles.

Quietly, Laura states, "I used to be telepathic when I was younger, but the gift changed into something else as I got older."

"Ah! Your uncanny ability to hear what I was thinking and finishing my sentence in the restaurant. Well, you three are special. I presume Melissa brought you to me. This can't be pure coincidence."

"Maybe luck played some part in our paths crossing," Laura says.

A shrewd expression shapes Michael's face. "Nothing is purely by chance in this world. I believe a grand design is taking place, and Melissa is the orchestrator and protector of you three. I sense her powers play a significant role here. Somehow, she's aware of my abilities to communicate with spirits. And I suspect she needs me to communicate directly with you." Michael exhales strongly and places the cider on the table. "However, I decided years ago not to meddle in the spirit world; it can be dangerous." Michael stares at the three women, sensing Melissa's powers around them. He sighs heavier. "Many malevolent spirits reside around us, but I'm sensing Melissa Gowan is a benevolent soul. The only danger here is to you three. I feel compelled to help if you're willing."

Tara still stuck on Michael's remark, *nothing is purely by chance in this world,* can't believe Melissa has been with them this entire time. She remembers emailing Cody the list with

Michael's name back in December. *Was Melissa guiding her actions at that moment?* It all seems so impossible. But a year earlier, no one could've told her she'd be surrounded by a family of psychic women on the run from a stalker, and now, the help of a shaman and a spirit. Her life is a supernatural tale. "Michael, how will you communicate with Melissa? What's involved?" Tara asks with burgeoning curiosity.

"The procedure is similar to meditation, facilitated by crystals, stones, and herbs. Staring at the unusual glow on the dining room walls, Michael's certain it's Melissa.

With that thought, Laura and Leanne turn their heads toward the dining room.

"However, with Melissa's strong presence, I'm sensing I won't need any of those tools," Michael continued.

"Can you help me see my vision more clearly?"

"I can try, Tara."

Chapter 24

Melissa Gowan

Charleston, SC, 1828

Sunday is the only day Melissa can escape the Alcott estate and visit her sisters. Today, she visits young Nathan Cox to celebrate his first birthday. Her sisters have secreted Nathan successfully in their home. Not many people come or go from the premises, except servants, who were told the child's mother died in childbirth. Around the servant's quarters, speculation abounds. They can't understand three white women taking care of a black child and raising him as their own. The child's heritage is evident given Nathan's coloring and features. Some even wonder if one of the Gowan women had an affair with a servant. They wouldn't dare ask questions. They're just content the child's safe from harm.

Nathan Cox sits upright in his crib, bouncing with laughter as the two Gowan women tease with a toy. Seeing Melissa approach, the child squeals joy recognizing her instantly. Melissa loves the child, her grandchild, and sees both her son and husbands features developing in Nathan's face. There's no doubt Nathan is an Alcott. Melissa glances at her two sisters and states, "In one hundred and eighty-seven years three of us will thrive again—three who carry the gift of past, present, and future at the same time. Tara, Laura, and Leanne are the key to continuing our family's gifts. We have to protect them from harm."

Since Nathan's birth and Melissa's vision of the gifted three's danger, she understands her role is to guide and protect them from harm. She'd seen Leanne in the room when Nathan was born and felt her powers. Today, she and her sisters will use their gift to guide the girls, using Nathan as a channel. "Are you ready?" Melissa asked prompting her sisters to action.

A medallion Melissa and the Gowan women carved from stone and crystal, sit in the middle of the room—the circle enclosing a square, enclosing a triangle. She places Nathan in the center and takes her sisters' hands, using Nathan's essence and the medallion as a channel through time.

Melissa watches Tara sleep, hoping when she wakes to guide her to the sacred-seven-stone pendant. From the moment Tara jumps out of bed, Melissa follows her every move. Minutes later, as Tara anxiously pulls outfits from her closet and ponders her attire for the day, Melissa finds the pendant, passed down for generations in the Gowan family. The necklace was given to Nathan Cox to pass to his progeny. Melissa wonders how she'll get Tara to wear the stones today.

Melissa stands close as Tara studies her outfit in the mirror, and repeats several times, "The jewelry box." Tara feels something tug at her mind but thinks it's her own instinct to lighten the dull tan dress with jewelry, unaware Melissa is guiding her. Tara forages through the jewelry box, while Melissa cast a brilliant glow over the stones, leading Tara to the sacred-seven pendant.

Determined to help Tara capture her vision, Melissa guides her all morning, following as she walks to work. Melissa hurls a warning causing Tara's cell phone to vibrate. She waves light from the phone toward the stalker across from AHD. As Tara stands on the balcony, Melissa waves her essence over Tara's pendant directing light into the stalker's eyes. She senses the chills run down Tara's spine and hopes she'll foresee this man's intentions.

Fear blocks Tara's mind, and Melissa realizes Tara won't see the vision today. She'll seek other means to speak with her. Melissa saw the men in the girl's lives. She's aware of Michael Anders special gift. She needs his help to save the girls. Tara sits at her computer, and Melissa repeats Michael Anders name over and over until his name registers in her subconscious mind. Tara, unaware of her actions, highlights Michael's name on the architect list and emails the list to Cody.

Weakened, Melissa awakens to her sister's watchful, worried eyes.

"Are you okay," they asked.

"Yes, but the girls need more help, but not today." The energy required for Melissa to remain in the future is much too draining.

* * *

March 14, 2015 (Present) Michael Anders Home

Minutes later, Michael opens his eyes to the girls' shocked expressions. Michael still senses Melissa's presence. He realizes she won't relent until she speaks to the girls. The need to help them has grown, now that he understands the trouble to come. "Melissa has been with you three the entire time. I suspect every intuition you've felt since December 15th was prompted by Melissa."

Chapter 25

Nathan Cox

Charleston, SC, McGowan Estate, 1843

In the Gowan sister's home, the only home Nathan's ever known, he takes solace in the private library among books he's read many times, escaping scathing slurs and watchful eyes of servants. Names they'd never say in front of the Gowan sisters—yellow baby, misfit, house nigger—are only a few insults they sling with loathing. He doesn't understand their hatred. From what he sees, the Gowan family treats them well. He assumes their hatred is because of his mixed blood.

He was told by Melissa he's of her family but never learned the fate of his mother. She only said her whereabouts must remain secret for your protection. He dislikes the secluded privilege. His speech and mannerisms belong to a white world. He respects and loves the Gowans for protecting and providing for his needs, but remains conflicted surrounded by hardworking servants.

Nathan peers out the library door for servants. With no sign of their presence, he rushes from the home to the carriage house—his art studio. One day, out of boredom, remarkably, he'd picked up a brush and started painting. The Gowan sisters noticed his potential and helped him cultivate his talent.

At the easel, Nathan finishes a painting of Melissa Gowan. He's certain the portrait will please her. Nathan sketches the Gowan sister's necklace—a geometric crystal in the shape of a circle, enclosing a square, enclosing a triangle. Striving to capture the precise brilliance of the pendant on his palette, he mixes silver, pink, and white until the necklace shines opalescence mother-of-pearl.

A young servant girl named Anna, his only friend, peers inside the room. She joins him when she's certain he's alone. Anna has been drawn to Nathan since her first day in the Gowan home. She'd heard gossip in servant quarters that he's begotten of a slave girl and one of the Alcott men. She too was conceived by a slave-owner but not the Gowan family. She's simply a servant in the home, not treated as a family member.

Nathan notices Anna's awestruck gaze at the painting.

"Can you paint me," she pleaded.

"Only if you let me keep it," he replied.

He directs Anna toward a chair across from him, and she sits fidgeting with her dress.

"Can you remove the wrap," Nathan asked.

With a shy glance, Anna unties the bow, and the cloth unravels. Massive reddish-brown curls disentangle and escape about her shoulder. He's seen her hair on several occasions and has dreamed of painting her natural beauty. Anna sits unmoving as Nathan studies her face. Their eyes meet, and a smile creases her face. With only minutes to pose a day, she relishes the few minutes in Nathan's presence then runs back to resume her duties as a servant.

Days later, when the painting is complete, Anna's eager to see her portrait. Uncovering the artwork, Nathan's met with an unexpected kiss, and a bashful thank you before she runs from the carriage house, back to being a servant. He hides the painting with a cloth among his other work. The portrait of Anna is his favorite; hidden out of sight of the Gowan sisters.

"Ma'am, how was your trip?"

Melissa smiles at the servant as he helps her from the carriage. "The paintings sold well this trip. I accomplished a lot for the boy this time," she said and continues straight to the carriage house where Nathan spends most of his time painting. Inside, Nathan sits on an old, wooden stool in front of the easel.

"Nathan, good news; your work was a huge success in Baltimore. Your admirers are looking to buy more of your paintings." Melissa couldn't sell Nathan's work in Charleston and found a Baltimore Maryland gallery where black artist's work is publicly displayed.

"We sold the Pink Lady piece," Melissa exclaimed. She opens a satchel and produces an artist bill of sale and a check. "This is yours; for you and your family. The money will go into a special trust." Neither of Melissa's sisters married or conceived children except for her. Nathan is basically their son. "One day, you will inherit our estate," the sisters had revealed on several occasions.

In disbelief, Nathan stares at the check and the large figure he hadn't expected, never for his artwork. "Ma'am, thank you," slowly escapes his mouth. Trustingly, he hands it back to her. Melissa peers around the space at Nathan's countless drawings, wondering where his talent flows from. In the near corner sits an unfinished sketch of her and her sisters. Nathan captured every detail eerily as if they'd sat for the portrait, but they hadn't. It's perfect, but none of the pieces are as brilliant as the Pink Lady. She browses

through one painting after another and stumbles on
a covered canvas. With a quick peep, she spies Anna's
portrait. She'd noticed Nathan's fondness for Anna
and isn't surprised the painting is hidden. She fore-
saw Anna and Nathan's future together and Anna's
portrait hanging in the McPherson's home. She covers
the drawing quickly without Nathan noticing.

March 20, 2015 (Present) Village at Northstar

Leanne wakes from her dream. Since the evening at Michael Anders, visions of Nathan Cox grow more frequent and vivid. *Is Melissa trying to show Nathan Cox's complete history?* She recalls Anna Cox's portrait hanging on the McPherson's wall—*the original artwork Nathan hid years ago.* Still fresh in her mind, Nathan Cox's strong jaw and prominent brow are unmistakably Alcott features. His hazel eyes were those of his descendent—Nyla and Tara. *The Pink Lady ...* Suddenly, she realizes AHD's headquarter is where Nathan Cox grew up. *The Pink Lady is the original Gowan home.* Unknowingly, Tara recalled the name from some childhood dream or memory. Otherwise, she couldn't have known Nathan called the home the Pink Lady all those years ago.

* * *

"I know the catalog doesn't show them in yellow ... I've always placed custom orders." Impatient, Laura asks, "Can I speak to Ken? This is Laura Alcott at AHD," she says tapping a pen on the table irritably.

Quietly, Leanne enters the room while Laura negotiates the color and patterns of chairs for the new Dream Home. Inspired by Michael's designs, Laura dove into sketching and hunting the perfect furnishings nonstop.

Slinking to the kitchen, Leanne spots a large, woven basket filled with scrumptious assorted pastries. She chooses a huge pumpkin muffin, pours a cup of coffee, and with Nathan Cox's paintings on her mind, she heads to the dining table. She wonders if Laura knows the Pink Lady's history.

Negotiating a yellow leather covering, Laura clinches the deal and ends the call with a satisfied smirk. "Morning, Leanne; I didn't hear you enter the room." Laura sees the muffin Leanne's eating and her stomach growls. "That smells delicious."

"Where did they come from?" Leanne asks, tearing the muffin into small, manageable pieces.

"They were delivered an hour ago from Michael's favorite bakery."

Leanne's lips curl puckishly. "So, when are you going to enjoy some time with Mr. Anders—Michael," she stumbled, finding it difficult saying Michael after taunting Laura incessantly with his surname.

"Well, honey, when you marry Adam, maybe I'll think about it."

"Ooh, we're sensitive this morning," Leanne teases.

Laura searches the basket of goodies, chooses a seven-grain muffin, and joins Leanne at the dining table. "Leanne, I enjoy Michael's company, but romance is impossible."

"How can you make such a definitive statement if you never try, Laura?"

"He's hours away by plane, sweetie."

"Well, you'll just need to compromise to make it work."

"I can't see either of us moving," Laura says, pondering both the Alcott estate and Michael's Mountain Home. "That's a big compromise."

Leanne surmises Laura's weighed all the pros and cons, so for the moment, she abandons the topic. "Laura, you won't believe the incredible dreams I had about Nathan Cox and the Gowan women last night."

That explains her dilated pupils, Laura concludes. "Your dreams are prolific lately. What did you learn last night?"

"Well, AHD is the original Gowan home." Leanne pauses; waiting for an expletive or slang from Laura's rich Southern vocabulary, but she receives a stoic pose. "You don't seem surprised."

"Well, for years, the Pink Lady has been a mystery to my family, even today. When I was a child, I heard the Alcott family practically owned the Gowan women. After Melissa's marriage to Zachary Alcott, a deal was negotiated, and the Gowan sister's received the home as a favor. My family never learned details of the pact," she says, taking a dainty bite of the muffin. "You know, till this day, I've wondered about the agreement with the Alcotts. I'd love to know what promise my ancestors made. But nothing's in writing; only the deed reflects Gowan ownership. One day, I overheard the house was destroyed during the Civil War, and the Gowan women moved to another Alcott home in Charleston. After the war, the Alcotts rebuilt the Pink Lady and resumed ownership."

"Well, Laura, the agreement was probably a verbal contract. We'll never know the circumstances, hmmm, unless I witness the conversation in my dreams."

"Well, I hope you do. Your findings will dispel years of suspicions."

"Laura, I believe Nathan Cox was part of the agreement between the Alcotts and Gowan women. The three sisters basically raised him as their own child. Did you know Nathan was a gifted artist? Remember Anna Cox's portrait hanging in the McPherson's home? That piece was drawn by Nathan Cox back in the 1800s. And I bet all that artwork Nyla has stored in the attic is Nathan's work."

"Hmmm … I vaguely recall a conversation between my mother and aunt about Nathan's paintings. My aunt believed his work was lost when the Pink Lady burned during the Civil War. Perhaps the Gowan sisters saved and protected Nathan's work all those years."

Fidgeting with her fingers, Leanne notices the muffin has dissolved into breadcrumbs. "I wonder how much Nathan's artwork is worth today. His work was well-known during his time. Nyla could be sitting on a fortune."

"Well, I doubt Nyla is thinking about selling them. After inheriting the McPherson estate and part of the Alcott estate, the McPherson family doesn't need money. Nyla probably wants to preserve the work as a family heirloom."

"Maybe you're right." Leanne looks toward the quiet office, wondering what happened to Tara's usual business chatter. "Speaking of the McPherson's and dreams, has Tara had any more visions of our stalker?"

"I don't think so ... The last couple of days, she's been so frustrated. She left earlier to get help from Michael. Hopefully, he can unblock those childhood memories."

Leanne recalls frightful fragments of Tara's first vision. She hopes for their sake, Tara's premonition emerges from hibernation and soon.

"Laura, I've meant to speak to you about something."

"What, sweetie? You sound so serious."

"Well, at Michael's home, I retrogressed and saw what transpired between you two before I entered the room. I captured Michael's thought about Daniel—that he still watches over you. I realized you'd heard it as well when I saw the expression on your face. How're you coping with this information?"

"Frankly, I'm just relieved I didn't imagine Daniel's presence. I thought I was becoming one of those delusional widows clinging to their dead husbands. It's satisfying having validation of what I've suspected for a while, and knowing it wasn't my imagination."

"Laura, since Christmas Eve, I've wanted to tell you, but I wasn't sure if Daniel was a spirit or just a past essence. At first, I was confused, but the way he stared at you across the kitchen island and his presence when you opened Callie's gift, convinced me it was his spirit."

"I heard your thoughts, sweetie, but I knew you were looking for confirmation before you said anything."

"So, you're okay with your husband's spirit watching over you?"

"His presence is comforting … But a little unsettling. I'll need to let him go soon. I believe Daniel is still here because I'm not ready."

"Laura, the moment you find peace with his death and move on with your life and another man, Daniel will be at peace as well."

Chapter 26

Childhood Memories

March 20, 2015, Michael Ander's Home

Tara lies on the small sofa soothed by Michael's tranquil ancestry room. Although fearful of what's about to happen, she tries to keep an open mind, hoping Michael's technique will pull the vision from hiding. Michael enters the room with a foaming cup of tea and places it in her hand.

"Tara, from what you've told me about your traumatic childhood vision, I believe it's left you fearful of your gift and blocked your premonition. So, today, I need you to relax. This herbal concoction will calm you and put you in a lucid dream state."

Tara sniffs the foamy tea. A floral potpourri of cloves, jasmine, and unknown herbs tickle her nose. "Are the herbs like a drug? My body is sensitive to stimulants."

"Don't worry. These herbs are soothing and medicinal. You'll be fine."

Tara's brows arch. "Okay, Michael, I'm putting my body and mind in your hands," Tara says half-heartedly. She stares at the cup, raises it slowly, and then takes a small sip. A bitter, grassy flavor coats her tongue. She waits a moment, hoping the tea takes effect, but nothing happens. After several sips, she believes the herbs aren't working.

Michael notices Tara's pupils dilating. Soon, she'll enter transcendence. "Tara, the tea consists of psychoactive herbs, which will induce dreams and visions. I'm going to help you recover consciousness you lost as a child.

"What's the name of the psychoactive herb?"

"The tea contains Silene Capensis, which is an African Dream Root and minute portions of other herbs. Don't worry; I've used them before. When you're finally relaxed, I'll feed you suggestions; much like psychiatrist when they hypnotize their patients. I'll use my voice to guide you toward the day of your vision."

A few minutes later, every muscle in Tara's body relaxes as if she's never experienced relaxation in her life. Waves of light extend in long bright lines from the corner of her eyes. Unexpectedly and alarmingly, she feels weightless with no sense of bodily control. Soon, she looms high above the sofa. Blurrily she stretches her arms above, trying to grasp and stop her floating body from moving higher. In the background, she hears Michael's voice.

"Don't be afraid; let your mind and body go. Close your eyes Tara and follow my voice. Just relax. Remember when you were six and seven years old."

Her body is all air. Desperately, she tries to hold on to something concrete, the sofa which she can't feel, and the walls her arms melt through. Finally, she's levitating in one spot, not floating upward. She closes her eyes and holds onto the only concrete element, Michael's voice, which grows fainter and fainter until she's in her childish form.

Objects and people tower above. She walks speedily toward the city bus holding Nyla's hand and adjusting the floral-printed, mini jumper which twists and turns awkwardly around her small frame. Nyla pulls her onto the first step and leads her toward two empty seats, where she climbs up with difficulty. Her legs dangle off the chair, far from the floor, and she swings them back and forth, extending them straight out, admiring the purple-floral sandals.

Beyond the purple bouquet, her eyes meet an elderly woman sitting across from her. A sharp pain insults Tara's body. She cringes, inches closer to Nyla, and lays her head on her arm. The old woman catches Tara's eyes. Her illness invades her body. Tara flinches with her pain and turns her gaze on a young man seated in the back of the bus. A throbbing headache smacks her. She closes her eyes as a deluge of pain and ailments rush into her small body. She begins to cry and scream. Fearful and unsure what's wrong, Nyla tries to comfort her, but Tara screams louder and louder. Nyla shouts at the bus driver to let them off and frantically hails a taxi. The moment they're in the cab's back seat, Tara's pain subsides. Nyla comforts her to sleep.

Michael's voice pierces her mind. "Tara, remember your vision when you were seven. Where were you and what were you doing?"

A blender whirs. Nyla sings in the kitchen. Lemons and chocolate fill the air. Seated on the floor of her bedroom, a dollhouse looms over Tara. Just as she places her favorite dolls, Laura and Leanne, around the miniature coffee table, a veil cover her eyes. She emerges in a large room where a woman arranges furniture.

Laura's adult form amuses Tara. Laura stands in front of a fireplace admiring and pondering artwork above the mantel when a man entering the room startles her... Michael.

"Exquisite!" Michael exclaims.

Laura shakes her head. "No, something's missing." She rushes past Michael into the foyer filled with a flotsam of boxes, drags a yellow, wooden chair into the room, and places it in front of the window. "Perfect!"

Tara hovers about the place and notices with clarity every detail. A brown sectional and four plush creamy chairs surround a large, deep stone fireplace. Windows enclosed the room on every wall, showcasing pine trees and mountains in the distance. Sliding glass doors open onto an outdoor patio lined with Adirondack chairs around a long fire pit. Snow floats gently around the home, filling the interior with a glow. Tara sees everything in precision as if she were physically in the room.

Sparks burst from the chandelier then dims. An unworldly female figure shines with bluish-white luminescence. The door to the foyer opens, and a young woman enters.

"Time for the last group photo shoot; come on guys, out front."

"Michael, go ahead. I'll join you in a minute," says Laura.

Unaware of the manifestation, Laura examines the room one last time. The ethereal female hovers near trying to warn Laura. On the granite island, spectral hands brush over a knife igniting a sparkle, but Laura dismisses the shimmer. The presence moves quickly, casting luminosity on the window into Laura's eyes. Laura looks up and catches a male reflection approaching from behind. But there's no time to react. Laura's knocked unconscious.

The ghostly woman follows as the man drags Laura through the foyer and into the garage. All the while, Tara follows yelling Laura's name, but no one hears. The man drags Laura to the back of the home, through pine trees, and beyond. The ethereal woman turns to Tara, pointing toward the back of the home. Tara believes she wants her to follow. Immediately, Tara's consciousness blurs, speeding her to another time inside the home.

She lands in a chair between Laura and Leanne, bound with tape in the great room. Laura's bloody head rolls unconsciously to the side. She's strapped to the same yellow wooden chair she dragged into the room earlier. Leanne, bound and angry, shouts, "You murdered them," but she freezes with a realization and fear. Again, Tara jumps ahead in time. A gunshot rings out. Leanne slumps in the chair. Tara catches their assailant's feverish eyes just as he fires another shot. Her chest singes. An earsplitting scream rings out, then darkness.

Tara bolts from sleep, grasping her chest.

Quickly, Michael seizes her teetering frame, restraining her motion. "Tara, I'm here. I've got you," he says, allaying her fear. "Don't move. The herbs are still active."

Tara's rapid breaths quieten as she drifts into another dream state. Michael perceives she'll sleep for some time, recapturing lost memories of her youth. He takes a throw from the sofa's edge, drapes it over her, and remains by her side with vigilant eyes.

Chapter 27

Knowing

March 20, 2015, Village at Northstar

Reeling from the herbal brew's effects, Tara sways on unsteady feet as Michael leads her into the Ritz Carlton suite. Surprised by Tara's weakened state, Laura rushes to her side, and helps Michael place her on the sofa.

"Ladies, Tara's progress is remarkable. Honestly, I'm worried. Is there any more news from Cody?"

Laura captures Tara and Michael's thoughts. Instantly, she's overcome with fear. The sound and sensation of a gunshot, searing pain and darkness linger in Tara's mind. Laura notices Michael's expression and senses alarm. She exhales deeply and harnesses her fear. "I spoke with Cody a few days ago. The news isn't good. Our stalker checked out of the Constellation and Cody discovered he's using a fake identity."

"Is he still working with the private detective?"

"Yes, they're checking out a clue in Boston."

"Have you or Leanne capture more images of this guy?"

"No, Michael. When we left Charleston, our visions stopped." Laura notices Tara's glazed eyes circling the room. Soon, Laura's swaying with her dizziness.

"Don't worry," Tara says, seeing fear on their faces. "There's time. From what I foresaw, this all happens after the Dream Home is built. That gives the private detective more than enough time to uncover our stalker and for us to receive more visions." The ceiling begins to spin. Dizziness makes it impossible to remain upright. Tara drops her head awkwardly and closes her eyes. Now the spinning is a quick descent through a swirling dark chasm. She opens her eyes swiftly.

Noticing Tara's inability to focus, Leanne wonders if Michael gave her too much of the potion. "Those must be some powerful herbs you gave her."

Michael, perplexed by the lingering side effects, frowns curiously. "Nothing out of the usual; I gave her the smallest possible dose. She did say she's sensitive to stimulants."

A dry laugh escapes Leanne's mouth. "You should see her when she drinks alcohol. No tolerance whatsoever."

Laura rushes to the refrigerator and brings Tara a bottle of water.

Noticing concern on their faces, Tara makes light of her dizziness. "Guys, I'm okay. The Ferris wheel is coming to a gradual stop. I'll be fine soon."

"Tara, drink the water. The liquid will dilute the herbs in your system."

Tara knows Laura and Leanne feel her dizziness, and undoubtedly, want it to stop. Tara swallows the water and cups her mouth, hoping the liquid stays down.

"Laura, can I see your iPad."

"Yes, but why?"

"You'll understand in a minute. I rarely see your preliminary sketches until your final design is complete, but after my vision, I can describe in detail each item you've sketched and more. I know the exact location of every room and almost every piece of furniture you'll pick." The gunshot flares in her mind. Tara realizes Laura and Leanne have captured horrifying images. She noticed Laura wince a second again when the gunshot fired in her mind. There's no sense disguising her fear. "For weeks, I've recognized the home's mountain style in my dreams, but I didn't have all the pieces until today." Tara continues to describe the house and furnishings in detail before looking at Laura's sketches.

Laura stands with mouth agape. Leanne recalls the yellow chairs Laura negotiated earlier on the phone.

"I also know the three of us will die in that room if we don't stop this man."

Chapter 28

Melissa Speaks

March 25, 2015, Michael Ander's Home

Unease invades Michael's mind as he wraps up for the night. Sipping tea, he peers at Donner Lake, with the prescience of Melissa Gowan around him. Since the girl's visit, he's unable to escape her presence, but he's managed to block Melissa's entry into his body. Having served as a medium since his wife's death, he's unprepared for the toll it exacts, leaving him physically and mentally exhausted for days.

"Not yet Melissa," he mumbles, and takes a sip of tea.

Three years ago, he'd used his gift to say farewell to his wife. He'd promised Asia never to communicate with the spirit world again, but she would approve of him helping his friends. The pain of that night resurfaces, remembering the void he'd felt when her spirit left. Tonight, Melissa Gowan's presence is just as dominant as his wife's had been. He can't ignore her much longer. At night when he sleeps, Melissa seeps into his unconscious mind. He's blocked every attempt she's made, but her energy grows stronger and soon she'll break through when he's at his weakest.

Tonight is that night. As he sleeps, Melissa embeds Michael's receptive mind with words only a medium can hear. Unaware of his actions, Michael shuffles to his office bolstered by spectral arms. A dual choreography styles Michael's nimble hand. Melissa Gowan and Nathan Cox ply words and artistry, directing Michael's hands like a brush along a canvas, capturing every feature of the stalker's face. Long after Melissa and Nathan's visit, Michael remains in deep sleep—a pen, detailed drawing, and note poised at his hand.

The next morning, Michael wakes slumped over his desk with an excruciating headache and no memory of the previous night. His vision adjusts and focuses on the pen in his hand, and a sketch of a strange man. Below the picture lays a note from Melissa Gowan written in a Spencerian penmanship. Instantly, Michael realizes she'd visited while he'd slept, but Melissa's unconventional communication is baffling. *Why didn't she use his voice to communicate verbally with the girls?* Michael puzzles over Melissa's choice until he's read the entire note.

Tara, Laura, and Leanne,

I'm happy you've found Michael. I know you're aware of the danger you're facing. As your protector, I can only provide clues to guide you through your ordeal. I cannot say who this man is. I can only reveal where, when, and how you will meet your fate. With the awareness of these three facts, you can outwit him. Because my essence isn't linked with your assailant, I cannot determine his name, his past, or any personal history. This is something that will come to you because his actions affect you directly.

Tara, your visions are growing stronger, and you've already foreseen your fate; this man means you bodily harm. Use what you have seen to fight him. I must tell you this man is mentally ill and will not stop until he destroys AHD. Leanne, your gift is also critical here. You can see where he comes from. His past before

Charleston will provide missing pieces. Laura, you believe your gift of telepathy is gone, but it only lays dormant and still resides in you. Telepathy will save your life if you can summon your gift at the right time.

Girls, I wish I could tell you more, but this is your fate. This challenge must happen for you three to become who you're meant to be. I'm your guide; follow my clues—the light and any unusual indications that shine brightly will be my guide for you. Tara, Laura, and Leanne, I've given you many signs along the way. Some you heeded and others you didn't. Girls, I'm still guiding you; follow your instincts. October 10th, 2015 in the Dream Home is the day you will be challenged. Laura, be alert at 2:22 P.M.

Girls, you cannot change the design of your premonitions, you can only call on your talents to thwart this man's plans. Changing any aspect of the vision will lead to serious consequences.

Michael, forgive me for using you as my vessel. There's another presence protecting you who would only allow me to speak to the girls in this fashion. She protects and still watches over you.

Melissa Gowan

Michael smiles with moist eyes. Melissa was influenced by Asia wielding her protective arm. Michael studies the drawing, relieved the girls have a concrete image of their stalker and comforted by his wife's protection.

Chapter 29

Closer Than You Think

April 3, 2015, Martis Camp

Taking his usual morning stroll around Martis Camp, Tom peers at mountains beyond the golf course, breathing in the crisp morning air. For days, he's lived a fictitious life in the wealthy community, waiting for signs of the Dream Home construction crew. Today, as he finishes his morning trek, an entourage of trucks, cranes, and vans crawl the narrow roads toward lot 795.

So, today it begins.

He pauses and watches as vehicles pack AHD's untouched three acres. Just as he resumes his walk, the camera crew van follows, prepared for the long, arduous task of daily filming. Tom remembers online virtual cameras filming day and night, every second captured of prior Dream Home constructions. Heading back to his rental, he takes a seat on the deck, spies on the construction crew, and ponders his next move with a malicious grin.

They have no inkling how close I am.

A few feet away, a man and child pause to adjust the boy's ski as they prepare for a cross-country trek. Childhood memories prick Tom's consciousness. He quickly dismisses images of his father with the scene before him. Standing from his crouch, the man speaks inaudibly while the child nods in acknowledgment. The man demonstrates how to use the ski poles, and the child mimics awkwardly with a giggle. Obviously, it's the child's first adventure on cross-country skis, as he moves clumsily beside his father. Soon they vanished down the snowy trail.

From his messed-up mind, Tom remembers only pain not happy moments with his father, not one precious instance, just anger, fear, and pain. He touches the white crescent scar dissecting his brow, flinching as if his father's violent fisted blow just brandished the wound.

Chapter 30

A Tormented Child

April 27, 2015, Martis Camp

Tormented by dreams of his family, Tom lifts his weak body from the spot he's lain tortured for several days. He forages about the dark room searching for his mobile, finding it beneath the bed where he'd thrown it several days ago. The voice in his head stirs. He exhales annoyance.

She's not going to believe you the voice taunts. *She'll see through your lies, Tom.*

He hesitates, envisioning a barrage of questions from Ellen. She'll question why he hasn't called and what he's been doing. He'd already prepared answers—lies and more lies for her imagined queries.

He dials his home number and the phone rings five times before voicemail picks up. *Why aren't they answering?* Quickly, he glances at the time. It's seven in the morning on the East coast—the time Ellen prepares breakfast for the boys. Dialing the number again, he leaves a brief message and returns to bed. Pulling the covers over his head, sleep arrives with more haunting dreams.

August 1979, Boston

*Tom lies in bed with a pillow over his head, try-
ing to block harsh accusations slung from his father
at his mother. A loud thump echoes from the living
room, and Tom knows his father's thrown his mother
to the floor again. He covers his ears but shattering
glass slips through his fingers. Furniture falls with a
bang. Footsteps clomp and vibrate as they approach
his room. He waits fearfully for his father to appear
wielding another belt.*

*Tom sits unemotional as the belt lashes at his and his
brother, Sean's flesh. Defiantly, Sean fights back and
escapes from the apartment. Tom bites his lip to contain the pain, tasting blood as his father throws one
final blow, knocking him unconscious.*

*Opening his eyes, Tom listens for sounds of his fa-
ther in the apartment. Certain he's gone; he lifts his
bruised body and steps fearfully into the living room.
Surrounded by toppled furniture, his mother lays unconscious. He rushes to her side tearfully screaming,
"Mom, wake up … Wake up."*

Tom rolls fitfully in his sleep as dreams of forgotten pains materialize. Scars of his mother and father discarded with age now
seep into his memory.

October 1979, Boston

*Entering the small dimly lit apartment, stale beer,
cigarettes, and burning food foul the air. Sean runs
toward the smoke-filled kitchen, turns off the stove,
and throws the burning pan into the sink. An eldritch
quiet fills the apartment. The usual TV chatter and
his mother cooking are absent. Low moans fill the
back room. Tom takes Sean's hand as they approach*

*their parent's room down the hall. Fearfully, they en-
ter. Their mother, balled in a fetal position, shivers,
and rocks with despair. In a corner chair, their father slumps with his head to his chest. Blood splatter
marks the walls. On the floor, a gun lays below his
dangling arm. A loud scream punctures silence. Sean
rushes from the apartment. Tom, frozen with shock,
cradles his mother's rocking body.*

A loud mournful moan escapes Tom's mouth as he rolls in deep
sleep.

October 1979, Boston

*Tom dashes through the lobby door onto the sidewalk
screaming, "Sean, come back, come back," as a man
claiming to be Sean's real father pushes Sean into the
car. Sobbing intensely, Tom falls to his knees as the
car whisks Sean away, leaving him … taking him …
escaping his grieving mother. Spiteful, harsh voices
multiply in his mind, taunting as he sobs. "You've got
your father's blood, you'll grow up just like him …
You're just like him."*

Ephemeral images of Ellen weeping over the children and the
boy's blank-eyed stares flit about his dreams. He tries to wake,
but can't. Soon he dreams of his mom.

October 1979, Boston

*Tom guards his mother's motionless body, pushing
food through stiff lips. Blankly, she stares through
him like an apparition, food dribbles down her chin.
The doorbell rings; Tom ignores it hoping they'll go
away. Keys enter the lock, and he hides in the closet.*

Horrified, his aunt and uncle gasps when finding his mom lying in filth and unresponsive. The closet door opens. His aunt stares at him like a lost puppy. A low moan penetrates the walls as two uniformed men lift his mother's body onto a stretcher. Tom bolts from the closet with piercing screams, running after his mother.

"Tom, she needs help. They will take care of her in the hospital, and you will stay with us until she gets better," his uncle explained with a steel grip.

His uncle wrestles him through the front door while Tom clings to the doorjamb, peering at the apartment ... at the tattered sofa, RCA TV atop plastic end-tables, and his mother's favorite red sweater, hanging from the worn recliner. The door closes, the image freezes, the last image of his first home.

Wrestling fitfully, Tom wrenches himself from sleep and bolts upright, an image he'd forgotten knots his stomach. That frightened boy seems like someone else. But every so often he rises in dreams, reminding him who he used to be.

Finally, hunger and thirst pull him from the edge. He peers through window shades and flinches from sunlight. Unaware of the day or time, he taps his cell phone—April 27th, 11:05 pm. Turning on the television and flipping through channels, he pauses when a house taking shape behind a young reporter catches his attention. "AHD's Dream Home construction is underway in the Martis Camp community," the woman states. Annoyed, Tom flips off the television and heads to the shower.

* * *

April 27, 2015, Dream Home Construction Site

Needing a break from the hotel and their daily ritual, the girls decide to visit the Dream Home construction site. The SUV carries them through winding roads along Martis Camp's golf course. Since the session with Michael, Tara revels in newfound energy, feeling lighter than she's ever been. Melancholia she'd borne every night since childhood suddenly vanished, escaping with salvaged long-repressed memories, leaving her more exuberant than she's felt in years. *More alive* she thinks, and I'll fight for the girl's lives.

Just as the car winds past lot 793, the rental home, a bright light sparkles off the windshield. They turn their heads like a rippling wave, searching for their spiritual guide's clue. After reading Melissa's note, they're heeding every intuition. They're certain she's trying to tell them something at this exact moment.

Chapter 31

The Cover-up

May 28, 2015, Ritz-Carlton, Tahoe

Cody stares at his mobile, contemplating calling Jake, the private investigator and anticipating his call for hours. During their last conversation, Jake said his team's investigating a gap in Sean Cavanaugh's history—an unverified period between his move from Boston to Newton, Massachusetts.

The phone rings. In a heartbeat, Cody answers, "Jake, you find anything new?"

"Nothing yet, Cody, but my staff is still working the timeline between Sean's birth in Boston and his move to Newton. Looks like someone went to a hell of trouble to erase Sean's biological mother. Her name's missing on all his records, even his birth certificate."

"Hmmm ... I wonder why? He wasn't adopted, right?"

"Well, the father took Sean from his biological mother at twelve. The woman he was married to when he took custody adopted Sean. The adoptive mother's name is on the birth certificate, not his birth mother. Unfortunately, both Sean Cavanaugh's parents are deceased. Finding his biological mother will be tough."

"Tough but not impossible; someone's bound to know Sean Cavanaugh in Boston. Keep looking, Jake."

"Often parents' names are concealed for critical reasons, Cody. My firm's handled several cases of hidden lineage for ethical or medical reasons. I've seen wealthy families hide a child's true lineage to preserve the family fortune. A few years back, I handled a case of a child born in prison. The mother didn't want the child tainted by her past, so her name was stricken from records. Cody, we need to consider Sean's biological mother may never be found, but I'll continue searching."

"Jake, what about social media, college records, DMV, hell, even the IRS; there's got to be some public record of Sean."

"Already hit those records. My staff is thorough."

Cody sighs deeply. His patience wears thinner by the minute as he deliberates the stalker's identity and the girl's safety. He wishes he could just wipe this man from the girl's lives forever. "Have you checked Sean's school in Boston? They must have his records on file."

"I'm already working that angle. My staff contacted the Administrator. I'm just waiting for permission."

"Make sure you pass around the stalker's sketch. Someone may recognize him."

"Cody, let's hope so. By the way, who drew the picture? It's so detailed I'd swear the guy sat for a portrait."

"Well, you won't believe me if I told you. Let's just say the girls have unique abilities."

"Well, the artist did an excellent job. We should find something with this."

"Jake, no matter what the hurdles, keep me posted."

"I will; hang in there. We'll get this guy."

Cody's sure they'll find him, but will they find him in time? *"Keep them safe, Cody."* Marion and Anson Alcott's request resounds through his mind. Years ago, he was told, *"One day you'll need to protect the family treasure."* He didn't know what treasure they meant at the time, but now realizes it's the girls. For years, he's known about the clairvoyant Alcott women and realizes the gift's future heritage depends on the three's survival.

The private detective's words invade Cody's thoughts. *There have been instances where wealthy families hide a child's true lineage to preserve the family fortune.* For whatever reason, the Alcotts wished for his bloodline to remain a secret. He's questioned their motives for years but has respected their wishes. Marion and Anson have been in his life since his birth, taking care of him like parents. *"They mustn't know who you are,"* repeats in his mind. Contemplatively rubbing his chin, Cody swivels his chair toward the snowy scenery and ponders why his kinship must be hidden from the girls. *"Keep this stone on you always,"* the Alcotts had warned. Cody rolls the Moldavite stone in his hand and ponders the girl's reaction when they discover he's also a descendant of Nathan Cox.

Chapter 32

One Piece at a Time

July 14, 2015, Lake Tahoe, Ritz Carlton

After three months, the Dream Home construction is well underway. On the computer, Tara stares at a live webcam; amazed seventy-five percent of the home is complete, leaving only the East wing to be constructed. No extraordinary expenses have cropped up. The budget's on target this year. *Everything's perfect, well, except for their stalker.* She sighs. How can anything be perfect with looming destruction? Given the fire and smoke in her vision, she wonders why they've continued with construction. *It doesn't make sense to build the home when a deranged man plots to destroy it ... I hope we can stop him in time.*

Tara swivels her chair toward the window and stares vacantly at mountain views. Her mind whispers, *October 10, 2015*—the ominous date. She pivots around to her calendar and counts the number of days till the fated meeting with their stalker. She exhales deep, closes her eyes, and quiets her mind until deafening silence alarms her. Thank goodness Cody didn't listen to me earlier she thinks, recalling her silly protest.

"Cody, I'll be okay. There's no need for security."

"Tara, I'm not leaving you here alone; so, stop being stubborn."

"Okay, big brother, I'll stop protesting. You just make sure Laura isn't out of your sight today," she'd snapped back.

Obviously, without security, she'd be a nervous wreck. She'd never admit she was wrong, although, she's relieved Cody took extra measures and placed the second guard inside the suite. Stark silence contrasts morning's noisy bustle. She recalls Laura and Cody deliberating over her designs, and Leanne's excitement about afternoon plans with Adam. Even with their chatter, Tara's sharp intuition settled on Cody. For days, she's felt a familiar aura about him. Cody's been like a brother since the first day they met. His acceptance of Laura's talent is bewildering. He's never perturbed when she reads his thoughts, and he's never questioned her abilities.

Does he know?

Tara recalls all the times Laura's read her mind. She'd found it peculiar and annoying, but never thought she was clairvoyant. Maybe Cody has done the same. Anyhow, Melissa Gowan's letter warned to heed every instinct, and she's noting every instinct about Cody.

Staring at her watch, Tara recalls an earlier vision and ponders Leanne and Adam's outing. She'd seen Adam's arrival hours before he reached Tahoe, and hoped Leanne hadn't sensed her knowledge. She'd tried to conceal her thoughts and not spoil the surprise. If Leanne sensed anything, it wasn't apparent. When Adam arrived at the hotel, Leanne's surprise appeared genuine, or she's just an excellent actress.

Tara had seen Adam's plans before he whisked Leanne from the condo. She glances at her watch, knowing at 1:15 pm Adam will propose to Leanne over lunch at Manzanita's Restaurant. She'd foreseen Adam pulling a diamond ring from his jacket and Leanne feigning surprise. Tara also sensed Leanne's mixed emotions, but the dominant emotion will triumph. Leanne will say, "Yes," with certainty to Adam's proposal. Elated, Adam will place the ring on her finger and jest, "I knew you'd say yes. I guess I'm psychic too," causing Leanne to laugh and cry as she admires her diamond-clad finger.

Tara's amazed at how vivid her visions have become; some stronger than others. She opens the dream journal and examines highlighted entries. Melissa's words play in her mind. *Use what you've seen to fight him.* In her childhood vision, Melissa had beckoned her to follow Laura and the assailant behind the home and through the pine trees.

What did she want me to see?

She turns the page to an earlier dream ... the black and white spotted dog magnet securing a note on a stainless-steel refrigerator. *What does it say?* If only she could read it. *Maybe it's a critical piece to the puzzle.* Twirling a loose curl about her finger, suddenly it dawns on her. *Leanne!* She'd said in her visions, every detail is enlarged with microscopic vision. *She can read the note!* Tara writes next to the dream: *Tell Leanne.*

She scours the journal, memorizing every action, every detail, hoping the knowledge will help her and the girls on the fast-approaching, fated day. She recalls warnings from Melissa she didn't heed back in Charleston, and the ones she did—the sacred-seven pendant, light shining off the stalker from the piazza, the architectural list. *Did I miss any other warning?* She wonders as she recounts her step that warm morning.

She returns to the vision when they're bound to chairs in the Dream Home. She wonders why Leanne is yelling, *"You murdered them." Them? Who's them?* Has their stalker killed before, or is Leanne referring to their impending doom? *If it's their stalker's past, who did he murder?* She remembers Leanne's expression of sudden realization and the stalker's instant anger. Is Leanne's discovery the reason he swiftly pulls the trigger? Precipitously, Tara writes: *What did Leanne see? She mustn't reveal it to the stalker.*

Dread seizes Tara's mind. *He's killed before!* Thoughts of their stalker lurking about and overtaking security spurs Tara to her feet and out of the office. In the main room, the guard sits reading. He peeks up when she enters the room.

"Is everything okay?" He asks.

How the hell can I be okay with a man plotting to kill us, she retorts inwardly, but contrary words exit her mouth. "I'm good," she says with a grateful smile. *Cody was right*. She's relieved she's not alone in the condo.

Chapter 33

August 15, 2015, Boston

The petite school Administrator shuffles into the room, tugging her close-fitting dress with one hand and holding Sean Cavanaugh's records in the other. As she sidles stiffly behind the desk, the dress inches up her thighs and pouches around her waist.

Jake inhales deep, sensing the tight outfit choking her breath. He exhales and says, "Thanks for taking the time to see me."

"I'm sorry it took so long to get back to you. Generally, giving out student information is prohibited unless you're a parent or have a judicial order. There're privacy rights the school must abide, but after much consideration of what you've explained, I spoke to the previous Administrator, and she pulled some strings. However, she could only acquire basic information. This is a copy of Sean's file received from the Archdiocese. Records show he attended South Boston Academy for six years until he transferred."

Jake examines the paperwork and notices the surname Mallory. "So, is this the mother's maiden or married name?"

"Well, Mallory is the name on file," she says, sifting through the folder. For a moment, she appears perplexed. "Hmmm, strange," she murmured, placing her hands on her lips. "There's no information on the mother, just the father's name, Peter Cavanaugh." She rummages through several documents. "Hmm, the mother's name's whited-out on all the forms. Since the father's surname is Cavanaugh, I assume Mallory is the mother's maiden name," she says knitting her brows and pulling a faded paper from the file. "This was Sean's address while in attendance—17 Bowen Street, which is just a few blocks away. Perhaps the landlord can provide more information."

As Jake jots down the address, he suddenly remembers the stalker's sketch and pulls it from his messenger bag. "Does this man look familiar?"

The young woman studies the drawing with a shake of her head. "No, but I'm the wrong person to ask. I've only been here a year. The last Administrator retired a year ago after forty years."

"Do you know where I can reach her?"

"Well, yes, but I'll need to call her first. She might be reluctant to talk."

"Well, let's hope she consents, and she has a damn good memory."

* * *

On the way to Lisa Fulcrum's apartment, Jake wonders if she'll remember Sean after so many years. On Beacon Street, he rushes up the brownstone's steps and rings the doorbell. A statuesque woman with dancing eyes and a welcoming smile greets him. She appears in her forties rather than her sixties. A few graying hairs, smoker's lines above her lips, and yellowing teeth are the only indications of aging. He hopes her mind's retained resilience.

She opens the door and welcomes him into her home. "Can I offer you something to drink," she asks with a strong Boston accent.

Jake declines and politely thanks her for allowing him into her home. "Mrs. Fulcrum, I understand you were the Administrator at South Boston Catholic Academy for forty years. That's an impressive amount of time. Congratulations on your retirement."

"South Boston is where I spent my life, but I couldn't wait to retire. Now, I'm happy just to enjoy retirement with my husband. I saw so many children come and go from South Boston, and I've always wondered what became of their lives."

Her sincere tone suggests emotional involvement with the students—perhaps the reason she spent so many years at the school. "Well, your students are why I'm here. I'm hoping your memory of the seventies is strong."

"Well, there're students I'll never forget, especially Sean Mallory. When Amy called and told me you were asking about him, I became concerned. Such a troubled family he had."

Jake withdraws photocopies of Sean's school pictures and spreads them on the coffee table.

"Oh, that's Sean I'll never forget him, such a smart child. It's so unfortunate what happened to his parents?"

"Can you tell me about them?"

"Well, it was rumored Sean's father was ill … I believe schizophrenia or one of those mental disorders. Every day, I feared for those children because of the physical abuse in their home. They'd come to school disheveled and covered with bruises. With no luck, we sent Social Services to their house several times."

"Children? So, Sean had a sister or brother?"

"Yes, a brother. I believe half-brothers. They looked like twins and favored their mother."

Now we're getting somewhere. "Do you remember the brother's name?"

"Oh, my, now I believe Jim or Tim ... My memory is declining with age, but that sounds about right. The brother was different ... So, so, painfully shy and antisocial. He seemed afraid of the world at times—poor child."

"Do you happen to recall the mother's name?"

She shakes her head as if she can't bear the thought of the woman. "That poor soul, I'll never forget her. I believe after her husband committed suicide, she went into a terrible depression, and the family institutionalized her. She not only lost her husband but Sean. I heard Sean's real father pulled him out of the home. A year later, she was committed, and her sister took Jim."

"School documents have Mallory as Sean's last name. Do you remember if Mallory was his mother's maiden or married name?"

Lisa Fulcrum sits straight, takes a sip of the steaming tea, and roles the name Mallory off her tongue several times. She frowns and puckers her lips as if the actions will extract information from her fading memory. "I'm inclined to say her married name, but there were rumors she married neither of the children's fathers."

Sudden pain settles in Jake's stomach. *Poor kids ...* Now he realizes the stalker may have inherited his parent's mental illness. "Mrs. Fulcrum, thanks for taking the time to speak with me. I have one more item to show you, and I'll let you resume your morning." He hands her the drawing.

Her jaw drops. "Oh, my, this is Jim."

"Are you sure?"

"No doubt in my mind, this is Jim Mallory. I remember his eyes and his mouth. I'll never forget the scar. One day he came to school all bruised with a black eye and a deep gash above his eyebrow. He said a couple of boys beat him up, but we'd seen his injuries too many times and realized it was his father's doing."

With a pained expression, Mrs. Fulcrum gazes at the picture for a long time. Finally, as if she can't bear the face much longer, pushes the sketch across the table. "May I ask why you're looking for Jim Mallory?"

Before the words form in Jake's mind and before they exit his mouth, he hears Mrs. Fulcrum's fearful question.

"Oh, no, what has he done?"

* * *

Moments after leaving Mrs. Fulcrum's brownstone, Jake pauses in the middle of the sidewalk, pulls his mobile his from his pocket to call Cody, but changes his mind, deciding to wait until he's uncovered everything on Jim Mallory. Instead, Jake calls the young Administrator at the school. "Hi, Amy, this is Jake again. Can you check Jim Mallory—Sean's brother's file."

"I'm glad you called back. Mrs. Fulcrum already asked me to check the records. She thought she might've given you the wrong name. Sean's brother's name is not Jim, but Tom, Thomas Matthew Mallory."

Hours later, Jake and his team have checked every single Thomas Matthew Mallory located in the Boston area with no success. Records show Tom's mother died in the nineties at the sanitarium. His aunt and uncle passed away several years ago. The only concrete evidence he has is a name, age, place of birth, and relatives, all leading to a dead end. There's no public record or driver's license under Thomas Matthew Mallory. Jake remembers Lisa Fulcrum saying the mother hadn't married either man. Given the lack of information on Tom Mallory, Jake wonders if he'd taken his father's surname. But what is it? Jake knows one place he can find public records and makes his way to Boston Public Library.

He flips through digital obituaries and articles from 1979. With no luck, he continues ... "Come on ... October third ...

fourth ... fifth ... October 6, 1979 ... Here we go." A small obituary no more than a paragraph long, announces the death of Patrick Matthew Fallon, who leaves behind two sons, Sean and Thomas, and a wife, Sienna.

"Gotcha now, Tom Fallon ..." Pulling out his cell phone, Jake calls information looking for the number and address of Thomas Matthew Fallon. Flabbergasted by the number of listings in Boston for Thomas M. Fallon, he heads back to the hotel and settles in for a long afternoon. With the help of his staff, he calls every Thomas M. Fallon in the directory.

Chapter 34

A View from the Rear

August 27, 2015, Martis Camp

A week ago, the construction crew vacated the Dream Home site, leaving every windowpane glazed, eaves and rafters framed, shingles nailed, walls plastered, molds crowned—every fixture in place. The Dream Home stands structurally sound, ready for Tom to bring it down. Today, Tom spies through binoculars on the interior design team, camera crew, and photographers as they enter the home, working on its completion and photographing every interior and exterior angle of the home. All-day, vans from various furniture stores arrive. Movers, guided by the design team, haul boxes of furniture and accessories inside appropriate areas of the home. Pine trees separating his rental home from the Dream Home block a portion of his view. From the deck, the back of the garage, the east end, and parts of the front yard are visible. At certain angles, faces of team members he's become familiar with are distinguishable.

Tom treads through pine trees to a hidden spot—a thicket of trees where he hears and sees activity in the front yard. He spies Laura standing beside a truck, directing deliverymen unloading a massive stainless steel refrigerator and double oven. As men unload furniture, Laura squeals with delight.

An antique looking credenza slips and she exclaims, "Be careful, we don't want to order this item again. It'll take weeks."

For hours, furniture in all shapes, colors, and sizes make their way into the home. Meanwhile, Tom lies hidden, dreaming of ways to destroy it all.

Several hours later, Tom returns to the rental deck and resumes his post. Gradually, temperatures drop as fading sun cast spiky shadows across the deck. Soon, the design crew will wrap up their day, and Tom will enter the rental's warmth.

Fortuitously, the garage back door opens. Tom raises the binoculars to his eye, spotting a man exiting the door. The man lights a cigarette, surveys the scenery, and blows long whirls of smoke into the air, enjoying every nicotine breath. The man inhales and exhales quick puffs, and peeks inside intermittently. *Ah, smoking's prohibited in the house,* Tom surmises. The man takes a deep, intoxicating drag like a much-needed breath of air, releases a thick toxic fume, and drops the bud to the ground with a furious twist of his foot. Moving further behind the garage, he squats to the ground, picks up a rock, and throws it through the pines. The rock lands mere inches from the deck. Annoyed and ready to protest, Tom opens his mouth, but his sinister companion chides. *Go ahead, if you want to be discovered.* Strangled words linger unspoken on his tongue.

Five minutes later, the man enters the garage, leaving the door slightly ajar. *Did he forget to close it? Or did he leave it open for a reason?* Thirty minutes pass and no one returns to close the door. In front of the home, cars and vans leave one by one, but the back garage door remains open.

Hmmm ... An opportunity?

You fool, the competing voice ridiculed.

He places the binoculars on the chair; and steps into the back-yard. Rocks and thistles crackle and crunch beneath his weight as he trudges cautiously toward the garage.

Go back! The taunting voice screams.

Defiantly, Tom moves toward the home with mounting adrenaline. At the back door, he pauses, listens for sounds, and then glances inside the four-door garage. Two black SUVs occupy one corner, and a workbench with paint cans, rollers, and brushes stands at the opposite end. Beside a baseball cap, lies a ring of keys.

Unbelievable!

Moving with speed, he races toward the keys. Male voices approach swiftly.

Won't make it, the voice says as he stares at the door he just entered.

"But I'll make the storage closet," Tom mumbles. He snatches the keys, rushes to the closet, and pulls the door quietly. *Have they returned for the keys?*

Workmen approach.

He grasps his trembling hand, stilling rattling keys. His breath shallows and sweat wets his brow. Through the door slit, one man collects the baseball cap, heads to the back door, and pulls it with a click. The other man removes clanging metal cans from the wooden bench.

Have they forgotten about the keys?

Don't be stupid. They'll come looking, the voice swears.

The mudroom door opens, slinging voices into the garage.

"Good night all! Thanks for your wonderful help today. Get some rest. Tomorrow we've got much work to do."

"Goodnight, Laura."

"See you in the morning," several voices reply.

Tom peers through the slit, tensing at Laura's nearness and two accompanying men. Bits of strawberry blonde hair tied in a ponytail, a tan shawl, and dark-washed denim with a smattering of paint are visible. An intense silver sparkle from Laura's wrist-watch harpoons his eyesight, momentarily blinding him with white spots. He stumbles backward, pondering the uncanny, persistent light around the three women. SUV doors open and close, the garage door lifts, and the car pull away.

A few minutes later, several men enter the garage and get into the second SUV. Tom listens as the car exits and the garage door locks in place a second time. Slowly, he leaves the closet.

Don't be stupid. Someone could still be inside, the voice nags once more.

Heedful, he steps slow and quiet toward the mudroom door. Wide-angle peephole fishbowls the interior view. A foot turns the corner of a long hallway. A few minutes later, lights dim and the home glows a bluish hue. After five minutes, car doors open and close. The engine revs and the car drives away. Tom stares through the peephole, eyes roam side to side. The home looks empty, but he could be wrong. Fearing a shrill alarm sounding, he holds his breath, braces every muscle, and turns the knob. To his surprise, the door clicks open. No blaring alarm.

Like a child finding a box of sweets, delight steals tension as he steps inside. He pauses and assesses the mudroom, the laundry room, and the hallway beyond. Through the windows, outdoor lighting cast a bluish glow, aiding his view. The smell of new furniture, flooring, and paint permeate the interior. Plastic-covered wooden floors squish with each step. Treading lightly, he rushes straight to a closet at the end of the hall and listens for noise.

After a few minutes, he's certain everyone's gone. He exits the closet and examines the home, but the menacing voice squelches thrill. The sweepstake winner who wins this home brings thoughts of losing the Vermont Home. With new emotion and a deeper loathing, he surveys the space calculatingly, thinking of ways to destroy it and the Dream Team.

Tom continues toward the West wing, unaware Cody sits in his SUV in the front yard, waiting for Laura's assistant to retrieve her purse inside the home. Tom takes several steps through the foyer, oblivious of the woman around the corner. A sudden flurry of movement freezes him in his track. Taking a step back, he stops when he catches sight of Cody through the window. Fortunately, Cody's talking on the phone and looking in the opposite direction. Counting his luck, Tom rushes inside the hall closet, where he'll wait until they're gone.

Chapter 35

The House at the End of the Street

September 26, 2015, Dream Home

Laura stands in the middle of the great room admiring her work as an artist would a finished painting, inspecting every nuance of her canvas. Lost in thought, the design crew's activity appears white noise. She recalls Tara's description of the home, amazed every item is exactly as she foresaw. She'd ordered the furniture long before Tara's revelation and realizes Tara's vision had no impact on her interior designs. Laura glances around; aware they will meet their stalker in this room. The image of blood streaming down her face and her limp body tethered to the yellow chair is unfathomable. For an instant, she toys with the idea of removing the chair from the room, then scoffs at the absurdity. *It won't change my fate.*

Regardless, she can't help admiring her work. Laura inhales the room's beauty then flinches with the fiery image destroying it all. *This doesn't make sense. Why create this beautiful home just to watch it perish in a fire?* An urge to scream overwhelms her. *If only we could give this guy a taste of his own medicine.* Laura takes several deep breaths to center her mind, blowing steam from her mouth. She ponders why they can't see their stalkers location. The last couple of months he's simply vanished. Nonetheless, she senses he's still watching. Every move she makes is with caution. She's never alone, always with the girls, Cody, and her staff. No matter how tight security, Laura realizes fate is unalterable. Every intuition, every instant of danger she heeds.

She glances at the wall of windows and an overwhelming sense of exposure seizes her. Immediately, she wants to draw all the shades. She stares at the photographer taking pictures in the dining room, and her design team busy with final touches, and wonders why she still feels vulnerable surrounded by people. She walks to the window and finds the security guards still scoping the area from their SUV. Another guard sits diligently at the front entrance, watching people enter and leave the perimeter.

Laura sighs. *The home's almost complete*, except a few missing pieces in the family and guestroom upstairs. Laura's appalled items she ordered months ago are inexplicably on back-order. *As if the sweepstake can wait*, she scoffs. Her design process halted by other's mistakes she won't tolerate. Fetching the cell phone from the counter, Laura calls customer service, fuming and itching to scream at someone. She realizes her anger is misguided and should be at their stalker … *If only I could.*

"Yes, this is Laura Alcott from AHD. I have a few items on back-order. Do you have the delivery date?" Laura asks with a calm voice and waits as customer service checks the status. She prays it's already shipped.

Instead, the representative explains, "Custom orders can take a while. The computer is showing pieces still in manufacturing. Scheduled delivery is October tenth."

"October tenth! But I ordered these pieces in May!" Laura remembers negotiating the colors and can't believe it's taking so long. *Well, it's too late to stop the manufacturing process now.* Laura takes a deep breath to steady her temper. "Is there any way to expedite the order?"

Customer service assures her they will try. Irritated, Laura ends the call with growing frustration. She walks to the yellow chair and drags it from its fated spot; placing it in the foyer. Suddenly she can't breathe. *Air ... I need to get outside.* She rushes through the door, beyond the front yard, and onto the rolling paths of Martis Camp, unaware security is following closely. Laura strolls ahead; unaware Melissa Gowan is guiding her toward the home down the road.

In her mind, Laura calculates the number of weeks before the final order arrives—two more weeks. And she's struck by the date—October tenth, the date they'll meet their stalker. A quarter of a mile, Laura realizes she's wandered too far. A sudden fear overcomes her, and she swiftly assesses her surroundings.

Ahead, a bright light flickers off a light fixture. *It can't be the sun.* The sky's too overcast. It can only be Melissa. Laura stares at the Mountain Home, searching for signs of its occupants. For a moment, she surveys the backyard when a warning chills her entire body. Quickly she turns with a frightful heart leap, a gasp, and then a heavy sigh of relief, realizing the man behind her is security.

"Oh, God, thank heavens you're here," Laura says clutching her chest. Laura walks toe-to-toe with security back to the Dream Home, and glances back at the home down the road several times, wondering what Melissa's trying to tell her.

* * *

"Thank you for your service," Laura says to security and enters the hotel suite. Slipping out of her flats and placing her bag on the credenza, she heads toward Leanne and Tara's voices in the media room. Exhausted, Laura plops onto a large leather chair with a loud, "Whew! I'm in need of a big glass of wine and some good company."

Tara hits pause on the remote control, sensing Laura's frustration.

"Leanne, any more post from Mountainhigh899?"

"No, Laura, not for a month. He's disappeared off the face of the earth."

"Leanne's right; I haven't had a vision in weeks. Maybe he's given up and gone away," says Tara.

"We would sense his retreat, wouldn't we?"

"I don't know Laura; something's not right."

Recalling the earlier warning from Melissa, gooseflesh scales Laura's body. She pulls her shawl comfortingly over her shoulders.

Studying Laura's expression, Leanne straightens in the chair, "You had another clue from Melissa?"

Laura shakes her head. "Yes, earlier today in Martis Camp."

"What did you see?"

"I had a restless day, girls. I needed some air and went for a stroll, but I walked farther than I intended. Down the road, I noticed a bright light reflecting off a home's light fixture. The skies were too overcast for such a bright sparkle … It was the same light that flickered from my chandelier back in December. Then I realized it was another sign from Melissa. Thank goodness for security. I panicked and almost ran back to the house, but security was behind me the entire time. I felt like I was sleepwalking. Something was pulling me toward that home."

Tara recalls the strange sensation back in December, guiding her actions as she emailed Cody the architectural list. "Laura, it was Melissa."

Leanne sits stoic, straight as a board in the oversized leather chair. She wonders what the house down the road has to do with their stalker. "Something's wrong here. Does anyone live in that house?"

Laura slides back, engulfed by leather, mulling over the fact she's never seen anyone come or go from the home. "I believe so, but I've never seen the owners, only that Jeep Wrangler pulling in and out of the garage. They've never venture onto the property or the community. You would think they'd be curious about the Dream Home."

"Hmmm ... Well," Leanne says, removing the hairband from her wrist and securing her tresses into a signature ponytail, "Some people like their privacy."

"Perhaps, but there's a reason for Melissa's warning, and I'm not dismissing any signs from her."

In her vision, Tara recalls how Melissa guided her to the back of the garage. *Was she trying to tell me something? Does that house sit directly behind the Dream Home?*

"Tara, it might," Laura replies, hearing her thoughts. "That house sits on a curve, which would place its backyard directly behind the Dream Home. Do you believe Melissa was trying to show you the house in your vision?"

"She kept urging with her hand. There was something in the backyard she wanted me to see."

Worried, Leanne rises from the chair and paces the room. *Did he get through the gate?*

"How could he?" Laura replies.

"If he obtains a badge or one of the remote gate controls he could," Leanne says.

Tara stares at the two in confusion. "Okay, please stop the mental chatter and tell me what you're talking about."

"I'm sorry, Tara," Laura says, rolling her head in Tara's direction. "Leanne thought our stalker may have gotten through Martis Camp's security."

Tara wondered the same when she first drove through the gated community. She imagined several scenarios given their stalker's cunning. "Well, if he steals a badge or gate control, or if he's invited as golf club guest, he can get inside Martis Camp."

Leanne staring at the frozen movie screen responds dubiously, "He couldn't get a badge or automatic gate control unless he's a homeowner or club member. I seriously doubt he would join Martis Camp's Golf Club."

"Uh-huh ..." Laura says with a chortle. "If he's cunning enough to get inside each of our homes without keys; he's cunning enough to get through Martis Camp's gate."

"But something's not right," Tara says with a scowl. "How can he be in the home if the owners are there?"

"Well, he was in the Alcott estate, and Laura had no idea," Leanne says glancing at Laura with a scrunched up face. "Tara, he could be somewhere in the vicinity and the only way we'll know for sure is to have security sweep the area, or get the homeowner's permission to search the premises."

"That's a good idea, Leanne. I'll see what Cody says tomorrow. But, right now, all I want is to enjoy the company of my dearest friends and forget about our stalker for a few hours. What were you ladies watching before I entered?"

"House at the End of the Street," they mumble simultaneously with a gasp.

"Another clue from Melissa," Laura says with equal astonishment.

Chapter 36

Got Your Man

October 1, 2015, Boston

Jake's faced opposition at every turn unearthing Thomas Matthew Fallon. He's searched every Tom Matthew, Thomas Matthew, T. Matthew, and Tommie Matthew Fallon in Boston and still no luck. Nevertheless, he's not giving up. He's taking another approach to finding AHD's stalker. Earlier, he thought Tom Fallon might have been adopted by his uncle; therefore, his last name would be Spencer—Thomas Matthew Spencer. With time running out, he's following his gut instinct, taking a leap of faith on a hunch. Jake realized Spencer is also a common name in an Irish town like Boston, and his assistant has been working for several days checking every Thomas Spencer in the Boston area. Jake's phone rings. Recognizing the office number, he instantly answers.

"Hey, Clara any success with the Spencer list?"

"We got him!" Clara exclaims. "This is his number and address," she continues reading the information.

Jake's face brightens. "Sweetheart, you're the best! You deserve a raise."

He dials the number, and immediately, a woman answers.

"Good morning, Mr. Hayley's office."

"Yes, is this management?"

"Yes."

"May I speak with the manager?"

"Who's calling?"

"I'm a private investigator, and need some information on a previous tenant."

"Please hold," she says.

Jake hopes the manager will take his call. He doesn't want to circumvent his authority and acquire information through other means.

"Sam Hayley, how can I help you?"

Jake explains the urgency in finding Tom Spencer a previous tenant. Despite the manager's objection to providing information over the phone, he agreed to meet at his office in thirty minutes. Jake jots down the address and with lightning speed, jumps from the chair, and rushes through the door.

* * *

Jake steps out of his parked car onto 780 Boylston Street. Thomas Spencer's old apartment is located in the Avalon at the Prudential Center—a tall high-rise in the Back Bay area. At the door, he's greeted by the manager's assistant and led through a tiny reception area into the Manager's office. A graying middle-aged man with a paunch greets him with a handshake and directs Jake to a small chair facing a desk and colorful wall. A mosaic of pictures accosts Jake's view. Obviously, they're family photos. Sam Hayley's in every picture. A large photo of him kissing a woman, presumably his wife, is in the center of the collage. Other pictures show several children blowing out birthday candles, posing at high school graduations, family outings at the beach, boating, and fishing trips. On a boat deck, Sam Hayley stands topless, holding an enormous fish with his belly bulging over baggy shorts.

Jake nods his head at the wall of pictures. "Large family."

"Yes, my pride and joy," Sam says, turning his head toward the wall.

"I see you do some fishing as well."

"Yeah, it's my only form of relaxation from this place. Family and I take the boat to Mattawamkeag River in Maine during the spring and summer and do a little fly-fishing."

"Sounds wonderful ... " Jake points at a photo of Sam holding a large fish proudly. "How big is the fish?"

"That's my biggest catch yet ... An eight-pounder."

"Aww ... Is that right," Jake mumbles, uninterested and unimpressed, but he figures a little friendly banter will engender more information.

"Well, one day I'll have to give it a try," Jake says, easing into the topic of Tom Spencer. "Thank you for seeing me on such short notice. As I told you on the phone, it's urgent I locate Tom Spencer. I'm hoping you can provide some information."

"Well, I prefer not giving out tenant information, but this looks serious from what you've told me. After your phone call, I had my assistant pull Mr. Spencer's records. He lived here about six years, got married his second year, and shortly after, his wife was in the family way."

"So, he has children?"

"Yes, two sons. I worried about those boys. Many of the tenants complained about screaming and fighting in the apartment. I believe he abused his wife, but we couldn't help. She simply refused to file a complaint."

Ah ha! Tom is repeating the cycle of abuse.

"Mr. Spencer was a strange man. He always appeared disoriented."

"Do you know what happened to the family, or where they moved?"

"Some people are just plain lucky. Mr. Spencer won some Lotto or sweepstake and moved away."

Jake's eyes widen. "Does AHD Dream Home Sweepstake ring a bell?"

"Actually, that sounds about right."

Loudly, Jake exclaims, "Got him!" Ccaught off-guard, the manager flinches. Eager to report the news to Cody, Jake jumps from the chair and shakes the manager's hands. "Thanks, you just made my day." And he rushes out of the office, fishes for his cell phone, and quickly dials Cody's number. "Cody, I got your man. He's one of your sweepstake winners—Thomas Matthew Spencer."

Chapter 37

Behind the Pines

October 1, 2015, Martis Camp Dream Home

An autumn chill swiftly replaces Lake Tahoe's summer. With October tenth only nine days away and no trace of their stalker, the girls consider Melissa Gowan's last clue—the house behind the pines. At their request and without delay, Cody and security visited the home down the road, but the owner didn't answer. Without the homeowner's permission, checking inside is impossible. Nonetheless, the girls discovered the home behind the pines is a beeline from the Dream Home's backyard.

While Laura finishes details inside, Tara and Leanne secretly journey toward the house in the distance. An hour earlier, Tara was certain a light shone in an upper room, but as they draw near, every room appears dark. Stealthily skulking out of sight, they tiptoe toward the deck and peer through French doors, but daylight casts a reflective glare making the interior imperceptible.

Desperate for a better view, Leanne strays toward the side of the home. Above an outdoor generator, a window is slightly ajar. Hoisting her weight atop the steel box, she stoops beneath the window. From her crouch, she rises and peeps over the windowsill, spying a laundry room on the other side. Certain no one's near; she throws her leg astride.

"Leanne! No! Are you crazy? Get away from there!"

Startled, Leanne wobbles on the ledge. "Shhh! someone could hear you."

"What are you doing?" Tara asks.

"I'm just going to check the first floor."

"Are you crazy? He could be inside."

"I'll be careful."

"It's too dangerous—"

"We won't get another opportunity. Just stay and keep watch."

"This is foolish," Tara grumbles just as Leanne slips inside.

On top of the dryer, Leanne pauses and listens for sounds beyond the adjacent pantry and kitchen. Only silence echoes through the dark abode. On the floor, next to the dryer, a hamper of dirty laundry spills onto wooden flooring. Sliding off the dryer, her ankle grazes the basket, throwing her into a trance. Instantly, she's the stalker.

Withdrawing and piling scorching sheets atop the washer, she stares through the window into the dark night, glimpsing a gaunt, pallid reflection.

Frightened, Leanne wakes, stumbles over the basket, and lands on a mound of dirty laundry, marinating in a foul stench. Again, she's assaulted with the stalker's essence. Scooting backward, she hustles to disentangle limbs and glides forward on a damp T-shirt. A cloying musk assaults her nostrils sending her into another trance.

Weakened with fever, she moves toward a night breeze flowing through the window, letting air cool sweaty flesh. She removes the drenched T-shirt and pants and throws them atop the laundry basket.

Gripped with dizziness, she claws the doorframe. A
bitter liquid rises in her throat ...

Leanne wakes with a lurch and tight grip to her throat. Her face blanched with the phantom illness. Still, on her hands and knees, she slides forward, accidentally brushing a finger against clothing, triggering a maelstrom of images. Colliding retrogressive dominoes send her helter-skelter, backward in time.

> *A powerful thrust lands her in a car seat beside a strange woman as she states, "Mr. Cavanaugh, several vacant lots are available. How much land are you looking for, and what square footage are you seeking to build?" A view of the Sierra Nevada Mountains and the Martis Camp's golf course appears. Another surge thrust her behind the wheel as she drives behind a Northstar bus. A swoosh of light and she walks the aisles of an airplane, searching countless passengers. A sweeping leap and the domino images crash to a halt. She stares at the Vermont home through a rearview mirror.*

Leanne wakes aghast, supine on the floor, and buried in laundry. With haste, she scrambles to her feet, scoots atop the dryer, and out of the window.

Tara, beside herself with fear, breathes a sigh of relief when Leanne reappears in the window. "I'm having a heart attack out here." Noticing the ghastly pallor of Leanne's face, she races to her side. "What happened?"

"Let's go," Leanne says, grasping Tara's arm and pulling her along at a quick pace.

"What did you see in that house?"

The illness they sensed in Charleston invades Leanne's body as they rush through the pines. Abruptly, she halts, a statue ossified in time.

Lying on the ground with binoculars, she spies on Laura in the front yard, watching as she directs the delivery of furniture into the home.

Beside her, Tara sways on frozen feet.

The stalker shoves Laura through snow-covered pines with a gun pressed in her side. Manic voices resound frantically in both their minds. Fearful of the stalker and the gun, Laura can't block his thoughts.

Snapping out of her trance, Leanne's feet tingle with warmth. She peers down at the spot he'd laid. At that instant, Tara recovers from her vision.

"Let's go, Tara."

"What did you see, Leanne?"

"I'll tell you when we get back inside."

Tom

Tom refuses to leave the rental since Cody and his men's appearance at his front door. At the time, he thought they were just looking to speak to the neighbors, but now, spying Tara and Leanne in his backyard, he fears they know he's in the home. Tom rushes to turn off the light, hoping they hadn't noticed. With the binoculars, he follows Tara and Leanne as they near the rental. When they drop out of sight, he makes his way downstairs.

A sudden flurry of noise emanates from the laundry room. Tom cautiously inches toward the door. With the sound of a dull thump, he rushes toward the open window, peeks outside and catches a glimpse of Leanne and Tara speeding from the house. Suddenly, they stand frozen. He ponders their curious stance. Something about their rigid pose unnerves him. He wonders why Leanne stares down at her feet then pulls Tara away. It's the same spot he's kept vigil of the Dream Home staff. Noticing the laundry strewn about the floor, he wonders what they were looking for. Something tells him they're aware he's in the house. Now he worries they'll find him before he makes his move. *I have to act and soon.*

The Girls

Leanne and Tara enter the Dream Home just as Laura completes a phone call with Cody. An inscrutable blankness covers her face. The only emotional cue is a tremble in her voice. Before Laura ends the call, Tara and Leanne sense her unease.

"Okay, Cody … We will," Laura murmured.

"What did Cody say?" Tara asks.

Laura's emotionless visage now erupts in shock. "Girls, we should have known."

"I already know, Laura. I saw our stalker a few minutes ago," Leanne utters.

"Who is he?" Tara asks, realizing Leanne's vision is why her complexion is pallid.

"He's the Vermont Dream Home winner," Leanne and Laura answer concurrently.

Tara shakes her head. "No, no he can't be. I remember that man. Our stalker looks nothing like him. He's heavier, stocky, with thick, wavy brown hair—this guy's totally different."

"Remember his illness, Tara. Maybe his infirmity has changed his physical appearance."

Besieged with chills, Tara's instincts warn the stalker's too close for comfort. "What does Cody recommend we do, Laura?"

"He wants us to stay here with security. We'll be safer. The private detective is contacting the family in Vermont. Hopefully, they can get information from the wife." Laura pauses and stares in alarm, sensing frightening images and thoughts from Leanne and Tara.

He's already here.

He's in the home behind the house.

Cody

Cody stares at the eleventh sweepstake winner's file and the Spencer photo in his hand. He recalls meeting the family two years ago. At the time, they appeared an ordinary family. *What's happened? What's made you so angry Tom?* Standing under the portico of the beautiful Vermont home, they all assume a smile in the photograph. *A smile for show*, Cody thinks, pondering the wife and children's fear. He recalls Tom's constant watch over his wife and Ellen's cautiousness. Reticent but polite, she'd let Tom control every conversation. Even when asked a direct question, she'd let Tom answer. At the time, Cody thought she was just shy. But now, he clearly understands. Ellen feared him. After Jake's revelation of neighbors' complaints of abuse, he's worried for the family.

"What happened to make you so angry with AHD?" Cody mumbles. He searches the file for a telephone number, hoping the number hasn't changed. The phone rings several times. A joyous voicemail greeting sails through the phone of a presumably happy family.

"Sorry, the Spencer family can't come to the phone," says Tom.

"Leave a brief message, and we'll call you back," says Ellen.

"Have a happy day," exclaim the children, followed by cheerful giggles.

Cody leaves a brief message but perceives Ellen won't return his call. Tom's stronghold over his wife may be powerful even in his absence. He prays she summons the courage to return his call. Perhaps she can clarify Tom's issues and prevent him from harming the girls.

Chapter 38

Running Out of Time

October 2, 2015, Lake Tahoe Ritz-Carlton,

Standing on Ritz Carlton's balcony, Tara anguishes over the season's first snow and summer's quick ending. Usually, the sight of snow brings joyful childhood memories. But not today, flurries resemble snow in her vision—of the fated meeting just eight days away. It's perplexing they hadn't sensed Tom Spencer's nearness—right behind the Dream Home. Tara glances at the girls seated around the fireplace, examining and memorizing every aspect of October tenth from her dream journal. She closes the sliding doors and joins them by the fire.

"This is so frustrating. I still can't believe Tom Spencer rented that home and Martis Camp refuses to do anything about him."

"Well, Cody tried, sweetie," Laura says with a sigh and head jiggle. "Management won't do anything without proof of wrongdoing. As far as they're concerned, he's paid his rent and upheld community rules."

"Tara, we're on our own. We just have to pray Melissa is still guiding us," Leanne says.

"Hmm, if we'd paid enough attention to Melissa's warnings we could've solved Tom Spencer's identity without a private detective," says Tara.

Leanne ponders Tara's clues and decisively shakes her head. "No. I don't believe so. They were random clues with no meaning whatsoever—the glow in your office and home, the light on the rim of the cell phone, and the light bouncing off your pendant. Your chill, as you stared at Tom at the gate, is the only intuitive warning that made sense."

"Neither of us could've deciphered the danger," Laura says reflecting on Melissa's warnings.

"I did. Nyla's early phone call; she never calls before noon. She told me to heed my intuition. I should've perceived the call as a warning."

Laura frowns, remembering the nasty cut from the staple. "Tara, you weren't the only one who missed Melissa's clues. She sent a warning my way in December. The signs were all around me—the flashing Chandelier, the glow and blood smear on the Vermont Dream Home photo. What was so vague then is so obvious now. Girls, there's something else … The chandelier cast a light on the French doors, and I swear I saw a figure staring back at me. But when I glanced a second time, it was gone. I believe Tom Spencer lurked at the back of the home that morning, and Melissa was trying to warn me."

Leanne glances at the girls with a sudden realization. "Melissa sent me a warning as well. But it was inexplicable. My computer kept flashing in and out, and a long beep rang out when Mountainhigh899 posted a response on the blog site. I thought it was a computer issue and called the tech guys."

Silence blankets the room with memories of December fifteenth. Personal and professional concerns precluded their intuition. Laura's preoccupation with Daniel impeded her senses. Leanne's heated conversation with her father obscured her perception. And Tara's concern about locating a new site for the Dream Home hindered her abilities to identify Tom as a threat.

With reverence, Tara contemplates the enormous energy Melissa expended to travel to the future and warn them. Her efforts fell on deaf ears.

"We weren't ready, honey," Laura says, sensing Tara's concerns, "but we are now. Girls, we have our stalkers' name and information, but we need to know why he's trying to hurt us? Why is he angry with AHD? And how do we stop him?"

"We've done nothing wrong! Tom Spencer's problem is personal. He's delusional … his issues are a figment of his sick mind," Leanne countered.

"Yes, he's delusional, but whatever he believes we've done is real to him. That's the problem, sweetie."

"Uh-huh, well, his illness may well be our end."

"God, that poor family, I've been worried about them since the discovery. Cody called Ellen's mother, but she hasn't had any contact with her daughter for three years. She said Tom prevented her from having any relationship with her." Imagining Ellen stuck with this monster, Laura perceives the fear she must live every day. "Well, girls, our survival depends on our gifts at this point. We need to use our knowledge of October tenth to overcome Tom Spencer."

Searching journal pages, Tara recalls the moment before Tom fires the gun. "Leanne, when we're bound to those damn chairs, I believe you have a vision of Tom. You scream. *You murdered them.* Tom becomes outraged by your comment. I wonder what you saw or will see."

"Tara, I wish I could tell you, but I can't control when my visions come. If I had an object of Tom's, it would help, but we don't. Damnit! When I was in that house, I should have taken an item of his clothing. That was the perfect opportunity … Damn, damn, damn it!"

"Leanne, you were too fearful to think clearly at the time. But what if we perform a group shushing like we did in Charleston?"

"Tara, remember we had the bloodstained letter and keychain. We have nothing to help me see what was in your dream."

"You have me," Tara says. "Come on, let's just give it a try. It can't hurt."

"Okay, we can try this evening."

"Girls, even if Leanne doesn't see the vision in time, we have one another. Remember, our combined gifts are strong as a whole. We're aware of what will happen on the tenth. Tom will knock me unconscious and drag me to the house behind the pines. And somehow, lure you two into the Dream Home. So, what if we don't have all the details, we have enough to fight back. Why don't we use this information to set him up?" Laura, more determined than ever to defeat Tom at his own plan, tries to inspire hope in the girls for once.

"You're right, Laura. Using what we've seen is a wise choice besides involving the police, which I've contemplated a lot lately."

"Leanne, from what we understand about fate, it can't be altered. Remember what Melissa's letter said, any change will cause greater consequences," says Tara.

Consequence ... Leanne wonders what affect one element of change will have—more death, endangering other's lives. The vastness is unfathomable. "You're right, Tara. This is so frustrating, the waiting, the uncertainties..."

Laura frets over being struck unconscious. The thought is terrifying and she's not going to let that happen. "Girls, we can work with information from Tara's dream. Melissa gave us the exact date and time he will appear. So, without changing anything leading up to 2:22 pm, we should assume our usual routine on October tenth, and be ready to attack when he grabs me. All we need are the right weapons to stop and restrain him."

"You mean a gun … Where are we going to get a gun?" Immensely fearful of guns, Tara wouldn't in a million years dream of using one. But now, after all that's happened, she'll use any means to protect her friends.

"I saw a gun in Cody's glove compartment. Laura, since you're closer to Cody, you can somehow sneak the weapon out of his SUV without him knowing."

"I'll try Leanne; we only have a week, so I need to do this soon."

"Laura, how're we going to prevent Cody from finding out about this, or any of our staff?"

Laura knows Cody will disapprove of their plan. "Girls, we don't tell Cody. We have to keep this secret as best we can. Remember Tara's vision, I'm alone in the house. No one else is in the vision. So, if events happen the way they're supposed to, we shouldn't worry about Cody or the staff, we only need to be ready to protect ourselves."

Leanne reflects on Melissa's note. *This is your fate. This challenge must happen for you three to become who you're meant to be. I'm your guide; follow my clues, the light, and any unusual indications that shine brightly will be my guide for you.* "You're right, Laura, we can't change anything. From what Melissa told us, this vision must happen. We just need faith in Melissa's guidance. I believe she's telling us to use our powers to overcome Tom. If we bring in security and involve Cody, things might end worse for all of us."

"Fate is set. It's irreversible, Nyla would always say. She said don't toy with destiny, just be prepared when the time comes."

"Exactly, Tara," Leanne replies.

Cody … Tara ponders intense vibes she sensed from him earlier. Instincts about him have grown stronger the last few weeks. "Girls, something's been bothering me for days."

Immediately, Laura catches Tara's thought. "What's wrong, honey?"

"Is Cody aware of our gift?" Tara already knows the answer by the expression on Laura's face.

Laura was hoping to reveal her findings later—the Moldavite stone in Cody's blazer. She still wonders if he'd intentionally left the jacket for her to discover. At the exact moment she'd returned it, his thoughts exploded in her mind. His demeanor quietened and he'd stared keenly, awaiting a response. *Cody wanted her to discover his bloodline.* Without the stone's protection, Laura sensed everything he'd hidden for years. She's tried to keep his secret, but with Tara's suspicions, she can't.

"Girls, Cody's been aware of our clairvoyance a long time. A promise to the Alcotts bound him from disclosing his knowledge and his secret."

"Secret?"

"Tara, Cody is also a descendant of Nathan Cox."

For years, she'd pondered Cody's strong jaw, brows and hazel eyes that resemble Tara's. "I've always thought Cody was related to the Alcotts and suspect Daniel knew of their blood ties as well."

Tom

Hiding in darkness since his visitors in the backyard, Tom wanders feverishly around the rental where he's been a prisoner for days. Unable to leave the property for fear of being found, he's caged in the luxury rental, and delirium grows worse by the minute. Cabin fever and uncontrollable madness steadily drive him to his climactic plan.

In the kitchen, he prepares another unappealing meal from a can—the diet of a sick man. He glances about the luxury rental and thinks he should be eating elegant meals worthy of preparation in the high-tech kitchen. He recalls Ellen's constant need to please him with gourmet meals, and his sons' stiff faces as they pretended to be a normal family around the dining table. He aches with memories of his five-year-olds' palpable fear whenever their eyes met—the same fear he held as a boy whenever his father looked at him. Despite extreme effort to be different from his father, his son's eyes revealed his failure. He doesn't want his family fearing him. Emotions just take control, and he can't stop them. He's aware the only thread holding his family together is the Dream Home. Ellen would have left him long ago if they hadn't won the sweepstakes.

Back upstairs in the bedroom, he peers through binoculars and spies two men prowling behind pine trees in the backyard. A feverish chill crawls over his body, and a deep, hacking bloody cough escapes his raw throat. Despite days of rest, fever, chills, and weakness still invade his body. He curses the untimely illness. Until his energy returns, all he can do is watch from a distance. Time is running out, and he grows desperate by the hour. He returns to the solitude of his bed. *Soon I have to make my move.*

Chapter 39

Old Things New Again

October 8, 2015, Michael Anders Home

For several months, Laura's practiced telepathy, a gift she thought she'd lost years ago, until Melissa Gowan's letter. Michael Anders, once again, is her faithful subject, and circles about her, preparing the area with soothing crystals. Entranced by his athletic physique and the sculpted denim contour of his legs, she's unaware Michael's caught her ogling eyes.

Furtively, Michael smiles but hopes Laura's attraction won't interfere with their session. He continues placing blue Chalcedony, Apophyllite, and Ulexite crystals and stones around her to strengthen telepathic impression and mind control.

Only two days away from the fated day, and Laura worries her gift is unperfected. She hopes her attraction to Michael isn't too distracting. Incessantly, she twists the Herkimer diamond ring she started wearing months ago to strengthen her telepathy.

Placing the last crystal in the circle, Michael sits across from Laura. "Do you remember the sensations you felt when you used telepathy as a child?"

"Wow … It was effortless as a child. I would sense thoughts, or send thoughts without even trying … It simply just happened. I'd glance at a person, and somehow they'd receive my message. Oh, I almost forgot. Right before I used telepathy, an unusual lucidity preceded my thoughts." Laura remembers the sharp, silent clarity, and the sensation of time abruptly halting right before she sent her message.

"Your gift was pure when you were younger. You need to capture that same sense of clarity—dispel all the stuff clouding your thoughts."

"I'll try, but it might be tough."

"You're defeated already, Laura. Just relax, forget everything, and concentrate."

Laura stares beyond crystals into Michael's eyes and tries to relax. She ponders a message to send telepathically, but the hint of dark hairs trailing his forearm breaks her concentration. Laura rapidly blinks Michael's image from thought. *This is going to be tough.* Silencing her mind, she hurls six words to Michael.

Your presence puts me at ease.

Mentally, repeating the words over and over, she waits for Michael's response, but nothing happens. *Is my attraction clouding clarity? Okay, Laura, focus on nothing but your words.* Ignoring Michael's handsome features, for several minutes, she peers deeply at bright crystal hues.

I know you hear me; now tell me something, Laura.

She hears Michael's words. With a penetrating glare, she delves deeper into the gem's radiance. Closing her eyes the afterimage imprints on her mind. Again, she propels a thought to Michael.

Your presence puts me at ease.

"Likewise, I also desire you, Laura," Michael replies.

Quickly, opening her eyes, Laura catches Michael's affectionate gaze and her pulse races. She glances away, nervously gnawing on her bottom lip.

Realizing his attraction may interfere with her abilities, Michael turns his attention to her efforts. "Good, Laura. So what was different this time? How did you feel?"

"Well, I was more focused, and the message was the only thing on my mind. Everything around me evaporated as if I were the sole existence—me and my thought.

"There you go; all it took was deeper concentration. Your gift is still potent; you just forgot how to use it."

Laura, thrilled with her effort, eagerly urges Michael to try again. The last couple of months, she's amazed at how comfortable she's become using her gift with him as her subject. However, she's not surprised attraction has swelled to desire. Neither has acted on impulse, but Laura senses Michael's restraint weakening. She wonders how much longer before he acts.

Okay, Laura, concentrate. The real test of her gift is to influence Michael's action which is much more challenging. When she was a child, mind control was usually prefaced by some emotion—anger, fear, elation, sadness. *What emotion will trigger my gift today? Hmmm ... Lust, desire? Certainly, erotic thoughts will help.*

Again, she stares into the crystals. She tries to separate her mind from her physical body and surroundings. The crystal's soft hues and calming vibrations are hypnotic. Soon, she's light as air, her essence—a single thought and pure desire.

With clarity, she sends a suggestion. *Sit next to me.* The message takes a few seconds to register, but he does. With closed eyes, she senses his heat beside her.

Michael's aware mind control appears without one's knowledge, but he doesn't question the sudden desire to sit next to Laura, believing it was his idea. He waits for Laura's thought to invade his mind.

Pick up the blue crystal, Laura projects. Once again, he obeys her suggestion. She opens her eyes and contains her laugh. "You can put the moonstone down now," she says with a chuckle, "but I like sitting next to you."

"That was you?" Michael says in awe.

"Yep," Laura replies with a devilish grin. She senses Michael's desire, but his swift action takes her by surprise. He leans over and her head jerks; lips bumping Michael's with the sudden kiss.

"I hope the kiss was my idea," he whispers hungrily into her mouth.

Laura playfully bites his bottom lip. "Yep, that was all you, sweetie." His essence invades her nostrils—the scent of outdoors lingers on his skin and hair; commingled with the citrus pine of his cologne. The soft, sweet flesh of his lips arouses all her senses. Soon, surprise dissolves; replaced with erotic yearnings she hasn't felt since Daniel. Her body relaxes into Michael's. His desire invades her mind. Emotions and old abilities she thought she'd never experience again, are reawakened.

PART 3

Chapter 40

A Glitch in the Plan

October 10, 2015, 1:30PM

Standing in the Dream Home's front yard, Tara's oblivious to snowflakes melting around the buzz of excitement. Under white tents dotting the front yard, caterers pour bottles of champagne and prepare containers of food on linen-covered tables. Thoughtlessly, she takes a glass, then quickly returns it to the table. *Bad idea. Today I need to be hyper-aware.*

Tossing her eyes across the front yard, the film crew and photographer stealthily film unsuspecting crew and staff members enjoying the celebration. *How deceptive*, Tara thinks … *A perfect picture of accomplishment … it can change in an instant.* Nervously, she inspects the yard, wondering if Tom Spencer is watching. *If so, why can't I see his actions?* The moment she asks that question, Nyla's words enter her mind. *"You need to silence the mental chatter masking your gift."* And she knows fear hinders foreshadowing Tom.

She examines the beautiful façade and prays it won't perish by fire. Worries turn to Laura waiting inside for a face-to-face confrontation with a man who's caused dread for several months. Searching the yard, Tara notices Laura's assistant offer Leanne champagne. She declines, nervously fidgets with her fingers, and glances at Tara with a frown. Tara knows exactly what she's feeling.

Clutching the sacred-seven pendant, Tara forces a smile for the staff and crew. Closing her eyes, she tries to intuit an ethereal presence. *Is Melissa here?* From a distance, it appears she's praying. To some extent, she is. Still grasping the pendant, Tara makes her way toward Leanne and the design crew. Halfheartedly, she joins the conversation, but never disengages her attention from the purlieus of the yard.

Tom

Meanwhile, in the house behind the pines, voices compete in Tom's head as he executes his plan. Unaware of the Dream Home celebration, he's at once infuriated as a crowd emerges through the binoculars. But surprisingly, the back of the home which crawled with security for days is vacant. *Hmmm … Another opportunity.* He's certain the celebration will distract attention from the backyard.

Cars continue to arrive at the entrance. A black SUV pulls behind a convoy of vehicles. Three men exit and Cody Darling greets them with a formal handshake. Their stilted demeanor contrasts the festive crowd. He follows the men till they drop out of view. *Are they security?*

Vigorously, he paces back and forth in the kitchen. *Today is the day to make my move.* He ponders the black bag hidden in the Dream Home's storage closet and stares at the ring of keys on the kitchen counter. To his surprise, the keys he'd pilfered the first day in the home, not only opened the garage but also every door on the premises. Days later, he'd made his way back inside, leaving a bag filled with supplies and two cans of gasoline.

In rapid successions, Tom runs his hands through his hair. Clarity sparks renewed energy he hasn't felt in days. He continues to pace, more energetic than before, preparing for action. For several minutes, lucid thoughts flit through his mind; instilling mettle to proceed. He glances through the sliding door—eyes fixed on his destination. Questions raid his mind. *Are the official-looking men inside? Are the items placed in the garage closet still there? Will my plan work?* He stops pacing, mortified by a gaunt reflection in the glass cabinet. Piteously, he looks away.

Preparing to leave, he dons a black jacket and baseball cap to disguise his face. Taking a knife from the kitchen, he places the blade in his back pocket. On the back deck, flurries float but never touch the ground. Cool air he hasn't felt in days, revives his energy as he treads through snow-covered pine. Like a final march, he continues tree-to-tree, hoping the illness doesn't return.

The dark antagonist taunts again. *You will fail Tom, just as you've failed with everything in your life—just like your father did. You won't succeed; so give up now.*

The reproach fuels anger. "I'm not my father!" Tom screams.

The rebuff is harsh and judgmental. *You're worse than him. Tom, think. What happened in Vermont?*

Tom dismisses the battle stockpiling in his mind. Unsure of the probing voice's intent, he turns his attention back to his mission. As he grows closer, a dull drone hums in the front yard. He waits a few minutes, eyeing the door to the garage, hoping no one appears.

Dashing toward the rear, Tom inserts the key and opens the door with ease. He rushes toward the closet where the black bag is hidden, relieved it's still there. Inside lays a handgun, duct tape, and several locks and chains—tools to execute his plan. Securing the pistol in his back pocket, he surveys the dark corner and two cans of gasoline, exactly where he'd left them.

A few minutes later, he exits the closet toward two small windows on the garage door. In the front yard, a crowd eats and drinks merrily under white tents. In the center of the gathering, a film crew captures the celebration. Tom searches the yard and finds Tara and Leanne engaged in conversation with two women under the tent. Tara appears distracted. Her eyes scan the yard, every other second and she throws Leanne sly glances.

Where's Laura?

Tom watches Cody Darling direct two young caterers. He's relieved the stiff men he'd seen through the binoculars are serving food and champagne and aren't security.

At the mudroom door, Tom listens inside the home. He calculates his next move—a beeline to the closet under the staircase, where he'll wait before he makes his move. Tom glances at his wristwatch; surprised to find its 1:50 pm. *Time is moving too fast.*

Slowly, he opens the door and enters the Dream Home—a silent monument, bordered by worshippers at its gate. Tom rushes toward the closet under the stairs. Lucky for him, the noisy plastic is gone. A man enters the foyer just as he steps into the closet. Swiftly, Tom closes the door. He plants his ears to the doorjamb and listens as he enters the great room.

"Exquisite!" the man exclaims.

"It needs something else," a female voice replies.

A flurry of movement in the foyer grows close. Tom worries someone's heading toward the closet. He peers through the door slit and catches Laura dragging a yellow, wooden chair toward the great room.

"There, perfect!" Laura says.

In the center of the stair hall, the mysterious Alcott medallion, similarly positioned in the Vermont home, glows brightly. Unnerved, he looks away. The front door opens. Tom freezes.

"Time for the last group photo shoot, come on guys out front," a woman exclaims.

"Michael, go ahead, I'll join you in a minute," says Laura.

The sound of movement and the closing front door confirms Michael's exited the house.

She's alone. My timing is too good to be true.

Wary of others entering, he waits a few minutes before making a move. The dark antagonist taunts, *you're stupid! Honestly, do you believe you can pull this off? You go in that room, and they're going to cart you off to jail.* The antagonizing voice only makes him more desperate to act—invalidate its remarks. His heart gears like a racing engine. Adrenaline builds, *this is the moment.* Determined, he exits the closet without a sound and walks across the foyer.

At the end of the hall, in the great room, Laura peers out the window. Tom advances through a flotsam of boxes and home accessories; swerving in and out, trying not to collide with cartons. He fails to notice through the window, Cody heading toward the front door. In an instant, the door swings open, missing Tom's face by a few inches. Now facing Cody's posterior, swiftly, he pulls the knife from his pocket, pointing it at Cody's back.

"You move, and this goes straight through your spine."

Laura

Again, for the hundredth time, Laura glances at her wristwatch. She can't believe the ominous hour is almost here. In seventeen minutes, Tom will be in the room behind her. To calm her fears, she walks to the window and gazes about the room for signs. "Melissa, please be here," she whispers, all the while hoping their plan works. *Everything must be the same as the vision. Otherwise, a chain reaction will happen,* she hears in her mind. She frowns at the yellow chair she'd dragged back into the room a few minutes ago, loathing it and what it presages. Regardless, all objects must be exactly as they were in Tara's vision.

Laura considers their plan with mounting doubt. *Please, please, girls, enter on time.* She fears the pain of Tom's gun knocking her unconscious. *Please, God, don't let me go through that ordeal.* In her mind, *2:22 pm* reverberates. *Melissa, I hope you're right.* She reevaluates the plan. Leanne and Tara will enter the room carrying a concealed gun at exactly 2:22 pm. *Maybe they should enter a minute earlier. Well, it's too late now. There's no time to change the plan.* She tugs at the Herkimer diamond ring; her finger stinging and bruising from the constant twisting and turning. She glances at the chandelier and the knife on the counter, exactly where it lay in Tara's vision.

Melissa, please be here.

Anxious to be done with this day, again, she stares at her wristwatch. Only a minute has passed. *Time is moving too slow.* Fearfully gazing out the window and biting her lip, she hopes Melissa's watching. Suddenly, in the windowpane, an unsteady figure approaches. The sun's glare distorts the image. Frantically, she screams in her head. *He's too early!*

No! Now, what do I do?

Gripped with fear, Laura braces her body. She can't let Tom knock her unconscious. The figure grows closer.

It's Cody!

She turns quickly; stunned to find Tom holding a knife at Cody's back.

"You scream, and Cody's dead."

Sheer anger suffuses Cody's face, and sheer madness consumes Tom's. Gripped with fear, Laura stands rooted to her spot.

Considering his next move, Tom glances about the room wild-eyed and poking a knife at Cody's back. He maneuvers his free hand toward the gun in his back pocket.

Cody catches Tom's reflection in the windowpane and realizes *he has to act at now.* With every ounce of strength, Cody springs forward, arches his waist, angles his legs, and reaches for Tom's arm. But Tom's too swift and pulls the knife back, sending it forward forcefully into Cody's waist.

Cody groans and grips his side. Blood oozes through his hands, saturating his sweater bright red. Tom menaces above him ready to strike again.

"No!" Laura screams. Immediately she clasps her mouth, fearful of the knife in Tom's hand. She looks down at Cody, wanting to help him but she can't, but her scream stopped Tom from striking again. He turns and stares at her—eyes trance-like. Removing her hands slowly from her mouth, Laura glimpses her wristwatch—2:09 pm. Panic sets in.

They're going to try to stop you. You realize that don't you, the voice in his head warns. Tom pulls the gun from his pocket and wields it in Laura 's direction. "You move, and I'll shoot," Tom says. Tom takes the end of the gun, and with a swift blow, knocks Cody unconscious. Blood swiftly spreads through his sweater and pools to the floor. Frenziedly, Tom paces about Laura, grabs both her arms, folding them behind her back. His mind explodes with manic thoughts. Several voices battle to gain control.

You idiot, leave her.

No, I've already done damage.

What do you do now, Tom? Where will you take her?

You fool! It's not as simple as you thought, huh!

What? Are you taking her from the house?

You'll be caught!

You idiot … Idiot!

"Shut up!"

Laura's blood freezes with Tom's tortured howl. *Oh my God, those voices!* Suddenly, Laura recalls the bevy of thoughts when she touched the blood-smeared photo. *He's really demented.* The voices taunt incessantly, making it impossible to channel mind control.

Now what Tom? What do you do with her? She'll scream the minute you get her outside, the voice teases again.

"Enough!" Tom howls, and pushes Laura through the foyer, into the garage, behind the house, and through the pine trees.

All the while, Laura screams in her head.

Tom, stop!

Let me go! Tom, drop the gun!

But mind control isn't working. You've got to remain calm, Laura. She takes a deep breath and tries to quiet her fear. *I have to stop him.* But the voices in Tom's mind infiltrate her thoughts, making it impossible to remain calm.

Take it easy. Calm down, calm down, Laura repeats. Stumbling through pines with a gun lodged in her side, and Tom's painful grip makes telepathy impossible. Manic voices roar through Tom's mind, holding her fearful and thwarting her gift.

Leanne and Tara

It's 2:21 pm and Tara and Leanne prepare to enter the home. Scanning the area, they watch security roam the yard. Tara searches for Cody, finding him nowhere in sight. When they're sure no one's looking, they enter the foyer. An eerie stillness blankets the home. Alarmed by deafening silence, Leanne shakily withdraws the gun from her handbag. The moment Tara steps inside the house, her eyes veiled over with visions of Tom shoving Laura toward the house behind the pines, onto the patio, and through the door.

Leanne enters the foyer and staggers with Cody's pain. Overcome, the gun slips with a dull thud to the floor, pulling Tara from her trance.

"We're too late!" Noticing Leanne on the floor, she rushes to her side. "You okay?"

"Yep, but Cody's hurt," she says grimacing with pain.

"He's got Laura," Tara says, and she swiftly sweeps the gun from the floor, rushes to the back of the garage, and through the pines. Helplessly, she watches Tom shove Laura through the door with a gun at her back. The door slides behind them.

Slumped with Cody's pain, Leanne stumbles into the great room toward his unconscious body. Reaching into her bag, she grabs her cell phone and dials emergency. "A man's been stabbed! We need an ambulance fast. Please hurry!"

Chapter 41

Consequences

October 10, 2015, Tahoe Forest Hospital

Several hours later, Leanne, Tara, and Michael wait anxiously for news on Cody's injuries. Furrowed-browed, Michael paces the hospital corridor, checking his mobile incessantly. Finally, he stops pacing, places the mobile in his coat pocket, and joins the girls in the lounge.

Staring into space, and gnawing her fingernails to a nub, Leanne worries about Laura in the arms of a madman. Tara, glaring at her cell phone, rereads for the hundredth times a text message Tom Spencer sent moments after he snatched Laura.

> *Laura's with me. If you bring anyone with you, she's dead. We're waiting for you at the house.*

God, poor Laura, I can't imagine her fear. How're we going to pull this off? No matter what, we have to help Laura and soon. Michael's voice pierces Tara's thoughts.

"What happened? How'd this guy get to Laura so easily?"

"I don't know … It happened so fast, Michael. We didn't have enough time to stop him." Tara loathes persistent lies she's told since the ambulance arrived. With Tom's murderous threats, she's had to conceal everything to prevent Michael and the police from interfering.

Tara's relieved from more lies when the doctor enters the waiting room. She jumps from the chair swiftly. "How's Cody?"

"There's considerable blood loss, but he'll recover just fine."

"What about the head wound?" Michael asks.

"Well, he suffered a minor concussion. We'll monitor him for twenty-four hours. Otherwise, Cody's in good shape and should be up and about soon," he says, backing away with a smile.

Michael's cell phone buzzes and he yanks it from his pocket. His eyebrows knit as he checks the display and unfurls as he places the phone back in his pocket. "Is there any news from the police?"

We haven't called the police. We can't. It will change my premonition Tara thinks. "Nothing yet, Michael," Tara says, detecting a change in his demeanor.

"Michael, I called. They're doing everything they can," Leanne says—spouting untruths she'd never mouthed, but given the circumstances, dishonesty is necessary to save Laura.

Michael detects not only Leanne and Tara's fear but also their lies. The previous day, Melissa warned him not to interfere with their plans. *This is something they need to do on their own.* He prays Melissa is right, and the girls escape their plight unscathed. "Are either of you sensing where this guy's holding Laura?"

"No, nothing, Michael," Tara lied. Just as she's about to utter another untruth, Michaels' cell phone rings again.

"Excuse me," he says, walking toward the window. "Where are you? … Okay … Uh huh … Yes … About twenty minutes. My man is waiting at the gate," Michael says.

Tara overhears Michael's clipped, concise responses to the caller and suspects he's censoring his conversation. For an hour, she's pondered his constant phone vigil and wonders if the call is about Laura, but why the secrecy?

Leanne realizes this is the perfect moment to escape. "Michael, we're going to the lady's room, we'll be right back."

Michael turns, shakes his head, and then resumes the suspect conversation.

"Come on, Tara," Leanne says, pulling her toward the exit. In the parking lot, a simultaneous thought jabs their conscience. *The predestined night with evil begins.*

* * *

Behind the wheel, Leanne drives as fast as she can on steep snow-covered roads. Thoughts of Tom's text message, *if you bring anyone else Laura is dead*, angers her more than the message scares her.

In the passenger seat, Tara reassures herself they're doing the right thing by not involving the police. The sight of Cody lying unconscious with blood oozing from his sweater still perturbs her. *Why didn't I see the event before it happened?* She'd never forgive herself if he'd been killed. *But he's okay,* she thought with relief.

Tara peaks at Leanne's stolid expression, eyes straight ahead, and wonders what she's thinking. "Something's changed, Leanne. Cody wasn't supposed to enter that room. Why did Tom show up before 2:22 pm? What went wrong? We didn't change anything."

"Yes, we did," Leanne says. "Maybe we weren't supposed to enter the house at 2:22 pm. Maybe bringing a gun and failing to tell Cody about our plan shifted the vision. If we'd told him, he wouldn't be lying in the hospital with a hole in his side. Tara, I don't believe we're supposed to stop Tom. I think the vision has to play out entirely. Otherwise, any change causes greater consequences, such as Cody getting hurt. We have no choice but to see this through to the end."

Tara, no longer conscious of Leanne's words, stands in front of Laura bound to a chair in the Dream Home.

Tom's voice elevates as he rants and raves in front of Laura. Upset, he throws a wooden sculpture to the floor. Time speeds up, and Tom takes a vase, knocking Laura unconscious. Blood flows from her head. Suddenly, a bright light encircles Laura's body, blinding Tara.

The sudden light and lurch of the SUV pull Tara from her trance. Acting swiftly, she grabs the steering wheel and hits the brake, just in time to stop the car from swerving off the road. The SUV veers and glides to a smooth stop. Horrified, Tara holds firm to the wheel in amazement. The bright light in her vision was Melissa pulling her from her trance, just before the car went off the road. *Melissa saved us.* Beside her, Leanne sits frozen behind the wheel; eyes fixed straight ahead.

Soaked in a sweaty delirium, she taunts Laura raucously. Laura tries to appease and reason with her, but she grows angrier and walks out of the room around the foyer into the garage where she takes gasoline cans from the closet. She exits the garage, splattering gasoline in one long line down the hallways. In the great room, Laura's chair is not where she placed it. Angrily, she drags her back to the center of the room. Leanne's hands graze Laura's shoulder, and she wakes from her trance.

Immediately, Leanne's aware of the motionless SUV and Tara gripping the wheel. "Oh God! How—what happened?" She stammers, realizing she'd retrogressed while driving.

Tara exhales loudly and throws Leanne an *are-you-serious* look. "We're lucky. Melissa saved us from going off the road."

Chapter 42

Strapped to a Chair

October 10, 2015, Dream Home

Bound to the dreaded yellow chair, Laura sits in fear and disbelief. She never imagined this would happen. But now, she's living Tara's vision. *What went wrong? Why did he appear before 2:22 pm? This can't be happening. Okay, Laura, stop. This is your reality now. You either survive or die.*

After the frightful text Tom forced her to send to Tara—a part of Tara's vision they hadn't seen, she now grasps how Tom lures the girls inside the home. *What else haven't they seen?* Anxious for help to arrive, she peeks every-other-minute out the window. *I hope the girls have a plan.* Wincing at Cody's bloodstain at her feet, Laura prays the girls got him to the hospital in time. Losing another loved one, especially Cody, is unbearable.

In front of her, Tom paces back and forth frenziedly, talking to the voice in his head, and occasionally stopping to taunt her with angry slurs. Delirium has taken over his mind—irrational thoughts claim his reasoning. His strength wanes with fever and she senses he'll succumb to his weakening state. *Hopefully, soon,* she prays.

She remembers the stocky man she met two years ago, and can't believe this is him. Illness has consumed his portly figure; carving a thin, pasty version of his original frame. Round cheeks whittled hollow. Obscured bones protrude razor-sharp. Red veins lace canals through his eyes—two dark pebbles void of any life. His essence is of unspeakable suffering. Heated thoughts surface to a boil. Helplessly, Laura awaits another verbal assault.

Tom picks up a wooden sculpture and glares at Laura with burning eyes. Beads of sweat glisten his forehead. "You think you're clever with your little art pieces. Why do you think this is appealing? It's junk! This is a piece of wood for God's sakes lady! You think you can fool people into believing this is stylish. Well, Laura, I see through your trickery. You can't fool me." With brute force, he throws the wooden sculpture across the floor. It splinters and scatters into several pieces along the floor. Weakened, he drops to the couch directly in front of her.

"Do you know what you've done to my family?" He pauses; perhaps waiting for Laura to respond. "DO YOU HAVE ANY IDEA?"

Laura flinches, then brace for a brutal strike at any moment. Instead, he rises from the sofa and paces the floor. Laura senses an instant recollection, vague images of his family, but the menacing voice prevents him from seeing clearly. *Something's wrong, something horrific happened, but what?* Laura intuits Tom's intentions. He doesn't plan to return home to his family. He intends on dying in this place, but not before he kills her and the girls.

Again, the voice taunts him. *She promised you your life would change for the better, but it hasn't, Tom. So what are you going to do?*

Tom's agitation ensues. Incapable of protecting herself, Laura braces for his next action. *Maybe if I can get through to him, talk to him, calm that voice in his head, buy some more time before help arrives ... Laura, think ... Where're those words of wisdom you always dish out? Think!*

"Tom ..." A small frightened voice escapes. She refuses to show fear, and raises her voice boldly, "... I realize you're angry ... I understand your pain."

Tom turns around with snarled lips. "You'll never understand me, Laura. Don't play psychologist with me. You have no clue of my suffering. How can you with all your wealth! You'll never know my anguish or the burden of supporting a family without an income." Tom's eyes narrow. He approaches within an inch of her nose and whispers, "Never!"

His sinister tone chills. His illness sickens Laura to the core. The unrelenting voice prods and picks at his sensibility. *Be bold Laura; don't let him see your fear.* "My life hasn't always been easy, Tom. I struggled hard before I married into the Alcott family." Laura lifts her eyes for a response, but nothing. Suddenly her mind floods with childhood memories. "My family struggled when my father's business failed. Some days we didn't know where money would come from to feed us, but as a family, we helped one another. So, don't assume I'm too privileged to understand your pain because I do."

Laura's heart races with her recollection. The memory came out of the blue. She had no intention of dredging up old memories, but her mind clicked with Tom's. That period of her life slipped her mind until she read his thoughts. She remembers her mother and father always whispering in other rooms; forgetting her gift and her ability to read their thoughts. They could never hide their emotions or pain from her. She sensed their struggles long before her father revealed the business was failing. And saw through her mom's pretense of boredom. Her sole reason for taking the secretarial job wasn't out of tedium but to support the family until the family business thrived again. She vowed as a child she'd never struggle like her parents.

The room grows eerily quiet—no pacing feet or manic thoughts. Tom doesn't respond but stands unresponsive— the voice in his mind silent. At the window, he stares into the night. *Is he looking for the girls?*

No longer hearing his thoughts; Laura sits clueless of his next action. She deliberates tactics to appease him, her mind races with ideas, and lands on his earlier question—*Do you know what you've done to my family?* Obviously, he's seeking revenge for imagined wrongdoing. Considering he's unemployed, she assumes his motive is financial. Clearly, he can't afford the Vermont home any longer. She considers his wife Ellen and the fear she lives every day. She'd detected a hint of anxiety when they first met. Like a lioness protecting her cub, Ellen held strong to her three-year-old. Every word she spoke seemed guarded; fearful she'd say something wrong. *How stupid of me not to question the danger she was feeling, but it wasn't my place to pry into their personal lives. If only I questioned the situation at the time, things might be different.*

"Tom, think about your family ... Think about Ellen. They need you; don't do anything that will affect their lives forever."

Unresponsive, Tom stares with a steel shroud masking his emotions. *Something's wrong.* His mind is silent as if his conscious no longer exist. *What happened to the voices?* The quiet scares her more than the menacing chatter in his head.

There's an urgent need to solicit some emotion—remorse, sympathy—anything to penetrate his steely wall. *Laura, his issue is financial ... Of course.* She's confident she'll kindle interest. "Tom, the sweepstake agreement contains a release clause, providing you with two years to sell the home back to AHD. The sale would free you from financial burden ... You don't have to suffer. You'll receive the full market value of the house."

Cold replaces hot rage. Tom turns toward the foyer and states in a dull tenor, "You're on your high horse again, Laura, rushing in to save the day. I wouldn't sell the house if you begged me," he states and disappears through the foyer.

Alarmed, Laura glances around for something to cut her restraints. She realizes her efforts are useless. Barely able to move; the girls are her only hope. Tom's footsteps resound down the foyer and throughout the home. *What's he doing?* An acrid odor seeps around the corner. Laura's mind screams *fire!* The one thing she fears most in life. She squirms in her constraints and tries to move the chair toward the sliding door. As hard as she's trying, she only shifts a few feet—*futile, useless.*

At once, Laura realizes with Tom's silent mind, the absence of voices in his head, is the perfect time to summon her telepathy. She remembers Michael's words and tries to calm her mind and forget her surroundings, but the bitter odor holds her fearful. Regardless, she tries with all her might—hurling suggestions toward Tom.

Tom, stop! Don't move! Put the fuel down!

For several minutes she flings messages. The sound of approaching footsteps tells her telepathy isn't working. Laura opens her eyes, and Tom glares back with a terrifying expression. *Oh God, what now! Oh, no, I forgot to move my chair back.*

"Where are you going, Laura? There's no place to go," he says with ice in his tone. The odor of gasoline grows stronger as he approaches. "So, stop trying!" With monstrous force he grips the chair, dragging her toward the fireplace, in the center of the room. "I want you to see your burning masterpiece and witness everything you love destroyed."

Tom's threats stop. His knees buckle and he grasps the mantel. Making his way to the couch, his eyes roll to the back of his eyelid just as he passes out. The acrid odor gusts around the foyer, stinging Laura's eyes and throat.

Come on, Tara and Leanne. Please get here soon.

On the coffee table, Laura spies the deadly knife Tom plunged into Cody's side. She peers to and fro from Tom's unconscious body to the knife, hoping he's cataleptic long enough to secure it. With her wrists bound by tape, her fingers are free to clutch the blade. Inching the chair close, she spreads her index finger and slides the knife to the table's edge. Just as she positions the blade between her fingers, Tom wakes, witnessing her effort. Springing from the couch, he grabs the first item he sees—a metallic vase with serrated edges. With one swift blow to the head, the metallic edge slices through her scalp, and the force renders Laura unconscious. Blood streams from her scalp down the edge of her face.

Chapter 43

Dream Realized

October 10, 2015, Dream Home

Tara and Leanne sit silently in the parked SUV. Tara cringes at the chilling familiarity of hovering snowflakes buoyed by winds around the Dream Home—creating a snow globe illusion—a beautiful scene fraught with evil intent. Leanne's aware the moment they step onto snow-covered ground, Tara's terrifying vision commences.

"Tara, I hope Melissa has our back."

"I hope so, too," Tara mumbles.

"Let's go," Leanne says with finality.

Simultaneously, they take a deep breath, open their doors, and step into a predestine night. With snow covering their sight and wind pushing at their backs, they head toward the back patio, desperate to save Laura. They sense Tom's hiding and waiting for their arrival, but can't foresee where. Tara's heart sinks at the sight of Laura bound unconscious, in the yellow chair. "My vision's come to life."

Leanne takes several deep breaths to suppress an ever-blossoming dread threatening her ability to retrogress. "I hope we know what we're doing, Tara."

Tara lifts her shirt, revealing the gun secured in the belt of her pants.

"Yes!" Leanne yelps low.

Tara angles around the patio doors. "She's so close, Leanne," Tara whispers. "If only we could open the door and pull her away."

"But's it's locked Tara, remember the chains."

"I know …" Tara senses eyes on them from somewhere inside. "Leanne, he's watching us."

With the next step, Leanne freezes, retrogressing a few seconds in time.

> Spying Leanne and Tara in the back of the house, she walks to the back porch, unlocks the chain, pauses behind the curtains, and withdraws the gun from her pocket.

Wanting to verify her vision's accuracy, Tara pulls on the sliding door and a jingle resonates inside. Immediately, her eyes veil over.

> In the great room, Tom steps from behind the curtains exit onto the back porch and march quickly behind Leanne immobilized in a trance. He strikes her from behind and catches her fall. Tara turns just as he knocks her unconscious.

Before Tara can shake off the vision, a dull thump pulls her from her trance. She turns and glares at Tom much too late.

"I've been waiting for you two," he says, exerting a hard blow to Tara's skull.

* * *

Tara wakes with a blinding throb in her skull and coughing from the caustic smoke. Blurrily, the room comes into view. Beside her, Leanne sits unconscious while Tom binds her legs to the chair. To her other side, Laura sits slumped as she had in her vision. Tara reaches over to make sure she's alive when Tom's booming voice roars in protest.

"Don't touch her!"

Tara jerks her hand and head away from Laura and cringes at Tom's frightening countenance. His gaunt pallor, and haunted eyes horrify her. She looks away, glancing about the hazy room. There're chains everywhere, at every entrance. *There's no escape!* Quickly, she runs through her vision and what she knows will happen, but this wasn't in her premonition. *Something's changed. The sequence of events is wrong, or did I skip this part? Maybe there's more I failed to foresee. I definitely didn't see Tom knocking us unconscious. Or was it a consequence?*

Nyla's voice echoes in her mind. *Don't act until you see the complete vision.* Tara hadn't seen everything. When she's in a trance, she's always pulled through time, similar to fast-forwarding a movie. *I skipped important parts.* Maybe they were supposed to tell Cody. Perhaps as Leanne said, they have to let the vision play out.

She peers at Tom as he continues binding Leanne to the chair. Suddenly, cold steel presses into her back—a slither of hope arises. *I have to retrieve the gun without him noticing.* Keeping an eye on Tom, she waits for the perfect time to pull the weapon.

Tom eyes Tara from his periphery, certain she's up to something as her eyes roam back and forth between him and the room.

Tara watches Tom wrap duct tape around Leanne's ankles. *I can't let him tie me up. We'll die if he does.* She has to act soon; before it's too late.

Finished with Leanne's binds, Tom moves toward Tara. She braces, ready to act when he draws closer. As soon as he reaches for her hands, Tara lunges, pushing him backward. He teeters on unsteady legs but catches his fall. Fumbling with the gun,

Tara tries to pull it from her pants, but it tangles in the loop of her belt, then slips from her hand.

The thud awakens Laura into a semi-conscious haze. Tara and Tom's figures move swiftly across the room. *Tara's in trouble.* Laura tries to find her telepathic mind, but the painful throb hinders clarity.

Tara races toward the gun, struggling to grab it before Tom. She rushes forward, but his swiftness is terrifying as he sweeps the gun up, pointing it at her face. The gun shakes uncontrollably. Sweat rolls down his forehead, melt into his thick brow and glide into his eyes. For the first time since childhood, Tara senses another's illness. Tom's sickness is both mental and physical. Suddenly, his infirmity invades her body.

"Good try, Tara, but we're not leaving here." With the gun, he motions her back to the chair.

Tara would rather die of a gunshot than fire. *I'm not giving up! I can't let the girls die.*

Leanne regains consciousness, and peers at Tom holding the gun at Tara.

"Leave her alone!" Leanne screams.

Leanne's anger goes unnoticed as he shoves Tara into the chair. Roughly, he binds her arms and legs with tape. As soon as he finishes with Tara, he moves toward Leanne.

Leanne squirms in the chair and screams, "What's wrong with you? You won't get away with this!"

"Stop talking, Leanne; it won't do you any good." Tom continues to bind her arms. His fingers brush her skin, and instantly, Leanne retrogresses in time.

Leanne stands in the Vermont home's spacious kitchen. Overwhelming pain tugs her senses—death invades the home. She moves beyond the kitchen into the master suite. At the entrance, she touches the door frame. Immediately, she's thrown to December tenth.

Overcome with nauseating sickness, she makes her way toward the master bathroom, drops to the toilet, and dry heaves over the bowl. Rising from the floor, she approaches the vanity and Tom's face stares back—a face etched with sheer madness. In a manic state, she pours the medication down the sink and leaves the bathroom.

In the master bedroom, she approaches the four-poster bed, where Ellen lies fast asleep. Lightly, she kisses her on the lips and swiftly takes a pillow, covering her face. Ellen wakes, pushing back with all her strength, trying desperately to escape the pillow over her face. Increasingly, she pushes harder, but brutal force overpowers her. Ellen's strength wanes; unable to overcome immense rage. She stops fighting and soon stills. Leanne senses her last breath, then darkness. In a trance, she presses the pillow into Ellen's face, although she no longer breathes. Instantly, Leanne collapses to the floor, her consciousness leaving Tom's oblivion.

Once again, he stands over Ellen, believing she's asleep. At that moment, Leanne's body shifts out of the room, through the huge kitchen, and down a flight of stairs. In another room, two children lay in their bunk beds, covered as if asleep. An unmistakable decay inspissates the air.

She touches the edge of the bed, and once again, Leanne travels to December tenth. She peers at the two children sleeping together in the same bunk bed and kisses them both on the forehead. She thinks how their security will soon be taken away from them. A surge of anger arises, and she can't control her actions. A tear escapes her eye, unaware she's smoth-

293

ering the children. She only wants to keep them safe, but the sickness is overpowering. Under her enormous rage,the children's feeble struggle is hopeless. Soon, they are eternally asleep. She stares for a moment and mumble, "I won't let them take this away from us."

Leanne makes her way to the dining room table and writes Ellen a note. On the refrigerator door, she secures the note with a black-and-white spotted dog magnet. Once again, She makes her way to the master bedroom, watching Ellen one final moment as if she were asleep. Walking quietly, she exits the home.

Leanne wakes with a deep sob, imbued with Tom's anger, and his family's last breath. She sits weakened and tearful.

Tara stares at Leanne's slumped form, tears streaming down her face. *She's seen something horrific to be in such tears.* Tara hopes she keeps her discovery hidden from Tom.

But Leanne's uncontrollable anger jets from her mouth. "You murderer! You murdered them! You killed your wife and children, you animal!" She screeches with a painful gasp.

Tom cast a baleful eye in Leanne's direction. "What are you saying?" He points the gun at her, and screams at the top of his lungs, "Close your fucking mouth!" He approaches Leanne with the gun pointed at her head. Waveringly, he backs away, his eyes never leaving her face. "My family is where they should be, in the home you gave them in Vermont."

He's had a psychotic break. He doesn't remember what he's done. Leanne looks away from his eyes, hoping he doesn't remember; fearing he might become more enraged.

Tom maintains his gaze on Leanne's face. *She's lying. Why would she say such a thing?* His mind settles on images of his wife and children sleeping in bed, and he remembers the last text he received from Ellen in Charleston. Walking toward the kitchen island, he fumbles for his mobile and scrolls through his text messages. He discovers Ellen's last text was on November 30th. *No, can't be ...* And again, with frenzied fingers, he searches for numerous messages received in Charleston from Ellen—the ones he'd ignored deliberately, and the ones he read. Curiously, he finds only one message from November 30th. Confused, he glowers at Leanne. "Why would you say something like that?"

Leanne contains her tears and rephrases her comment quietly. "You're murdering your family with your actions. Ellen won't take you back if you do this to us," she says, hoping Tom doesn't see through her lie. Smoke swells insulting her nose and eyes and triggering coughing.

Tom resumes a frantic pace, then stops and screams, "You're lying! Did you speak to my wife?"

Tom's angry howl causes Leanne to recoil. *If I tell him I talked to his wife, he'll believe she's alive.* "Yes, I spoke to Ellen. She's worried about you, Tom."

"YOU HAVE NO FUCKING RIGHT CALLING MY WIFE!" Raging forward with heavy footsteps, the floor vibrates under his surge. Immediately, the chandelier emits a bright glow around the girls. Stunned and blinded by the radiance, he stumbles, falling backward on the floor, blinking rapidly and covering his eyes. Scrambling to his feet, he steps back, from the light. The brilliance swoops in one luminous cloak, enclosing the three in a protective glow.

Staggered, Tom rubs his eyes, wondering if he's losing his sight. "Aaargh ... " escapes deep from his core. Blindly, he waves the gun in the air, determined to do harm. He can't see them, but he knows they're there. With one swift move, Tom points the gun toward the center of the light, ready to fire.

A small, distant voice screams in Laura's mind. She'd heard everything Leanne and Tom said. When she felt his vibrating steps, she summoned all her strength. At that moment, Tara turned her head toward Laura and witness her exude an immense strength in Tom's direction. Before he squeezes the trigger, Laura forces energy from her body, sending Tom a message. *STOP! FREEZE!*

Tom freezes just as he's about to pull the trigger.

Laura senses a power of another mixed with her own; a greater strength somewhere nearby. *Drop the gun, Tom!*

Drop it now! Another voice screams.

The gun falls from Tom's hands to the floor. He stands motionless.

A familiar voice in Laura, Leanne, and Tara's mind urges them to turn toward the patio. It's the same distant voice Tara heard in her vision. In unison, they turn, staring in disbelief at Callie and Michael. At the sight of her daughter, Laura smiles, knowing they'll be okay and lapses unconscious again.

Now with difficulty, Callie tries to get Tom to release the girls. *Untie the girls. When you finish, go to the couch and sleep.* Tom obeys and cuts the girl's restraints.

Smoke grows thicker, and fire consumes the east wing. Tara glances at chains securing the doors.

We're trapped!

Frantically, she hurries toward the couch and bends over Tom's sleeping frame. Rummaging through his pants and shirt pocket, she pats his body in a panic. "Where are the keys?!"

The fire is spreading fast. The same sensation she felt in her vision warms her face and arms. Overcome with smoke, Leanne lies unconscious at the back door, black soot trail her nostrils. Desperately trying to break the solid glass doors, Callie and Michael run about the patio, throwing everything in sight. Callie realizes her mistake; she put Tom to sleep before he unlocked the doors. Angrily, she bangs on the glass doors, watching as Tara's overcome by smoke.

A few minutes later, Callie screams with relief, noticing the sprinklers dousing the flames. Sirens blare into the driveway, and she runs toward the fire engine.

Chapter 44

Divine Justice

October 10, 2015, Dream Home

Moments later, drenched and sooty, Leanne and Tara breathe through oxygen masks while huddled with Callie and Michael around an unconscious Laura inside the ambulance.

An unshakable sadness consumes Leanne. *That poor family... Someone has to know!* "Michael, I need your phone," she urges in a strained voice. Seconds later, Leanne informs Vermont officials, "A man's murdered his family." She continues with details about Tom Spencer and the Vermont Dream Home's location.

Curiously, Tara asks Callie, "How did you know?"

"Michael," Callie says, smiling in his direction. He told me about Tom Spencer and explained Melissa Gowan had seen my gift of telepathy. Michael asked me to come to Tahoe as quick as possible. By the time my plane arrived, Cody had already been hurt. When we couldn't find you at the hospital, I sensed you'd be at the Dream Home."

Ahh ... Michael's cell phone vigil and suspicious phone conversation right before they left the hospital, was a call from Callie.

"Tara, I was afraid my telepathy wouldn't work, but Melissa believed in me."

"You did good, Callie. If it weren't for you, we wouldn't be alive."

"Tara, mom saved you. She managed to stop Tom just before he fired a shot. It was the combined strength of our gift that caused Michael to drop the gun."

"And Melissa ..." Tara says. "She totally blinded Tom with that light."

They both laughed.

Tara recalls how Laura appeared right before Tom froze. She realizes Laura used all her strength to save them. And without Michael's intervention, they'd all be dead. She whispers, "Thank you," to Michael.

Tara sighs and glances at the Dream Home. Fumes rise above the scorched and blackened east wing, but the home stands structurally sound. The west wing, which contains the great room, sits damp and smoky, but untouched by flames. "I'm happy the firemen got here before the fire destroyed everything."

"Tara, it wasn't the fireman. The sprinkler came on just as you passed out. I've never in my life been so happy to see water," Callie exclaims. "The fires never fully started. The sprinklers prevented the fire from reaching the west wing."

"Well, Cody did think of everything," Tara mumbles.

Moments later, in the back of the ambulance, the girls hold on to Laura's hands as they head toward the hospital. Blaring police sirens speed past with Tom Spencer asleep in the backseat, reminding Callie of her blunder. Nonplussed, she says, "I don't believe I can wake Tom."

"Callie, I wouldn't worry about Tom. You did what was necessary. When the policemen asked me what happened, I simply told them he passed out and never woke up, which is partially true," Tara says with a chortle. "Besides, what else could I say? I couldn't tell them the truth. They'd never believe us."

Still overcome with grief for Ellen and the boys, Leanne states ineffably, "Perhaps it's best Tom never wakes again. He'll never accept what he's done to his family. Call it divine justice—he put his family to sleep forever, perhaps he deserves the same."

PART 4

Chapter 45

A Vision Seen

December 15, 2014 (Present Day) AHD Headquarter

Images collide to a halt, gyrating speedily in reverse. In a dizzying whirl, the vision settles in Tara's consciousness. Teetering on the verge of collapse, she swiftly grasps the balustrade, her gaze still riveted on Tom Spencer at AHD's gate.

Tom Spencer!

It's still December 15th!

It feels like months have flown by but it's only been seconds since she stepped onto the piazza. Stunned, Tara watches Tom's bewildered expression as he turns and walks away.

Taking several deep breaths, Tara tries to slow her racing heart. Her temples throb and her eyes blink in rapid successions with ten months of information processed mentally in only a few minutes. Never has she experienced such a powerful mental surge, weakening every limb. Suddenly nauseous, she rushes off the piazza, into her office, and flings her coat and scarf on the desk. Coffee surges up her throat and into the trash can. She catches the sacred-seven pendant swinging about her neck, holding it back as she heaves over the trash.

The sacred-seven pendant ... Melissa Gowan ...

Tara peers at the walls aglow with Melissa's ethereal presence. She holds firm to the pendant, and whispers into the air, "Thank you, Melissa."

The phone rings. Tara recalls from her vision Cody's phone call with news of the Lake Tahoe location. *Cody ... He's okay; he's not lying in the hospital with a stab wound.* She's relieved, but waits for voicemail to take the call, and immediately calls Nyla.

"You finally saw," says Nyla, as if she'd been expecting her call.

"Mom, oh my God, I can't believe what just happened."

Nyla knew Tara would capture her childhood vision today. She realized there was a slight chance she might not see the future until it was too late. Her abilities depended on the sacred-seven pendant. The Rutile stone mixed with the energy of the other stones served as an antenna, opening Tara's mind to Tom's intentions. Nyla also recognizes this would be a massive effort of Melissa Gowan, to guide Tara the entire morning. Nyla glances heavenward with a smile. "Melissa, thank you," she whispers, just as Tara had a few moments before.

"Mom, the vision was so clear, so real as if I lived the entire ten months, but it was only a few seconds."

"Tara, that's the way visions happens when your gift is strong, and you allow them to occur."

"Mom, I need to alert the police in Vermont."

"Yes, you do. You also need to stop Tom before the chain of events occur, before he reaches Laura, and before he places the packages inside her home. But, yes, first you must call the police. It won't be easy explaining what happened. They will question how you know. Just be honest and without too much detail."

* * *

Tara calls information for the Vermont precinct. Her voice resounds surreal through the phone as she explains what's transpired. Urgently, she tells them, "There's been a murder." Providing only crucial details, she states, "I'm AHD's Managing

Director. One of our sweepstake winners, Tom Spencer, killed his family." She provides the address and vehemently demands, "You need to get to the Vermont home now!" She hangs up and urgently calls the Charleston police precinct telling them a man is heading toward the Alcott estate and will attempt to break into the home. She gives them Tom's description and his precise location.

Drained from the powerful vision, Tara takes a deep breath and collapses with relief into the chair. She sits in awe, amazed at what might have occurred. *The girls ... They're okay.* In only a matter of seconds, she learned much about her clairvoyant friends ... Her family. With an urgent need to tell the girls of her breakthrough, she swiftly types an email to Laura and Leanne.

> *Girls,*
>
> *We need to talk. It's urgent. Leanne, cut your dad some slack. When you're finished talking to him, come to my office. Laura, the police will be at your gate soon. Don't worry, just get in your car and meet me at the office. Oh, watch out for the sharp staple in your file drawer.*
>
> *TM*

Chapter 46

New Day, New Talent

December 16, 2014, Tara's Townhouse

Tara opens her eyes to a brilliant new day. It's no longer December fifteenth, and there's no longer a threat of Tom Spencer. Tom was apprehended by the police hiding outside the Alcott gate, his plan squelched long before he could start. Thoughts of Tom's poor family lying lifeless and undiscovered for several days sadden Tara. Tom refuses to believe they're dead. His psychotic break was so severe; he may never recall what happened. But the girls will never forget the horrific images.

Tara dismisses thoughts of Tom. On the ceiling, a spectrum of colors captures Tara's attention. She's never seen such brilliance. She casts her eyes about the room, searching for the source, but only the sun streams through the window. She recalls the glow from the previous morning. *Is Melissa visiting again?* But this glow is different. Every item in the room emits different shades of color. *How beautiful.* With renewed vigor, which ensued after the vision, Tara bounces from the bed and walks to the mirror. Her image exudes violet, blue, green, gold, and silver colors. Befuddled, she rubs her eyes and stares unblinkingly at the mirror. *What's going on?* She rushes to the bathroom, taking another peek in the vanity mirror. The colors are growing brighter. *Am I going blind?* She stares fearfully at the purple hue surrounding her head. She rushes to the phone and calls Nyla.

"Mom, something's wrong with my eyes."

"Describe your symptoms, honey."

"My body—I'm emitting colors! Everything is emitting colors!"

"Calm down, Tara. I think I know what's happening. You're experiencing lingering side effects from your vision of Tom. You probably triggered all of your abilities. You're no longer repressing your gift, so your natural abilities are finally appearing. I've seen this before. Stay where you are. I'll be right over, hon."

Chapter 47

Full-Circle

December 24, 2014, Alcott Estate

It's Christmas Eve once again, or so it seems. Tara and the girls sit in the family room around the Christmas tree, just as they had in her vision, but this time, the evening is calm without the threat of Tom Spencer. Tara, in continual awe of her new gift, blinks consistently throughout the night, watching brilliant hues change and deepen around the girls. Again, dark-violet, brilliant-blue, emerald-green, metallic-gold, and pink appears a deeper roseate tonight.

Tara has developed what Nyla calls mystic eyes brought on by her vision of Tom. The vision was so strong, the pigmentation of her iris changed permanently. Now and forever, a hint of gold tints her hazel eyes. Tara recalls the startling image in the mirror the morning after December fifteenth. At first, the colors surrounding her body were faint, but grow brighter with time. She now experiences life differently. All people and objects emit colors, ranging from bright whitish blues to murky dark reds. Tara has learned that various colors represent the physical, emotional, and spiritual state of people. Those she holds the deepest bonds with have similar colors, apparent from the colors the girls exude tonight. She wonders what colors she would have seen around Tom Spencer, perhaps murky-brown or black.

Curiously, Nyla and Tara researched and discovered color's meanings, especially purple. Dark-purple is the color of the psychic, the visionary, a person who is intuitive, futuristic, and magical. Royal-blue symbolized the third eye, intuitiveness. Emerald-green represents the healer, growth, and change. Metallic-gold denotes psychic energy and power awakened and activated. The gold intrigues Tara the most because the color is the brightest surrounding her body. She believes the meanings are accurate because the girl's gifts have grown more powerful.

Tara stares at the Moldavite ring on her finger, hoping it blocks her knowledge of Christmas Eve. But she fears the girls have already captured details of her vision. Anyhow, Tara hopes the night contains some element of surprise. She watches the night unfold just as Christmas Eve had in her premonition. Callie places a decorative gift on Laura's lap. The painting causes Laura's eyes to shimmer with tears of joy and sadness. And again, emotions swell in Tara. Under the tree, she spies the burnt-orange wrapping tied with tan, leather strings and displays the same surprise she had in her vision for the expensive leather tote. Tara waits for Callie's exaltations when she discovers the Amethyst necklace and blue Lapis-Lazuli pendant, and braces for Leanne's loud squeal of delight as she finds the iPad. The only difference this Christmas Eve is the absence of the mysterious silver gift wrapped with a blue velvet bow. Another variance, are three gifts from Tara wrapped in vibrant colors representing the psychic powers surrounding the girls—dark violet wrappings with decorative blue, green, and gold ribbons.

Tara sits back, admiring her friends ... Her family. She marvels at the magic in their lives. Surely, there will never be a boring moment with this group. Tara detects Callie's lavender aura deepening a darker violet. The green, blue, and gold are still faint but deepen every day. Her green aura, signifying a healer, is the strongest. Tara senses Callie will be the most gifted of the group, channeling her healing powers to cure many as a talented doctor. Leanne has grown to appreciate her gift, embracing old objects and the wisdom they contain. Tara catches Leanne's perspicacious gaze at Daniel's spirit beside Callie and Laura, watching over his family.

Somewhere in time, in the Alcott estate, Tara foresees Leanne and Adam playing with a little girl with feline, green eyes and jet-black hair, a carbon copy of Leanne, celebrating a distant Christmas. She foresees Laura's future and knows she will keep this magnificent home. The laughter of a new husband and daughter with strawberry blonde hair echoes across the great room. Tara smiles with the knowledge of the beautiful Tahoe Dream Home, which will bring Laura and her second love, Michael Anders together.

Hearing her name and the mention of husband and child rattling around Tara's brain, Laura sends a knowing wink Tara's way.

Tara also sees her future with a man named Ellison, who she met only four days ago. She promised when they met the second time, she wouldn't be so rude. On the edge of Laura's couch, somewhere in the future, a young girl with massive-wavy hair and eyes etched with gold opens a gift from Ellison. Tara's daughter averts her eyes and stares at Tara with a familiar glare of insight.

Tara breathes a sigh of joy and peers at her gifts to the girls, three leather-bound books containing their family tree. Additional pages were added for their daughters, three girls she sees vividly. Tara foresaw their future and the daunting challenge they will face—a challenge greater than their own; one that will save many lives in the future. Tara understands the true reason for Melissa's protection and guidance, to ensure the birth of their daughters—Ariel, Darra, and Destine.

Meanwhile, another celebration is taking place at Marion and Anson Alcott's estate. In their dining room, above the fireplace, hangs a painting of the Gowan sisters painted by Nathan Cox in 1855. The crystal medallions around their necks sparkle with luminosity, captured by Nathan's eyes. The painting watches over the gathering on this auspicious night seen so many years ago. The Alcott, McPherson, and Davis family sit around the long, stone dining table containing the original Gowan medallion.

"We've come full circle. The girls achieved their spiritual awakening," says Marion.

Lifting their wine glasses, they toast to overseeing the hundred and eighty-seven-year-old vision seen by Melissa Gowan, fulfilled. Nyla and Marion peer at each other with satisfaction; knowing Melissa Gowan had also seen this moment years ago as she protected the newborn baby boy, Nathan Cox. Melissa's vision of Tara, Laura, and Leanne has come to fruition, and the girls are safe and stronger than ever.

In this room, Zachary Alcott made a bargain with the Gowan sisters to protect Nathan Cox. In exchange, he provided homes and land, as well as a trust providing for the financial security of Nathan and his progeny. Melissa Gowan also held Zachary to another promise, to protect the three women in the future when the time came. Zachary Alcott's promise kept all these years, will continue to the next Alcott generation as instated in the Alcott Family Foundation. The pact between the Gowan sisters and the Alcotts will carry on as long as the foundation exists, or until eternity.

"It's only fitting to celebrate the Alcott-Gowan bond in the room it was conceived. And may the next generations do the same," Marion says, lifting her glass.

Nyla studies the medallion the Gowan women carved in stone almost two centuries ago. With her finger, she circles the medallion and says, "Female power, unity, wholeness, and spiritual transformation," just as Melissa had done many years ago.

Chapter 48

Pen to Paper

April 2020, Charleston, SC

The door opens sending a sliver of light across the dark study, illuminating Leanne's face as she sits immersed in the computer. She rereads her novel's final sentence—Nyla duplicating Melissa Gowan's action and words one-hundred-ninety-two years ago.

"Mommy, you finished?"

Leanne peers at her daughter's small figure in the door frame and throws her a smile. Her child, so intuitive for her five years, smiles back. "Yes, sweetie; I'm finished."

Ariel takes her hand, and Leanne realizes she'd been with Adam only minutes ago, but had seen her type the last word of her novel. Leanne squeezes her daughter's hand and lifts her onto her lap. They both stare at the final chapter of her book. "I need to change my characters names. Can you help me, sweetie?"

Shyly, Ariel shakes her head. "Yes mommy."

Leanne remembers Tara's revelation she'd write a book about her vision of Tom Spencer in five years. Leanne had replied, *"I started writing the day your vision happened on the piazza."* However, Leanne realizes Tara and Laura had already sensed when she'd put pen to paper. After her dreams of Melissa Gowan, she started writing fiercely and couldn't stop. Melissa Gowan also understands Leanne will be the storyteller of the family's history and guides her toward her next book on Nathan Cox's life.

Quickly, Leanne glances at her novel, clicks save, and then turns her attention to her daughter. Ariel smiles a silly grin Leanne's witnessed many times—a smile containing some unknown secret. She suspects Ariel sees apparitions, and like her mom will understand things way before her time. The Alcott medallion Leanne used for her book cover fades in and out.

"Melissa!" Ariel exclaims, pointing and giggling at the screen.

Astonished her daughter's gift is blossoming so early, Leanne squeezes her tight. "Yes, Ariel, that's right," Leanne says with a smile, grateful Melissa Gowan still watches over the family.

Acknowledgments

WITH MANY THANKS to Ouida Billups and James Billups for years of support and lending an ear through this endeavor. Special thanks to Julie Chan, Marsha Bullock, Mirna Hamilton, dedicated early readers, and other friends, Par Balkaran, Ernest Mossiah for your feedback. Also to fellow writer Larry Crockett, thanks for sharing valuable advice.

About The Author

An author with a rare mixture of Southern and Northern charm, E. Denise Billups was born in Monroeville Alabama and raised in New York City where she currently resides and works in finance and as a freelance columnist. A burgeoning author of fiction, she's published three suspense novels—Kalorama Road, Chasing Victoria, By Chance, and three supernatural short stories, Ravine Lereux, The Playground, and Rebound. An avid reader of magical realism, mystery, and suspense novels, she was greatly influenced by authors of these genres. She's a fitness fanatic, trained in ballet, modern, and jazz dance, and uses the same discipline to facilitate creative writing.

Thank you for reading By Chance. If you enjoyed the story, please leave me a review at the merchant you purchased the book. I appreciate your reviews which support my success as an Indie Author. Again, thank you for reading about the three gifted women of By Chance!

E. Denise Billups

www.edenisebillups.com